D0968427

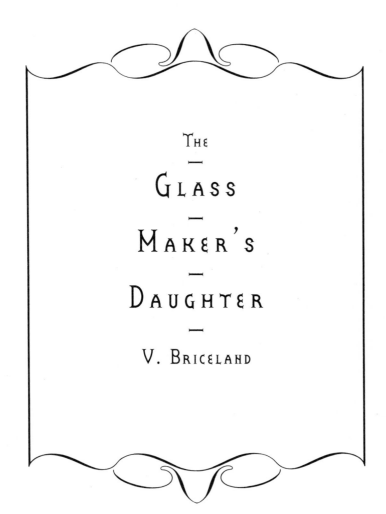

THE

GLASS

MAKER'S

DAUGHTER

V. BRICELAND

flux™
Woodbury, Minnesota

The Glass Maker's Daughter © 2009 by V. Briceland. All rights reserved. No part of this book may be used or reproduced in any manner whatsoever, including Internet usage, without written permission from Flux, except in the case of brief quotations embodied in critical articles and reviews.

First Edition
First Printing, 2009

Book design by Steffani Sawyer
Cover design by Kevin R. Brown
Illustration on cover and on page i by Blake Morrow/Shannon Associates
Map of Cassaforte by Jared Blando

Flux, an imprint of Llewellyn Publications

Library of Congress Cataloging-in-Publication Data

Briceland, V. (Vance)
  The glass maker's daughter / V. Briceland.—1st ed.
    p. cm.
  Summary: Sixteen-year-old Risa's disappointment over an unprecedented event is devastating, but the evil and destruction that follows the king's death show her that the god and goddess have special need of her talents and those of her new, lower-class friends.
  ISBN 978-0-7387-1424-0
  [1. Social classes—Fiction. 2. Kings, queens, rulers, etc.—Fiction.
3. Self-confidence—Fiction. 4. Fate and fatalism—Fiction. 5. Fantasy.]
I. Title.
  PZ7.B75888Gld 2009
  [Fic]—dc22
                                                          2008048138

This is a work of fiction. Names, characters, places, and incidents are either the product of the author's imagination or are used fictitiously, and any resemblance to actual persons, living or dead, business establishments, events, or locales is entirely coincidental. Cover models used for illustrative purposes only and may not endorse or represent the book's subject.

Flux
Llewellyn Publications
A Division of Llewellyn Worldwide, Ltd.
2143 Wooddale Drive, Dept. 978-0-7387-1424-0
Woodbury, Minnesota 55125-2989, U.S.A.
www.fluxnow.com

Printed in the United States of America

Acknowledgments

The original inspiration for this novel grew from a sermon delivered the Sunday after September 11, 2001, by Reverend Susan DeFoe Dunlap at the First United Methodist Church of Royal Oak, Michigan. For Reverend Dunlap's message of hope in a confusing time, I am most grateful.

This book would not have been possible without the aid of several people, especially the suggestions given on rough drafts by Patty Woodwell and Marthe Arends. Nor could I have done without the support and encouragement of Craig Symons. I also owe many thanks to early reader Brianna Privett, and to Michelle Grajkowski, the best of all literary agents. Andrew Karre and Sandy Sullivan, my editors at Flux, deserve great praise and all my gratitude for their amazing recommendations and hard work.

Many think I jest when I tell them that everything I know about writing novels, I learned in playwriting class. Yet whatever few good habits I possess in my fiction writing and rewriting processes I owe to the disciplined methods of Dr. Louis E. Catron, under whom I was privileged to study in the theater department of the College of William and Mary. Thanks to Dr. Catron's encouragement, I began writing regularly, and developed the ambition and confidence to write full time. It's with much gratitude, and with many fond memories of reading aloud my one-act plays with other students in his office, that I dedicate to him *The Glass Maker's Daughter*.

CASSAFORTE

A. Caza Cassamagi: The House of Scholars
B. Caza Portello: The House of Architects
C. Caza Divetri: The House of Glass Makers
D. Caza Catarre: The House of Book Makers
E. Caza Buonochio: The House of Artists
F. Caza Piratimare: The House of Ship Builders
G. Caza Dioro: The House of Weapon Makers

THE AZURE SEA

BOOK

—

ONE:

—

CAZA

—

DIVETRI

1

Of all the quaint traditions of the southern lands, perhaps the sweetest is to be found in the city-state of Cassaforte, where nightly its horns are sounded in a tradition that has been unbroken for centuries.

—Celestine du Barbaray, **Traditions & Vagaries of the Azure Coast: A Guide for the Hardy Traveler**

Sunset, on the balcony atop her family's home, was Risa Divetri's favorite time of day. Beyond the Bridge of Muro in the west, the sun tickled the horizon and set the city's canals aglow. Water and light rippled back to where Risa balanced on the balcony's wide stone rail, making it seem as if the setting sun were stretching its long fingers toward her. She thought of how molten glass had the same red-hot intensity when plucked from the heart of a furnace.

If someone could peer into her soul that night—her last at Caza Divetri—might they see how hotly it, too, burned?

In the twilight, the limestone balcony rail felt warm

and comfortable where she sat. Just below her stretched the upper branches of a gnarled old olive tree. If Risa dangled her legs, she could tickle the soles of her feet with its leaves. Far below, the tree's roots twisted among the rocks of the slope that dropped down to the canal, where a gondolier sang a slow, sweet tune as he punted by. Beyond the lone figure lay the Piazza Divetri, and then the cream-colored buildings of Cassaforte.

Standing beside her, leaning on the rail, Risa's father caught the gondolier's tune and hummed it to himself while he watched the city. Her mother, deep in concentration, sat nearby, on a bench erected upon the red and black tiles. Giulia Divetri always seemed to be smiling. Her long, dark hair, tamed by a silk cord woven through and around its length, fell like rope over her shoulder and down the front of her embroidered gown. In her hands she held her sketching board and a length of red chalk. Her fingers busily danced across the paper.

"Buonochio blood," said Risa's father, nodding at her mother's drawing. He gave Risa a private wink. "Fiery and artistic!"

"You married me for my bold blood, Ero," replied her mother, amused. She continued her sketching, capturing an image she later would render in one of her famed windows. "Would that I had more of it. See—I never capture the palace dome quite right." She held out the sketch board. Her perfectly placed lines outlined the rounded roof of the palace's throne room. A few more caught the two moons hovering above it, nestled squarely within two identical constellations.

"You have enough talent and fire for the both of us, love," he murmured. "I recognized it the first day I saw you—when you leaned from that window and called to me!"

"I felt bold that day."

"You were enchanting, my dear."

"I knew a good man when I saw one." Risa's mother's lips curved in recollection as she returned to her drawing. "Even if he did just happen to be a stranger passing on the street." The familiar story made Risa smile; she was happy to hear it one last time.

No matter what hour of day or season, a hush always seemed to fall over the city as the time of the rite approached. Some nights, she swore she could see the king's hornsman taking his place atop the palace dome, but her father said she was imagining things; although the dome was the city's highest point, the palace was simply too far away for her to spy such details.

"Risa?" As the streets quieted in anticipation, her father extended his hand. "Would you?"

Her face lit up at the invitation, though she couldn't trust herself to say anything. Not yet—not when she was trying to make her memory of this last evening perfect. Experience had proved, time and again, that opening her mouth only ruined things.

The dry heat of the tiles that seared her bare feet seemed to warm her heart as well. She loved this still and expectant moment of the day more than any other. Beside her, Ero was loosening the ties that held the Cassaforte banner aloft. He handed her the taut ropes, and together they lowered the rippling streamer to the ground, keeping pace in the nightly rite with Caza Portello to the east and Caza Catarre to the west. Once it was in her hands, Risa folded the rich purple and brown silk into its box. With respect, she knelt and slid the banner into its space beneath the pedestal, within which lay the Divetri horn.

It was her final night, she told herself with excitement. It was the last time she would help her father with the daily rite of fealty. Where there could have been sadness, she felt only joy. It frolicked inside her like one of the sacred deer in the royal forest, making her want to leap up and sing out. Tomorrow evening she would have a new home and be hearing the horns from far across the city.

She would no longer be merely Ero and Giulia's child once she was declared a daughter of the moons. She would not be a child at all, once she was accepted at one of the insulas and started to learn things. *Important* things. She would finally be living her life, like her older brother and sisters, instead of merely waiting for it to begin.

Scarcely had she climbed to her feet when a blow from behind sent her reeling. She staggered into her father, dimly aware of the giggles echoing from across the courtyard. "*Petro!*" she shrieked at the top of her voice. "You maniac!"

Wild and sudden excitement propelled her back to her feet. With a scream of laughter she took off, bounding after her younger brother in crazy circles around the upper courtyard. She only had this one final night to play with him, she reminded herself. It might be her last chance. "Touch me again and I'll strip you bare and throw you to the canal buzzards and let them shred you to the bones!" Her brother yelped in mock terror.

Giulia laughed. "She takes after you, dear. A Divetri with a mission is fearful to behold."

With a wink at his wife, Ero proclaimed, "And thus our little lady transforms back into the lionkit we know and love so well."

Her father had called her a lionkit so often that Risa wore the title as a badge of pride. People often commented on the similarities between Ero and his daughter. Her long chestnut hair, like his, seemed almost copper-colored in the sunlight. And while Giulia communicated her anger quietly, with flashing eyes and a dangerous tone to her voice, both father and daughter were known to shout their passions to the skies.

"Come back here, slimy wart!" she yelled after Petro.

"Never!" he caroled with defiance.

Around the balcony courtyard they chased each other. Petro dove headlong into Mattio, the chief craftsman of Ero's workshop, just as the man was emerging into the cool evening air. "By Muro's foal!" Mattio exclaimed, laughing in surprise.

"Sorry," Risa huffed as she dodged around the large-framed foreman to snatch at her brother. Petro dashed behind the skirts of their housekeeper, Fita, but the old woman was too busy to notice, quietly scolding one of the maids for wearing a dirty apron to the rite.

"Ah-ah-ah. Gently, gently," chided a middle-aged man behind Mattio. His nose was crooked from an old break. "This is a solemn part of the day." Cousin Fredo's expression was, as ever, pious and weary of their behavior.

"Indeed it is," agreed the housekeeper. She turned to the

red-faced maid. "Go change into something clean *immedi-ately*."

"Sorry, cousin," called Petro, slowing down. "I'm sorry, Fita."

"A-*ha!*" Risa cried in triumph. She seized him by the collar. Petro's yap of protest was cut short as she dragged him backward. "I've got you now, you little bloody scab on a beggar's behind!"

"Cazarrina," begged Cousin Fredo with deep dismay, addressing Risa by her formal title. His hand shot toward her shoulder, but she managed to wriggle from his grasp before he could give her one of his vicious pinches. "Cazarrina! Please! My nerves...!" He reached into the pocket of his surcoat to retrieve his little silver box of *tabbaco da fiuto*, with which he soothed himself. It was because of this creamy paste that their cousin's approach was always preceded by the disagreeable scent of tobacco leaves, cloves, and pungent pine oil.

"My dears," said Giulia from her bench, "it is nearly time. Grant your cousin's nerves a small period of rest. You may yell yourselves hoarse later."

Brother and sister exchanged glances. Cousin Fredo's nerves were his favorite topic of conversation. Smothering their amusement, they turned their gazes to the ground in an attempt to appear solemn. "We're sorry, cousin," they intoned. Fredo nodded stiffly and, using the tip of his little finger, dabbed *tabbaco da fiuto* onto his gums in the hollows over his two canine teeth. Seeming refreshed, he straightened his broad collar as they darted past him to the far end of the balcony.

"You've got something in your hand," said Risa, still giggling at Fredo's pomposity. "Give it to me."

"You mean this?" Petro produced a ball of stitched and stuffed pigskin from his pocket. "Catch!" he yelled. He had obviously intended to throw it at his sister, but when Risa grabbed him by the collar and spun him around, the ball arced high into the air and landed with a sickening thud against a casement of leaded glass. Giulia frowned, but the enchantments had held, leaving the glass unbroken. Any other window would have shattered from such impact, but thanks to the blessings fortifying their structure, Divetrimade glass could withstand even the fiercest storms from the Azure Sea.

"Not that," Risa said in a lower voice, while she tried to grab for the left fist Petro had kept clenched the entire time. "Your other hand."

"It's a letter," taunted Petro. "A *private* letter for you... from you know *who.*"

"Who?"

"*You* know," said Petro. With meaning he looked over at the craftsmen gathering near the doorway. She followed the direction of his glance. Emil, the youngest of the men in her father's workshop, stood behind Mattio and Fredo, his nose deep in a book. "He *looooooves* you. He wants to pay *court* to you."

Risa stiffened, torn between screeching with horror and laughing outright. "He does not!" she finally hissed. Emil was fine enough as the craftsmen went, but the loves of his life were sewn into folios and bound with leather.

"Pardon *me.*" Petro pitched his voice up a half octave

and pretended to toss imaginary hair over his shoulder. "I am Risa Divetri, Cazarrina. When I marry, my husband *must* be a man of the Thirty and Seven."

"I am *not* like that!" With a deft snatch, Risa seized the folded paper that was clutched in her younger brother's palm. "Hah!" she exulted, unfolding it. Though her brother had attempted to disguise his handwriting with the fancy script of his elders, his authorship was painfully obvious from the blots and the bits of quill feather stuck to the ink.

> *Dearest—*
> *When I think of you I could*
> *die, so deep are my feelings for you.*
> *I love your eyes, the arc*
> *of your brow, the quick*
> *smile that comes to your lips when*
> *I walk into the room. You are so*
> *beautiful—a near goddess!*
> *Marry me, please, please, please!*
> *—You know who*

Risa let her eyes run over the letter. To anyone other than herself or her brother, the message might seem innocuous enough, but with Petro, she knew better. She scanned the note quickly for its buried message. Then, with a squawk of outrage and no courtesy for Cousin Fredo's nerves whatsoever, she yelled, *"Duck nose?* You're calling me a *duck nose,* you little whelp?"

Petro was giddy with glee. Before Risa could strangle him again, he dashed off in the direction of his parents, gaining enough of a head start to turn a triumphant cartwheel.

"Someone is going to have a *broken* nose!" Risa shouted. She was not really angry at all, of course. She just enjoyed the noise of the roar as it flew from her lungs. Admittedly, there was also a particular joy in the sight of Fredo instantly clapping his hands over his ears.

"Gently, gently," he pleaded as she passed. "My nerves… Cazarra, please," he added, appealing to Giulia.

"Risa, what is this silliness?" her mother said as she approached. She held out her hand for the crumpled paper, then smoothed it out on her sketch board while restraining Risa's arm. "Your cousin is a sensitive man…" Privately, Risa knew her mother no more believed in Fredo's nerves than did anyone else in the caza. Giulia was always polite to Fredo, however, even in the most trying of circumstances.

"That brat who is allegedly your son called me a duck nose," Risa said, pointing to the letter.

"This note seems quite complimentary, though the script could stand improvement," said Giulia. "Where does it call you a duck nose?"

Risa ran her finger along the right side of the paper, pointing at the last letter on each line.

d u c k n o s e

"It's our secret code," she said. "See?"

Her mother raised an eyebrow. Risa could tell she was trying not to laugh, which would give Fredo reason to complain. Though he could not overhear them at this distance, he was studying them closely. "Very clever," said Giulia at last. "Quite ingenious. Aren't you a mite old for this foolery, however?" Risa bowed her head slightly. She had intended to keep this evening perfect, after all. "As a courtesy to your father's cousin and his…nerves, if you could restrain from murdering your brother until *after* the rite, I would take it as a personal favor." She folded the note and slipped it under her drawing, where neither of her children would be tempted to filch it.

A horn's rich cry resonated from the palace. It seemed to shimmer through the air as it drowned out Cassaforte's last few evening noises. The clop-clop of donkey hooves on the pavement, the cries of the gondoliers on the canals, and the friendly babble of the crowds all ceased at its musical tone. Risa's playfulness halted as well. The rite of fealty had been set into motion; it was time once more to think of herself as a sober young citizen, not a child.

Each of the cazas belonging to Cassaforte's seven great families had been built upon islands around the city's coast, Risa knew. The complex of bridges and canals that united them to the mainland, however, made it difficult to tell where the seven cazas began and the capital city left off. The cazas were separate from Cassaforte, yet of it, all at once.

From the farthest caza east, well beyond sight, came the silvery answering cry of the oldest family of the Seven. "Sweet Caza Cassamagi," breathed Risa, enchanted by the sound, as she was every night. Instinctively she reached for her younger brother's hand. If it was the two gods' will to separate her from Petro during the ceremony the next day, it might be the last evening they spent together for years to come.

Caza Portello, just east of their own island, was the second oldest caza in all of Cassaforte. As the call of Cassamagi's horn swept across the darkening sky, Portello's red and white silks climbed the flagpole. Cassamagi was known for its research into the discipline of enchantments; Portello was known far and wide for its architecture. Its walls rose high and proud, and its enchantment-strengthened bridges and spires rivaled Cassaforte's royal palace in grace and delicacy. When its colors reached the top of the pole, an answering cry, from its tenor horn, poured from Portello's heights.

At the cue, Ero began pulling the rope that would take Divetri's blue and green banner into the skies. He grinned, as he always did, to see the family's colors flying against the deepening twilight and to hear the silks snapping crisply in the sea breezes. Then, with two strides of his muscular legs, he crossed to the pedestal. He removed the large domed lid, green-blue with patina, and placed it on the ground. A brass horn lay atop the purple cushion within. Like a hunting horn, its tube was coiled upon itself until, after three turns, it flared into a bell.

Ero grasped the instrument and pointed it up to the heavens. He faced toward King Alessandro's palace. Risa watched with admiration as he took in a massive breath. Chest enlarged and feet braced, Ero blew into the Divetri horn.

Though she had heard the same velvet peal every evening of her life, its beauty and force always astonished her. As the single note grew in volume, it seemed to cast out a cord, invisible yet sparkling, that tied together Caza Divetri's inhabitants. It tightened around them all, then flew out in the direction of the palace itself, over the city and its buildings. To Risa it was almost a tangible sensation, that cord. She wondered for the first time if anyone else ever felt it. The others, however, seemed merely attentive, not enchanted. Why was it so vivid for her?

The velvety sound faded, though everyone remained still for another moment. The ancient rite of fealty had been completed. For another night, as it had for centuries, Caza Divetri would stand.

They listened for horns to sound from Catarre and Buonochio, book makers and artists, then from Piratimare and Dioro, ship builders and crafters of weapons. Seven cazas, united through this nightly rite with the country's most sacred relics and the symbols of the king—the Olive Crown and Scepter of Thorn.

After the cazas' loyalty had been proclaimed for all the city to hear, the palace hornsman played one last, long note. It lingered, then vanished into the sunset.

As the moment dissipated, everyone perceptibly relaxed. The craftsmen began to file out. The last to leave, of course, was Cousin Fredo, who lingered over his prayers to the god Muro and Muro's sister, the goddess Lena. Neither of the two moons adorning the night sky seemed to notice his muttered entreaties.

When the family was alone once more, Giulia ran her hand through her son's hair. "My youngest have grown up too swiftly," she sighed. Risa disagreed. She was not being allowed to grow up quickly enough.

"I'm not grown up," Petro asserted. "I'm only eleven. *Next* year, though!"

Ero laughed. "You're old enough, my boy. Old enough. Did you enjoy your last evening? Yes?"

"Papa." Petro suddenly sounded frightened. He was still

so young, thought Risa. Perhaps he was only now realizing that tomorrow he would be taken from the caza to live with the Penitents or with the Children, depending upon whose blessing he received. "What would happen if you fell ill after tomorrow? Who would blow our horn at sunset?"

From behind, Risa pounced on him and tickled him lightly. Petro squealed. The solemnity of the rite had faded, and she once more felt playful. "No one!" she growled. "No one would blow the horn or raise the banners, and then demons would devour the caza and it would no longer be ours!"

As she and her brother laughed, her father shook his head. His curls glinted in the dancing light of the raised brazier, whose flames illuminated the family's banner every night. "That won't happen, Petro. You know very well that Romeldo would come from the insula to take over my duties until I felt better. He's the oldest, and heir to the caza. Remember how I had the sun sickness once when you were younger? He came then."

"And what if Romeldo is sick?"

"Are you worried that we'll fall to pieces when you leave tomorrow?"

Petro hesitated. "No. Well, maybe."

"When you are big enough," said Ero affectionately, kneeling down and grabbing his son's nose with his fingers, "*you* may perform the rite and keep us all safe in our caza."

"I'm older than Petro!" Risa protested, not for the first time. "I could perform the rite!"

Without even looking at his wife, Ero replied just as Risa knew he would. "The protection of a caza is not the responsibility of women."

"Now, Ero," said Giulia, her gentle voice a contrast to his stubborn tones. It was an old argument between them. "You well know my good kinswoman Dana raises the flags as cazarra of Buonochio. Buonochio's cazarra has always done so, since the house's founding. In the past, Cassamagi ... "

Ero raised a hand. "In Caza Divetri, the rite of fealty is the cazarro's responsibility. It has always been so, and will always be." He got to his feet and winked once more at his daughter. "Women are good for other things, eh? Bewitching men's hearts, primarily. You'll learn."

He grinned broadly at his wife, who shook her head while returning the smile. "By Lena, you are an old-fashioned bull," was her only retort. Still talking, they moved toward the door that led down into the residence.

Risa stared after them, defiance dancing in her heart. "I am good for many more things than bewitching men's hearts," she said, voicing the opinion she dared not utter in front of her father. "After tomorrow I'll prove it."

"I don't think you could bewitch a toad, with your *duck nose!*" Petro cried gleefully. Before she could catch him, he dashed away after their parents, laughing at the top of his lungs.

2

It frustrates us to no end, my liege, to report that we are unable to
replicate the enchantments of the barbarian city, Cassaforte.
A married couple imbibing wine from one of its goblets is likely
to remain faithful until the end of days, and anyone reading from
one of its conjured books—though why anyone should wish to is a
mystery—retains the knowledge permanently.
Even their symbols of monarchy, the Olive Crown and the
Scepter of Thorn, are enchanted in such a way that none but the
true heir can lay hands upon them without dire consequence.
Sire, the people of Cassaforte are devils in human form.

—THE SPY GUSTOPHE WERNER, IN A PRIVATE LETTER TO
BARON FRIEDRICH VAN WIESTEL

Who do you think will grant you their blessing, the Children or the Penitents?" Petro asked. They lay upon the
matted floor of Risa's own chambers, staring out at the night
sky.

"It's the god or the goddess who grants the blessing during the Scrutiny, silly," she said automatically. Every six years,
during the alignment of the two moons with the twin constellations, every child of the Seven and Thirty between the ages of
eleven and sixteen went through the Ritual of Scrutiny. There
they were chosen by the moon goddess to study at the Insula

16

of the Penitents of Lena, or by her brother, the moon god, for education at the Insula of the Children of Muro.

"You know what I mean! Which insula will I end up at?" Petro's question had been on her own mind for some days now. The differences between the two insulas were, as far as she could tell, minimal. What mattered was that her life would be completely new and wide open at either one of them. "Mama and Papa were trained by the goddess' Penitents," Petro continued. "So won't we be blessed by them too?"

"Romeldo and Vesta are just as much their children as we are, and they were both chosen by the god," Risa pointed out. Her older brother and the younger of her two older sisters had been highly studious, one of the defining traits of those chosen to study with the Children of Muro. Their oldest sister Mira, however, had followed in their parents' footsteps; she was selected to join the insula of the Penitents of Lena, where she was now a master glass maker in its workshops. Many of the bright new colors of sheet glass that the caza had been using in its work were Mira's artistic innovations.

From a plate of snacks between them, Petro plucked a cracker spread with fresh honey. "I'm going to miss Fita's cooking."

"I'm going to miss Mama and Papa."

"I'm going to miss my room."

"I'm going to miss my studio," said Risa, thinking of her workroom next to her father's workshop, far away from the furnaces and hot glass workers. "At the insula I'll never have a private workspace until I'm a master craftsman."

"You're going to miss *Emil*," Petro teased, licking honey from his fingers and reaching for another of Fita's crackers.

"I am *not*." Risa kicked her heels up into the air. "I think you'll be chosen by the Penitents," she said at last, popping a nut-stuffed fig into her mouth. "Don't you?"

There was a long pause before Petro spoke again. "If I am, I hope you are too."

"Oh, Petro." Risa felt a sudden rush of affection for her little brother. He was only eleven. Though they often played and teased as equals, at times she knew that the five years between them made her an adult in his eyes. "I hope so too. Just remember, you have family at both insulas. Romeldo and Mira and Vesta love you too."

"But I hardly know them," Petro said in a very small voice. "They were gone when I was little. You've always been here." He reached for the plate.

"That's enough honey for you," she told him, taking it away. "You'll never sleep."

"I think you'll be chosen by the Penitents, too. You're artistic." He gestured to the cabinet in which Risa kept the finest of her own works. The cabinet once displayed the mosaics Divetri children had created during their early training in the glass arts, but of late these had been replaced by a number of beautiful round bowls Risa had created in the Divetri furnaces. Unlike the other objects created in her father's workshop, however, her bowls were not blown from hot glass. Nor were they pieced together bit by bit and held with cement or channeled lead, like the mosaics and windows for which her mother was famous. They were, in fact, altogether different from anything else the Divetri family had produced throughout the centuries. Some had geometric shapes in simple and colorful patterns; others were more complex renderings of glass cut into floral shapes and pieced together before being melted and fused in the furnaces. They were uniquely her own, and Risa was proud of it.

She smiled, now, at her brother. "Do you really think I'm artistic?" When he nodded, she hugged him tightly.

"All you need to do is learn the container enchantments and you'll be a junior craftsman. I've got a lot more to learn than you," he said.

"I want to learn a lot more than container enchantments," Risa said, feeling the excitement build inside her once more. "More than protection enchantments, too."

"But those are the skills the insulas teach glass workers." Petro stretched his mouth wide in a yawn. "Bowls and goblets have container enchantments. Windows have protection enchantments. Even I know that." Given that the natural purpose of a window is to protect people from the elements, Giulia's creations of lead and glass were reinforced with insula-learned enchantments that protected those within the caza from outside harm. No Divetri window had ever been broken or broached since its creation, not by a hammer or crossbow bolt or even one of Petro's many pigskin balls.

"Yes, you're right," Risa acknowledged. "But it's just so *boring!* I can't believe objects can only hold one kind of enchantment, that's all."

"Enchantments only work on an object's primary purpose. That's what Papa says."

Slightly frustrated at not being able to explain what she meant, Risa struggled for words. "Catarre's books are enchanted to aid learning, which is a book's natural function, but if I used a book for, oh, I don't know..."

"To hit me over the head! Then it would be a weapon and you could put a Dioro attack enchantment on it," Petro offered.

"You are so very silly!" She tickled him until he screeched with laughter.

They lay there, side by side, until their quickened breath subsided. "Risa?" Petro's voice was small and quiet. "I'm scared."

"I hope we're chosen together, by the Penitents. If we are, I'll watch over you, I promise," she whispered in his ear. She was rewarded by his tight and sticky embrace. "Now, off to bed. Lena will never bless us if you're snoring on your feet!" Together they rose from the matting and wiped cracker crumbs from their clothing.

"It's the last night we'll be sleeping here," Petro said, just before he left the room.

Risa already knew that. Though she loved the caza and all the people within its walls, she was anxious to begin her new, real life. With hands that were almost shaking from excitement, she opened the doors to her balcony and gazed out.

The scent of night jasmine, blooming on the opposite bank of the western canal, filled her lungs. As she twisted the key that extinguished the wall lantern, she caught a glimpse of herself reflected in one of her bowls. This was the last night she would see herself wearing her own comfortable clothes—a child's clothes. Tomorrow night, she would be wearing the robes of an insula initiate.

After tomorrow, she thought with a glow, everything will be very different.

3

It is a nation of nobodies, this Cassaforte—hopped-up peasants and tradesmen who, for no discernible reason, have assumed the responsibilities of aristocracy while shedding none of the trappings of their less-than-humble beginnings.

—Comte William DeVane, **Travels Sundry & Wide Beyond the Azurite Channel**

The yawn that Risa let loose threatened to split her head wide open. So gaping was it that she wouldn't have been surprised if someone had attempted to chuck pistachios inside (as children would be doing with oversized Pulcinella heads at the street fairs later that day). "What time is it?" she asked, as Fita pulled and prodded her down the stairs outside their residence.

"Five o'clock." The housekeeper was as grim at this early hour as at any other, Risa noticed.

"In the *morning?*"

"The kitchen maids are awake and at work much earlier

than this," Fita informed her charge, with another poke at her spine.

Risa was barely able to see the steps. The housekeeper had yanked her out of bed without any ceremony whatsoever—no sweet rolls, no early morning hot milk spiced with kaffè, not even enough time to wash her face, comb her hair, or make a quick use of the chamber pot. "I'm not a kitchen maid, though."

It was, as usual, completely the wrong thing to say. "That the day should come when a cazarrina should tell me to my face that she's better than me!" clucked Fita, fussing and fretting over Risa's nightgown as they descended.

"That's not what I—! No, never mind." Risa decided that mustering an argument would take too much effort. The sheer sensation of her bare feet slapping against the stone was jarring her awake, bit by bit. Though the early morning sky was still the color of cobalt, it was light enough that Risa could see a few of the workshop laborers carrying tightly bound bundles of wood to the furnaces. Smoke from their chimneys drifted toward the skies. The moons that had nestled so closely the night before had now parted ways and were sinking into the horizon, disappearing beyond the canals and the Azure Sea, sliver by silver sliver.

The kitchen maids might already have been up, but the birds were not. Birds had more sense. "You're right. I'm sorry," Risa mumbled. "I'm no better than a kitchen maid."

"I should say not!" agreed Fita, suddenly grabbing Risa's hand and yanking her from the bottom of the stairs in the direction of the lower bridge. "With your hair flying out every which way, you're more like a scullery wench!"

"You didn't give me any time to comb—!" Again, Risa had to calm herself. She tried a different tack. "Where are we going?"

"The Cazarro and the Cazarrina have summoned you."

"For what purpose?"

"I do not presume to know the business of the Cazarro and the Cazarrina." Fita's lips pressed into a prim and pious line. "But I believe it has to do with receiving the king's blessing."

"The king!" Risa was astonished. King Alessandro had been ill for longer than she could remember. When her brother and sisters had been inducted into the insulas six years ago, and the six years before that, they had received the king's blessing on the day before the ceremony. The Divetris had assumed, however, that given the monarch's infirmity, he wouldn't be making an appearance for Risa and Petro.

She now saw where Fita was leading her. They had trekked to the top of the old stone stairs leading from the end of the lower bridge to the lowest point of Caza Divetri—a wooden dock jutting out into the sea, where tradesmen could deliver the consumables and goods necessary for the workshops and day-to-day functions of the household. Her parents were already down there, wandering about on the dock's broad expanse.

"Risa, my darling, I've told you a hundred times not to run down those steps," her mother called before Risa's feet had even planted themselves on the wood. "You'll dash your brains out."

"She doesn't *have* any brains to dash out." Petro stood with his arms around Giulia, head buried against their mother's velvet gown. His heart wasn't in the jibe, as he was even more sleepy than Risa. Everyone seemed weary and worn at this early hour, Risa noticed. Though Giulia was as lovely as ever in soft maroons and yellows, Risa recognized the gown she wore as one of her morning garments, plush and comfortable and rarely seen outside her bedchambers. Petro had made some kind of effort to put on breeches and a shirt, but the latter was untucked and generous enough to come nearly to his knees.

"I'm too tired to kick you," Risa told her brother, joining him in hugging their mother, more for sheer physical support than affection. "Fita said the king was coming."

"Not the king. The prince."

"Prince Berto?" Risa opened her eyes fully. Some early morning mist remained hovering over the sea. "Really? So we're to have the royal blessing after all?"

"It was a surprise to us," said her mother. From the wry tone to her voice, Risa suddenly realized that Giulia was as inconvenienced as she was.

"Silly woman!" Ero was accustomed to being awake so early. He wore his daily work outfit—a plain shirt, heavy boots, sturdy thick trousers, and a massive gray apron tied multiple times around his substantial middle. "Complaining about a visit from the royal family! Wouldn't you like to see your children begin their education at the insulas with as much good fortune as the gods could shower down upon them?" The tart look that Giulia shot him was apparently reply enough. "I know you don't like Prince Berto…"

"What I don't like," said Giulia, stroking Petro's hair, "is how he keeps everyone in the dark about his father's health. The Buonochios were always very close to Alessandro."

In her confusion and sleepiness, Risa had not noticed that Fredo had come down to the dock with everyone else. Unlike the rest of the family, he was dressed in his holiday best—almost as if he'd gone to bed in his shiniest boots and embroidered surcoat, the bow of his shirt neatly tied around his neck. He stood at its far end, staring out and to the east, where the inkiness of the sky was lessening.

"Cousin! I think I see the barca," Fredo announced, commanding Ero's attention. Her father crossed the dock to look.

Giulia, however, still appeared worried. "Oh, dear." She forced Petro to stand on his own and attempted to smooth down his hair. Spotting a smudge of something, she withdrew a handkerchief from one of her pockets, licked it, and began to wipe off his face. Petro tolerated the attention with half-closed eyes.

When Giulia wheeled on her daughter with the self-moistened handkerchief outstretched, Risa had to put her foot down. "No thank you!" she insisted, backing away with both hands in the air. "I'll fix myself."

"Well, do what you can," said her mother, vaguely.

"Which won't be much," muttered Fita as she finally reached the bottom of the steps and wandered up to them.

The insinuation wasn't lost on Risa. She ran her fingers through her hair and attempted to gather it as neatly as she could in the back. Her nightgown would have to do; though not fancily trimmed or anywhere near as well-made as her more formal dresses, it was at least neat and plain and presentable, in that it covered her from neck to foot. Perhaps she could conceal most of herself behind Petro. The idea sounded good enough to her sleep-fogged brain, so she joined her family as they gathered at the end of the dock.

Fredo had been correct. Though she hadn't seen it before in the darkness, the palace's famous barcinoro was nearing at an astonishing rate. Its base was the length of perhaps ten to twelve gondolas. Unlike an ordinary barca, it had been gilded from its stern to the prow that curved up and out of the water; a fat cherub adorned the ferro projecting from its nose. Even in the dawn's modest beginnings, it seemed to gleam and radiate its way along the shoreline. All but the very back of the boat was covered by a steeply pitched roof, painted in the city's purples and browns. The city's banner flew from a golden standard at the top. Instead of relying on a lone punter, like a gondola, the king's barcinoro moved swiftly forward thanks to the work of twelve oarsmen hidden in the hold, six to each side, whose blades swiveled through the water in perfect unison.

It was so majestic and impressive a sight that the family waited in absolute silence as the vessel neared. The oarsmen changed the motions of their blades without any individual variation or hesitation, as neatly as any mechanical toy. The barcinoro slowed and began to turn in a counter-clockwise motion until it was parallel with the dock. As hypnotic to Risa as the smooth operation was, Petro seemed to find it boring. He let out a loud and noisy yawn.

"Respect your king and country, boy!" Fredo's voice was savage as he reached out to pinch Petro's waist.

Risa's eyebrows furrowed angrily as her brother let out a shrill squeal and accidentally stepped on her toe. "That hurt!" Petro complained.

"It's only the prince," Risa growled at Fredo, instinctively putting her hands around Petro's shoulders. Giulia, too, was trying to comfort her son, shushing him.

"The prince who is to be king when his father is taken by the Brother and Sister."

Risa had her cousin on that point, and she knew it. "Not until the king formally names him his heir. Until then, he is only a prince."

"There is no *only* when it comes to royalty," was Fredo's pious answer. "Any family of the blood deserves the same respect as its head."

Risa stared at him with dislike and wondered if he really was talking about the prince, or about his own position within the caza. "Pinch someone your own size," she warned him, "but not Petro. Not ever again."

Their eyes locked for a moment, both combatants fierce and unyielding. "Cazarra," he at last implored, reaching for the metal box in his pocket. "My nerves..."

"It is *my* nerves that concern me most at this moment, Fredo," said Giulia, bucking up Petro with a gentle caress at the back of his neck. Her lips quirked with displeasure in Ero's direction, for he notoriously declined to participate in any of the family squabbles that involved his cousin.

Perhaps, though, he was too busy watching the barcinoro. Two palace guards were tying it to the dock, while another two hoisted out a ramp of burnished bronze to form a sturdy bridge between dock and vessel. The barcinoro's surface was intricately etched, but Risa was too dazzled by the proximity of the golden boat to pick out the details. Then one of the palace guards, in his deep red uniform and long cape, stood forth from the others, cleared his throat, and declaimed, "Prince Berto, son of Alessandro, requests an audience with the family Divetri, of the Seven, on this most auspicious day."

In return, Ero bowed his head and replied, "My family would be humbled to enjoy an audience with the prince."

That, apparently, was their cue. The guards who had erected the ramp stepped aside, arms outstretched, to welcome them aboard the barcinoro. Ero and Giulia went first. The guards held Risa and Petro's hands when it was their turn. Risa was secretly happy that when Cousin Fredo tried to follow, the guard on the dock held up a hand. Fredo was not allowed on the golden barcinoro; like Fita, he would have to watch from the dock. As she boarded, Risa resisted the temptation to smirk in his direction, and instead turned toward the boat's covered bulk and waited for what was to follow.

Fortunately, they did not have to wait long. The deep purple curtains parted, their gold fringe drifting across the smooth planks of the boat.

"Bow," Ero instructed, quietly. Giulia's hands, resting upon her shoulder, pressured Risa down into a low curtsey. With her head inclined, Risa saw first one black boot, and then another, which quickly disappeared as Prince Berto's ceremonial robes were lowered over them. Pools of embroidered brown velvet puddled around the man's ankles as he came to a stop.

"Rise, family Divetri." Prince Berto's voice was not as deep as Risa had imagined it would be. Nor was it as commanding or, well, royal. To her ears, his nasal intonation sounded much like one of the quarrelsome merchants who made Fita's life an annoyance trying to wring extra lundri for a shipment of lemons. "Cazarro, I trust our visit did not incommode you all."

"Not at all, Your Eminence." Ero bowed once again.

"I would so dislike inconveniencing so prominent a family of the Seven." Now that she was upright again, Risa could see what the prince looked like. His nose was sharp and almost too large for his features; his brow was high and projected at a slant. There seemed to be almost no spare flesh on that face, so close was the bone beneath the skin. "But the illness of my father the king has prevented me from attending to many of my lesser, though not unimportant, duties." The hollow caverns around his eyes made them look almost ghostly, or as if he were the one who was sick.

"How fares your father?" asked Ero. Giulia tilted her head with interest.

The prince brought together the massive sleeves of his robes. For the first time, Risa noticed that they completely covered his hands. In fact, in those massive brown robes of state, Prince Berto looked a little like a scarecrow—a tiny, shriveled, apple-doll head stuck atop a farmer's voluminous festival garb. Did he even have hands? There was no evidence for it.

"Sadly, I fear he is coming to the end of his days," Berto said to Ero. His doll-head dangled forward for a moment, then rose again. "He allows only me to attend upon him, and refuses all others. As you can imagine," he continued, addressing Risa's mother, "it's so very tiring." Giulia murmured with appreciation. "What a lovely caza you keep, Cazarra," he remarked again.

"Why, thank you, Your Eminence." Giulia curtseyed prettily once more. Risa, however, was studying Prince Berto. His unearthly eyes, dark as polished obsidian and glittering even more brightly, were looking not at her mother but at the caza above, as the slowly rising sun illuminated its walls and structures. His eyes seemed to dart from the workshop chimneys belching out their smoke, to the warm glow of the kitchen windows, to the stairs leading into the main residence, all plainly visible beyond the courtyard at the end of the lower bridge. Strangely, Risa thought she could see greed in that glance, almost as if he wanted to reach out with his hands—if he actually had hands beneath those billowing sleeves—and grab the buildings, then stow them away in the hold of his golden barcinoro.

Then his dark eyes met hers. Risa froze, suddenly aware of how intently she'd been staring at him. She felt like a mouse scavenging the storerooms, suddenly confronted by the hungry kitchen cat.

To Prince Berto, though, she was apparently nothing. He'd barely noticed her. His eyes flicked away and softened as his eyelids lowered. "Let us attend to business then, shall we?" He gestured for Risa and Petro to approach.

"Kneel down before the prince," Giulia prompted, obviously pleased with their demure behavior so far.

Both Risa and her brother dropped to their knees, preparing to receive the blessing. Risa felt as if she were being smothered in velvet when the prince laid his hands upon her head, but at last he stepped aside. The purple curtains parted again, and one of the palace priests stepped from inside the enclosure. While the circlet around the supplicant's head was more elaborate than the circlets of the ordinary, insula-trained priests, his blessing was definitely of the ordinary—the almost generic, mumbled sort. He seemed sleepier than anyone else.

In fact, the blessing was over so quickly that Risa was almost surprised that the prince had bothered at all. Fita lingered longer over breakfast prayers. Scarcely had their knees touched the deck than it seemed that the priest was urging them to stand once again, and the guards began ushering them all back over the shining bronze ramp onto the dock. "It has been a pleasure," intoned the prince, "to see the family Divetri on the dawn of this special day."

"The pleasure has been all ours, One Most High." Cousin Fredo, reunited with the family, acted as if he'd been with them all along. "A most grand pleasure indeed."

One of the guards undid the knot in the barcinoro's rope. "A thousand gratitudes for your visit, Your Eminence," said Ero. Risa might have been mistaken, but she could have sworn that her father's face was as puzzled as her own at the brusqueness of their treatment. "Perhaps we will meet again soon."

The prince's only reply was a smile. Tense and noncommittal, it seemed. Once again, however, his eyes seemed to gallop over the landscape of the caza, devouring the sight hungrily. Still holding his sleeves firmly together, he stepped back behind the curtains. A guard shouted a command. As one, the twelve invisible oarsmen dipped their blades into the water and the vessel slid away, propelling itself in the direction of Caza Catarre.

"Well!" said Giulia, once the barcinoro was out of earshot. "The cheek!"

"Now, love," said Ero, already calming the tempest he knew was coming.

"I'm surprised he came at all, since he couldn't be bothered to give the children a blessing himself!"

"The prince is a busy man," said Cousin Fredo, watching the Barcinoro disappear to the southwest.

"He does have other cazas to visit," Ero added, still trying to placate his wife. He ruffled Risa's already messy hair. "Ours are not the only children receiving a scrutiny today. What did you think of the prince, little lionkit?"

Cousin Fredo sighed, his shoulders slumped. "A fine man, didn't you think?"

No. Risa didn't think that at all. "He was interesting," she admitted.

For a moment she thought about sharing her uneasy feelings, but she was distracted by the sight of her brother. He had pulled up the collar of his shirt until it covered his mouth and nose, and pulled his hands inside the cuffs. All she could see of him were his ears, bulging eyes, and hair. "Risa, look!" he said from underneath the fabric. "I'm Prince Berto!"

Risa's special day might have started hours earlier than she'd intended, but now that it was here, she couldn't help but be excited. Her mouth twitched at her brother's clowning, and then she laughed. "For the love of Lena, don't let Fredo see you!" she warned him, scampering in his direction.

Poor Cousin Fredo, still peering after the golden vessel. He seemed to be the only Divetri who had truly appreciated the royal visit.

ϙ

—

As every object has its intended purpose, let the sons and daughters
of the Seven and Thirty discover the purposes for which they were
born within the walls of two insulas. Whether they learn the trades
of their families, achieve scholarship, or pursue monastic lives, the
end result will be civil stability and a blossoming of the arts.

—ALLYRIA CASSAMAGI TO KING NIVOLO OF
CASSAFORTE, FROM A PRIVATE LETTER IN THE
CASSAMAGI ARCHIVES

க

Blue and green banners flew from every window of Caza
Divetri later that day. Leaning over the rail of her chamber balcony, Risa watched as servants decorated the tops of
the canal walls with bunting. Gaily arrayed were the servant
docks below, where bobbed a dozen gondolas. The day even
smelled festive. From the kitchens wafted so many fragrances
that it was difficult to identify one before it was replaced by
another. Duck. Roast pork. Red snapper baked in lemon
juice, its insides stuffed with sliced roast apples. Crushed
olives. A fruit tart. Baked custards. A hundred delicacies for
the feast to be served after the Scrutiny.

If she leaned out and peered around the corner, Risa could see Caza Divetri's two bridges to the mainland. The higher one was the grander of the two; it stretched from a piazza in Cassaforte to the gracious formal courtyard of the caza. The lower bridge was usually used by merchants and craftsmen, for it traveled more directly to the stable yard. Bell-arrayed vendors marched along the bridges and canal walls selling pomegranates and sugared apples, or comic broadsides printed with songs and poems.

Everywhere Risa looked, she saw that the capital city had donned its finest for the Festival of the Two Moons. Caza Catarre flew their red and green family colors as well as the purple and brown banners of the city. From the windows of the less wealthy homes and tiny shops that lined the canals and streets flew colorful streamers and paper flags. The Sorrendi family had gone to elaborate extremes for the occasion, arranging enormous displays of summer flora in boxes hanging from each window. The Sorrendis were of the Thirty—the most elite families in all of Cassaforte, save for the Seven of the Cazas—and thus were allowed to display the family arms above their door. Even now, Sorrendi servants hung out of an upper-story window, polishing the impressive brass crest. When the midday sun streamed into the piazza, it would shine proudly.

A servant squawked, pressing herself against the wall as Risa dashed down the stairs into the pillared room where the family was eating a late breakfast. Her feet slapped over the cool black and white marble. "It's here!" she sang at the top of her lungs. The wild animal inside her burst free of confinement, and she leapt with joy alongside it. "It's finally here!" she cried.

Her mother, who was laughing as she used a tiny spoon to put grape pits on a flat glass plate, held out an arm. "Restrain yourself, my love. We have company."

Not the prince again, surely. Whirling, Risa found herself facing a large, handsome stranger wearing a silvery helmet. He grinned at her. "Romeldo!" she yelled, as the man's features resolved into familiarity.

"By Muro, is that little Risa?" her oldest brother exclaimed. "Bare feet and all?"

With sudden self-consciousness, Risa looked down at her uncovered feet and legs. Only when he began to chuckle did she realize he was joking. Relaxed once more, she launched herself at him with a mighty hug, knocking her brow against his ceremonial headdress. "What are you doing here?"

Romeldo had been chosen by the moon god twelve years before, when he was fifteen. Though he still lived at the insula, soon he would be coming back to the caza daily to begin assuming his duties as heir. Risa had only been four years old when he left. She scarcely remembered a time when her brother had not worn the yellow robes of the Children of Muro.

"Why, I'm to scrutinize my brother. And you as well, you imp," Romeldo answered her. "It would be a neat trick if Mira is the scrutineer for the Penitents, this festival. Is she coming?"

"She will be here, but not to scrutinize." Ero bit into his toasted bread. "One of the Settecordi family will be performing the ritual."

"Renaldo Settecordi of the upper Thirty? I know him."

Ero snapped his fingers. "The very one."

Romeldo wrinkled his nose at Risa. "We had a rivalry at bocce. Of course, I won. Why are you still here, devil girl? Shouldn't you be busy dressing in your festival finery, Lady Barefoot Nightgown?"

Risa grinned at her new title. "But I've barely seen you!"

"You'll see plenty of me at the feast. And don't you *dare* make me laugh during the ceremony, young miss!" Romeldo winked at her. He reminded Risa of Ero in so many ways, from the long red-brown curls covering his head to his broad shoulders and confident nature. "What news is there of the king?" he asked his mother.

"I'm fashioning a new window for one of his chambers," Giulia said, sweeping her long dark hair back over her shoulder. "But though I've been given the dimensions, I've not been allowed in the room to see where it's to go."

"It has been over a year since anyone has seen King Alessandro!" Ero shook his head.

"We saw the prince this morning," Risa told Romeldo. He looked at her with surprise.

"For the blessing. He was not very forthcoming with details of his father's health." Giulia sniffed, obviously still put out by their abrupt treatment earlier that morning.

Risa reached up to her brother's head to adjust the headdress she'd made crooked. Romeldo spared her a friendly grin and fixed it himself before returning to the conversation at hand. "He has ailed for too long! Can no physicians heal him?"

"Not if he refuses to see them," said Giulia. "Or if the prince refuses to admit them."

"Now, Giulia." Ero might have been trying to shush his wife before her speculations grew out of hand, but Risa privately agreed with her mother. The prince did seem shifty. "The Olive Crown has granted Alessandro a long and prosperous life. It may be that he is simply ready to step into Muro's chariot and join his forefathers on the plains of the ascended. Now, child," he added to Risa, "run along, lest someone suspect you of trying to sway the opinion of our scrutineer."

"Only Cousin Fredo would suspect that," said Risa, not bothering to hide her scorn.

Her father's smile faded. "Our cousin is a good man. It's not his fault my uncle's ill-chosen marriage caused Fredo to be born outside the Seven and Thirty. He is still a competent craftsman and a Divetri, and as such demands your respect."

Her mother looked at the fruits on her plate. Romeldo averted his eyes to gaze through the pillars at the fountain splashing quietly in the sunlight. With a certainty she dared not speak, Risa knew they did not share her father's high opinion of nerve-wracked Fredo. Still, she lowered her head. "I'm sorry, Papa," she growled, trying to sound as if she actually meant the apology.

A sigh escaped from Ero's lips. "When you were born, I thought I would have my little girl forever." He gave her an impulsive hug that squeezed the breath from her. "Today is the day I lose you, little lionkit. You'll forget all about us once you're gone, I warrant."

All her excitement of the last week and all the anticipation for her new life could never erase the knowledge that she was leaving her parents. "You'll never lose me," she promised in a whisper. Moisture began to wick at the corners of her eyes. "Not ever. I'll make you proud, I swear. I'll always be a Divetri."

5

The savages of the desert sands south of the sea have their Madrasahs, the Vereinigteländer their guilds, the people of Cassaforte their insulas, and civilized countries their collegium and universitas, yet these all occupy themselves with one purpose: the betterment and education of otherwise idle youth.

—CELESTINE DU BARBARAY, TRADITIONS &
VAGARIES OF THE AZURE COAST: A GUIDE FOR
THE HARDY TRAVELER

⁊

Gondolas, flagged and flowered, congested the high-walled canals. Standing in the shaded garden room, Risa could see, dancing on the water, the decorated iron ferri that projected up from their sterns. By this hour there were so many people thronging the courtyard that scores of servants and well-wishers were forced to observe from the bobbing gondolas.

It was fortunate the garden room was elevated a few steps above the courtyard. Risa and her brother would have been unable to see the ceremony otherwise. Between them and the courtyard's center stood hundreds of elaborately coiffed women in their summer finery and men wearing brocade and velvet caps. Risa's memory of the last Scrutiny, years before, was little more than a blur of excitement and a vague memory of sitting on a window ledge and trying to see past all those colorful hats. The notion that she and Petro were now to be the center of attention turned her stomach to butterflies. Had her older brother and sisters felt the same way, peering through the window on their special day? Her father? Generations of Divetris before her had occupied this garden room on ceremony days, Risa realized. No doubt they had felt the very same pangs as she did. As comforting a thought as that should have been, it didn't at all quell her nervous excitement.

Petro was already standing on tiptoe, and would have climbed on a chair to see better had Risa not restrained him. Though none of the crowd knew they were in the garden room, she did not wish to run the risk of anyone spotting them before the appropriate moment.

"Your tunic is undone," she said, kneeling down to fix it.

"It isn't. I hooked every other button!" Petro replied. "No one will notice if the rest aren't done."

She finished fastening the rest of his buttons and smoothed down the plain black tunic. "*I* noticed," she said. "You look very handsome, though." She gathered back Petro's curls where they spilled from under his black cap. She was clad in black herself—in a gown, no less. Her aversion to gowns was well known in the caza; she preferred to work and play in simple leggings and a loose over-tunic. Her hair was usually restrained only for hot glass work, when she kept it collected in a net-like reta that fit snugly over the back of her head.

But today, her mane was woven with ribbons and taped into a complex coil at the back of her neck. When she had glimpsed her reflection in a mirror, an hour before, she'd barely recognized herself. Even with her snubbed nose and the slightly protruding upper lip she fancied made her look duck-like, when richly dressed and arrayed she looked almost like the subject of a Buonochio painting. This realization had actually made her look twice, pleased with the effect.

Petro's attention, however, was fixed upon two priests facing each other. Their arms were now raised to the sky, where the sun blazed at its highest point. "This is the day," Romeldo was intoning, "on which the chariot of Muro comes to rest in the Stable of Silver, before he again undertakes his journey of six years." Romeldo had lowered the faceplate of his helmet for this portion of the ceremony, and the mask of Muro, the god of the larger moon, smiled fixedly at the crowd.

Like Romeldo, Renaldo Settecordi wore a helmet that covered his face. Its faceplate had been molded in the familiar smiling face of Lena, the goddess of the smaller moon. "This is the day on which the chariot of Lena comes to rest in the Stable of Gold," he echoed Romeldo, "before she again undertakes her journey of six years."

The crowd gasped as the two priests thrust their ceremonial staffs to the sky. With an immense bang, which prompted Petro to cover his ears, sparkling fire shot from them and exploded over the crowd. Above the courtyard, visible despite the blinding midday sun, two spheres of golden fire hovered one above the other. The sparks formed constellations, surrounding them. Within an instant the glittering sparkles disappeared, though their brightness still lingered on Risa's eyes. Tiny particles of soot drifted onto the crowd. The shock of the sudden sound faded, but from across the city Risa still heard the retorts from other courtyards. It reminded her that in every household of the Seven and Thirty where lived a child between the ages of eleven and sixteen, the Scrutiny was even now taking place. She and Petro would be meeting the chosen others that night, in one or the other of the insulas.

Relieved laughter rippled through the crowd. A smattering of applause for the fireworks sounded from the gondolas, echoing between the canal walls. Risa considered wiping her sweaty palms on her gown, but decided against it. Why in the names of both moons did ritual dictate she had to wear a black gown at noon on a warm summer's day? It would be worse when they stepped into the sun.

With the hems of their long robes drifting around their feet, the two masked and helmeted figures—the Child and the Penitent—turned in the direction of the rest of her family, who stood the head of the courtyard,

"Who submits their children for the scrutiny of Lena?"

"Who submits their children for the scrutiny of Muro?"

"I—Ero, Cazarro of Divetri—ask that my children undergo the scrutiny of Muro. May he look into their hearts and choose them, should it be his will." Risa's heart raced as her father stood and spoke the words. Like the scrutineers, he wore a long and old-fashioned houppelande that stretched to his ankles. The turban of woven multicolored silks that enveloped his head made his beard look all the more stark against his face.

Equally beautiful was her mother as she stepped forward.

Giulia's hair, shining in the sun like ebony captured in silk cords, cascaded down the back of her patterned green gown. Sleeves of royal blue, embroidered with metallic thread, accented the gold circlet around her brow, from the center of which hung a single opal. "I, Giulia, Cazarra of Divetri, ask that my children undergo the scrutiny of Lena. May she look into their hearts and choose them, should she so will."

The two priests bowed first to her parents, and then to each other. Risa's breath quickened as her mother and father returned to their seats. Behind them stood her sisters: Vesta, wearing the robes of the Children, clasped her mother's shoulder in excitement, while Mira stood to the side, smiling as serenely as the goddess in whose name she had been chosen. Risa could not see Romeldo's face through his mask, but of course he too was present. Over the pounding of her heart, it struck Risa that they were together as a family—all the Divetris. She couldn't remember the last time she had seen all her siblings at once.

In a cluster nearby were the chief craftsmen: friendly Mattio, smiling as broadly as if she and Petro were his own children; Cousin Fredo, the tip of his finger rubbing *tabbaco da fiuto* into his gums, his surcoat piously arrayed with religious medallions; Emil, still dressed in his work clothes and squinting at the crowds in a bewildered manner. All the craftsmen and servants were part of the extended Divetri family as well—she was glad they were there for the proudest moment of her life.

"Once every six years, when the chariots of the gods come to rest, we their representatives travel through the houses of the Seven and Thirty to bestow their promised blessings upon the children therein." Renaldo Settecordi's voice, strong and clear, could have carried through the babble of any crowd; before this silent assembly, it seemed to thunder. "By the light of day, they shall be scrutinized. Tonight, bathed in the light of the moons, they shall be received into the company of the insulas, to continue their education and training."

Romeldo's voice, lighter yet equally as penetrating, could probably be heard from one end of the upper bridge to the other. "Let the children come forth. Let them be seen and judged." He removed his helmet and shook out his curls, while Renaldo did the same.

"Don't be afraid." Risa squeezed Petro's hand, aware of the irony that she'd never been so frightened in her life.

When the priests strode toward the garden room doors, the crowd parted silently. Risa pulled her brother back a few steps just as they reached the doors and pushed them open. The children stood there for a moment, framed in the entry-way. Hundreds of eyes stared in their direction. Even as the priests strode back to the courtyard's center, chanting, the crowd's full attention lay upon the two Divetris.

Risa suddenly panicked. What was she doing here? She loved the caza! Why did she have to leave? Why had she thought the ceremony would be exciting? It was exactly as she'd pictured it for years, but never once had she imagined how insistently her heart would be pounding, or how timid she'd become at this last moment. Only Petro's tug caused her feet to stumble into motion. She remembered herself. Though her jaw trembled with fear, she gathered the skirts of her gown with her free hand and walked through the doors.

Smells assailed her nostrils. A hundred perfumes barely concealed the heavy, rank odors of sweat and garlic from the crowd. There was the musk of hair pomades, the sharpness of clove powder that sweetened the breath. Brother and sister pushed through the aroma, taking step after step across the terra-cotta tiles until at last they were in the clear space at the courtyard's center. Everyone smiled at them. Risa knew that no matter what direction she turned, she would see face after smiling face for as far as the eye could see. She kept her eyes straight ahead until at last she and Petro reached their goal.

Renaldo Settecordi swept his arms in a dramatic gesture to keep the crowd at a distance. "Lena, luminous light of the heavens," he cried, raising his arms upward but keeping his face low. "Through my prayer I beseech you to grant me sight, so that I might know your will for these children." After a moment he raised his head and approached on slow-moving feet.

Suppressing a gasp, Risa immediately noticed his eyes. A film covered his pupils, giving him the appearance of an elderly man afflicted with cataracts. Still, he moved with purpose and deliberation in their direction. He placed one hand atop the other and held them inches above Petro's head. Her younger brother stared solemnly at the ground, his face a pasty white. Although she was trying not to gawk, Risa glanced up again at the priest. His lips moved in prayer for a few moments as he shut his eyelids. He fell silent.

It was as if he had heard an answer that was audible only to his ears. His eyes opened once more to look down upon her brother. They were no longer distant and alien, but very much unclouded and his own. With cupped fingers he lifted Petro's chin, and then kissed his hands in the traditional manner as he murmured a prayer. "Bless you, child," he said, keeping his voice neutral. The smile he wore, however, was genuine. He seemed to gaze upon her brother with affection. Risa would have been willing to wager the entire caza and her family's fortune that Petro had been chosen by the Penitents of Lena.

The priest's eyes glazed again as he moved in front of Risa. She lowered her head and tried not to think of the mass of people focusing all their attention upon her. On the top of her scalp she felt heat from the Penitent's palms as they hovered inches above. Just as he had with Petro, he murmured a private prayer to the goddess.

"Bless you, child," he said, raising up her chin at last. Though his smile was kind as he kissed her hands and murmured the prayer of blessing, his face wore an expression different than it had for her brother. *Oh Petro*, she thought to herself, suddenly understanding. *You've been chosen by the goddess and I'll be chosen by the god. I won't be able to go with you.*

Once the Penitent had stepped back, Romeldo swung out his arms and lowered his head. "Muro, giver of joy, I beseech you to bring me wisdom, so that I may choose wisely for you."

His eyes as unfamiliar and clouded as Renaldo's had been, Romeldo prayed over Petro. "Bless you, child," he finished. His expression was fond as he kissed his younger brother's fingers, but it held no special joy.

Risa was now all the more certain that she and Petro would find themselves, at the end of the day, in different new homes. She would return to the Insula of the Children of Muro with her brother. Perhaps tomorrow she would find herself working side by side with Vesta, who was only four years her senior. At the very last moment, as Romeldo's crossed palms hovered over her, she remembered she was supposed to be humbly looking downward. She jerked her neck toward the ground.

She waited for what seemed a very long time. "Bless you, child," she heard at last.

Risa looked up into her older brother's eyes, surprised at what she saw. He was puzzled. For a long moment he held her chin, his brows furrowed as if he didn't recognize her. Then he stepped backward.

It was time for the announcements. The crowd suppressed all noise to hear. "The Goddess Lena has chosen the Cazarrino Petro as one of her own," thundered Renaldo Settecordi. "Let him advance and take his place among her Penitents!"

A roar of cheering and applause erupted from the crowd. Risa's vision clouded slightly with tears at the sight of her brother's face. He looked as if he might be violently sick all over the courtyard, but at the sound of the Penitent's proclamation he breathed deeply, shuddered a little, and then stumbled forward. A wan smile tickled his lips as he realized more fully that he had been chosen. Finally he grinned, in real relief. Had he thought he would be unclaimed? No child of the Seven and Thirty had ever been denied the insulas.

Mira had stepped out, lifting high a turquoise banner behind Renaldo, who rested a paternal hand on Petro's shoulders. Showers of daisies filled the air as the crowd tossed handfuls of petals at the newly chosen one. As he crossed the courtyard, Petro peered through the cascade of white and waved at her, his little hat askew. Risa thought he looked genuinely happy for the first time that day.

After a moment of celebration, the crowd grew quiet once more, anticipating another announcement. Renaldo stepped back, gesturing for Romeldo to speak.

Romeldo, however, merely nodded back. His face was blank and expectant. After a long moment, he held out a hand toward Renaldo, as if indicating that he should continue. The other scrutineer seemed startled. There was a long pause as the two stared at each other. Romeldo still made no move to claim Risa for the god.

At last, obviously confused, the two stepped forward and began to whisper. Renaldo shook his head violently when Romeldo pointed in Risa's direction. The crowd began to murmur with surprise at the break from traditional ritual. Ero shifted in his seat, alert.

Risa grew more unsettled with every second of suspense. Behind the banner, Mira's face was as perplexed as her own. The smells of heavy perfume and sweat from the crowd seemed even more overpowering than before; bodies pressed in close on every side, obscuring her view of her parents. All Risa could see were strangers shaking her heads while looking directly at her. She must have done something wrong, though she couldn't remember having taken a step out of place or spoken when she shouldn't. The uncertainty felt like it would kill her if it lasted much longer.

Why did Romeldo delay? After a few more moments, the conversation between the scrutineers came to a conclusion. They both seemed dissatisfied with the other. With great apprehension, Risa watched as her brother at last walked in her direction. The same puzzled look colored his expression, but there was something else as well: pity.

He pitied her. Why?

With bended knees, Romeldo lowered himself down to bring his mouth to her ear. His breath tickled at her skin. "Sister," he whispered, clasping her shoulders. "This is ... difficult for me to tell you. I cannot believe it myself."

"What's wrong?" she asked. Fear choked her throat. She could not imagine what could be causing him to say these words.

He sighed, steeling himself to deliver the news. "You are unchosen."

Despite the heat and the heaviness of her gown, Risa felt icy cold at his words. "What?"

"You have not been chosen," he repeated. When she tried to wrestle free of his grasp, he held her more tightly. "Don't make a scene," he warned.

Her voice, when it came, was cracked with emotion. "Unchosen? No!"

"I am so sorry ... "

"What did I do *wrong?*" This nightmare was impossible. It couldn't be happening. No one was unchosen. Never. It was unheard of. She had spent her entire life waiting for this ceremony; she had imagined this hour the way some girls dreamed of their weddings. It was supposed to be the most perfect, happiest day of her life—a *when*, not an *if*.

Her brother's mouth still pressed against her ear. "You've done nothing wrong, little sparrow. Nothing. The gods have their reasons to—"

"Romeldo," she whispered, ashamed at the desperation in her voice. "Go back and tell them Muro chose me. You can just *tell* them. It doesn't even have to be true." With every word she willed him to obey.

"I cannot."

"You're my *brother!*" she cried, more loudly than she intended. Her throat was tight with pressure. "Please!"

"Risa, I cannot. It doesn't work that way. My vows—"

"This isn't happening!"

Ero and Giulia had hastened over to them as they talked, expressions of concern and bewilderment on their faces. In the distance, echoing over the canal waters and through the streets, Risa could hear sounds of cheering from nearby parts of the city. Other families were celebrating. Their own court-yard was deadly silent. Risa scanned the faces nearby. So many were familiar—servants, distant relatives, neighbors, family friends. They had all come to see her elevated. Instead, they were witnessing her humiliation.

"What's wrong?" asked Ero in a hushed voice.

"She has not been chosen." The words seemed to echo across the silent courtyard.

"That doesn't happen," Ero countered. His face was pale. "It's never happened. Every child of the Seven and Thirty has always been welcomed at the insulas."

Romeldo cleared his throat and straightened up. "Please, sir. Don't make this any more difficult—"

"Is this a joke? You must be mistaken!" So hoarse and angry were Ero's words that Giulia clutched his arm. "Pray again. Pray again! Or you are no son of mine."

Romeldo raised an eyebrow. "The gods do not trifle with their priests, Cazarro," he said, emphasizing Ero's title to drive home his graveness. "Settecordi and I received the same response to our prayers. Both the god and his sister spoke to us to say the child is not needed at their insulas."

During the argument, Risa's tears had begun to flow. She realized her face was red and blotched, and that the tears would puddle on her gown and cause the silks to pucker. She knew that weeping so publicly disgraced her family. Yet she felt as if Muro and Lena had reached down from the heavens to tear her still-beating heart from her chest. How could they be so cruel to her at what was to have been her proudest moment? What had she ever done to them? It was unjust—worse, it was vicious.

"If the gods don't need me," she shouted, savagely clawing at the tapes woven in her hair, "then I don't need the gods!"

"Risa!" Romeldo looked thunderstruck.

As she ran into the residence, shoving with tear-blind eyes through the crowd, she heard her father's sad and heavy voice behind her. "Let her go," he said. "Just ... let her go."

Ribbons and loose hair fluttered behind her in her flight. Let the people gawk! She didn't care if they saw her tears. No humiliation was worse than the sadness in her father's voice when he had spoken those dismissive words: *Let her go*. She had failed him badly. She had failed the family and its name.

Through the dining hall she ran, nearly colliding into immense tables laden with all manner of succulents. The Divetris and their friends would feast later to celebrate Petro. It was to have been her banquet too—had the gods wanted her.

They did not. If even the gods turned their faces away, then she was not needed or wanted by anyone. She was a freak. An embarrassment.

Through grand hall and vestibule her quick feet took her, up stairs that never seemed to end, then through hallway after hallway until at last she reached the safety of her own chambers. She thought slamming the door would give her satisfaction. It did not. Once it was latched tight, she sank to the floor and once more began to cry. Her face and gown were already soaked with salty tears. Moisture flowed from her nostrils. She did not bother to wipe her face.

"Risa?" A soft knock sounded on her door a few minutes later. Giulia's voice, muffled, came through the wood. "Risa? My darling..."

She did not answer. For long minutes she sat there, face buried in her skirts, scarcely daring to breathe. At last she heard her mother's slippered feet gliding away. She would never answer, no matter how hard they knocked. No consolation could soothe her heartbreak. Nothing could erase the echo of her father's disappointed words: *Let her go.*

6

*You wish to disagree with the King? Then stand up on the
Petitioner's Stair and make your case without rancor. Do not
choose the path you propose! The rite of fealty must be completed
without hesitation or regret! If you do not ... well, remember the
fate of Caza Legnoli, my brother, and tremble.*

—Arnoldo Piratimare, in a letter to the Cazarro Humberto
Piratimare (from the Cassamagi Historical Archives)

At the back of the caza grounds, near the sea wall, the
furnaces of the Divetri workshop blazed. Every day
they were fed bundles of densely bound wood, enchanted
by the Cassamagi to blaze with a blinding white flame. The
great ovens were ventilated in a method that produced an
even, smokeless heat while maintaining a steady temperature.
Many of the workshop's large blown vessels had to remain in
the furnaces for a day or two at a time. If they did not cool at
a slow and predictable rate, they ran a risk of shattering.

Risa's own bowl had remained in the furnaces for over a
day and a half. Every few hours she'd moved the foot-wide

ceramic mold in which it rested farther and farther away from the heart of the annealing kilns, until finally it was cool enough to slide off the smooth stone shelf. With a swift motion, she picked up her work. The glass bowl warmed her hands instantly, but did not burn them. She blew off the powdered sand separating the glass from the mold, then looked into the reflective surface.

It was beautiful. Plucking a creation from the heat always reminded Risa of the mid-winter Feast of Oranges, the celebration when once a year, children would wake up in the morning and find their blankets littered with fruits and candies and small gifts. Parents told the very young that the trinkets had been left there by an orange tree that sprang up at the foot of their bed while they were asleep, then withered overnight. Risa had outgrown the Feast of Oranges even before she was Petro's age, but whenever she removed one of her works from the furnace, she had that same itch of anticipation—the desire to see if she would be well rewarded.

Today she had been. Despite the layer of powder and some smudges left by her own fingers, this bowl was among her very best. With some of Mira's own cobalt blue glass as a base, Risa had cut two layers of varying softly curved waves and fit them together in an undulating pattern that soothed her senses. Caught beneath a cap of melted clear glass, the bowl looked as if it had been held under the waters of the Azure Sea itself and, when lifted out, captured its gentle inland waves.

The warm summer air cooled the bowl as she carried it through her father's extensive workroom, bent on returning to her own tiny studio. For the past week, Risa had been unusually shy about talking to either of her parents. She had not emerged from her bedchambers until hunger forced her down to the kitchens a full day and a half after her disgrace. With every step, she had cursed her weakness—she would rather have starved to death than appear in public again. Fita had taken one look at her stained and tear-streaked face and sat her down and fed her plate after plate of food. It was probably left over from Petro's banquet, but Risa did not pay that any heed.

At every opportunity she told herself she did not care that the gods had rejected her. The truth, though, was that it bothered her like a toothache, always throbbing with a dull pain. She thought of the rejection every time she saw the gods' visages smiling down at her from the steles decorating the caza, or with every servant's oath that invoked their names. She thought of it when she looked out upon the city and saw tattered decorations from the Feast of the Two Moons flying from gondolas or floating in the canals. Most of all, she thought about it during lonely, quiet moments when she missed her younger brother and wondered what he was doing.

After her self-imposed exile, her parents were cordial and kind. If anything, they seemed determined to pretend nothing at all out of the ordinary had taken place. They carried on around her just as they had on previous days, talking about their work and gossiping about other families within the Seven and Thirty. Of Petro they made no mention, nor did they discuss the Scrutiny. Save for the fact that she alone was left at home, it was almost as if that day had never happened.

With every hour's toll of the bells in the Palace Square,

however, Risa knew that it had happened. She tried not to imagine her parents' conversations when she was not around—whispered dialogues about how proud they were of their other children, shushed admissions that Risa had been their one disappointment. She tried to banish these thoughts into a cupboard in her mind, muffling them with denial and slamming shut the cupboard doors. Too often, however, they crept through the cracks to haunt her.

"You're looking well today, Cazarrina," said Mattio as she scurried by. The large, gentle man stood up to greet her from over the cullet bucket full of crushed glass. It was too late to pretend she hadn't heard him. Mattio was her favorite craftsman; he had always played with her and encouraged her to develop her skills. Her father had taught her how to cut glass with a diamond-tipped stylus, but it was Mattio who had made her practice over and over again until she could cut even complex curves without flares or accidental breaks. It had been Mattio who taught her how to keep an eye on hot glass to gauge its temperature, and how to make certain that different colors of glass would bond with each other. From Mattio she had received her first lessons in glass blowing. He always praised what he found right with her creations and pointed out what could be improved.

"Is that a new bowl?" he was asking now. "Might I look?"

Shyly, she handed it to him. He ran his fingers around the piece's edge. "Very smooth and even." He nodded, impressed. "Very few visible bubbles." Grasping the bowl by the rim, he held it up to the sunlight streaming through the workshop door. "Beautiful colors. You've done well, Cazarrina!"

Risa flushed with pride at his praise. But it was an unaccustomed sensation, feeling good. While gratification should have flooded through her like a cooling river, now it only sliced like a hot knife, making her more aware how ragged her grief had been during the past few days.

"Cazarro!" cried the craftsman, wheeling about and calling to Ero.

"Mattio, don't," Risa begged. She had been trying to move through the workroom as quickly as possible, before Ero could see her. Her father was the last person she wanted to talk to.

"Come look at what your daughter has done," Mattio called.

Ero looked over from a furnace, pole in hand. At its end glowed a glob of glass. Cousin Fredo reached out to take the pole and nodded for Ero to step away. Her father held up a finger to indicate that he needed a moment more. From a bucket of water, he withdrew a branch, cut from one of the family's olive trees that very morning. Its finger-long, silvery green leaves glistened and dripped as with both hands, Ero raised it into the air. The water prevented the wood and leaves from immediately bursting into flame as he brought the branch close to the white-hot, liquid glass. Then the branch began to steam as Ero used it to trace the signs of the gods in the air, his lips murmuring the prayer that would bless the glass before it took its shape.

Risa felt a tingle of energy in the air as the enchantment took hold. Her father returned the olive branch to its bucket and Fredo plunged the rod back into the furnaces. This rite, this ceremony of creation, should have been her birthright, she realized. It never would be. For the rest of her life she would only stand at arm's length while feeling the enchantment pass into her father's vessels. The realization made her heart even heavier.

Wiping the sweat from his brow, Ero made his way across the workroom. "She has an eye for color, your girl," said Mattio, proffering the piece.

Risa flicked her eyes to the floor as her father scanned it. "Very pretty," he conceded. "Interesting technique." She looked up with hope. He meant what he said, but then he ruined it by adding, "Do you not like traditional glass blowing, little love? You were advancing quickly with the art."

"She is a very good hot glass artist when she wants to be," Mattio replied. "Better than most of our apprentices when they begin. It's in her blood."

"Then I don't understand why she..." Ero paused to rephrase his thought. "You should join us at the furnaces more, Risa."

Risa grew more and more resentful as the pair of them talked. It was obvious that as pretty as her father found her experiments, he thought them a waste of time. She chewed back her anger and said to the floor, "I'll never be like you or Romeldo, Cazarro."

"There's always the window art, like your mother," Ero suggested. "Perhaps if you spent more time with her—"

Risa raised her head and stared at him, her heart now leaden. "I'm sorry to be in your way."

Ero sighed with frustration. More sweat dampened his brow. "Daughter, I have tried to be patient this week. It frustrates me to watch you ignore the Divetri arts—"

"Now, now," chided Mattio, playing peacemaker. "Risa is no stranger to either glass blowing or to the construction of leaded windows."

"Yet she flaunts training and family by turning her back upon them both," Ero suddenly thundered, his temper flaring at Mattio's challenge. "Hundreds upon hundreds of years of Divetri tradition!"

"I want to do something different," Risa explained angrily. Like her father, her temper could erupt without warning. "I want *one* thing that is mine only."

"No one wants *innovation* from Caza Divetri," shouted her father. "Pretty your trinkets may be, but no one will buy them. You waste your time on such oddities. The Seven and Thirty want vessels as we have always made them, blown and shaped by hand and blessed with the traditional enchantments."

"Enchantments I will *never* be able to perform!" Risa spat out. Each word was bitter on her tongue. She gestured to the olive branch her father had wielded in the ceremony moments before. "Because in all of history, I alone of all the seven cazas, and I alone of all the thirty great families of Cassaforte, have been rejected by the insulas!" With savage satisfaction she noted that her candor had brought about a stunned silence in the workshop. Even Cousin Fredo and Emil, at the other end of the room, gawked at her. "You think I waste my time, Cazarro? Perhaps I do. Thanks to your stupid gods, I have nothing *but* time to waste."

Ero held up a hand to stop her from saying anything further. "Do not speak ill of the gods. They watch over you even now!"

"Do they?" Standing up to Ero seemed to electrify her.

She felt energy in the air; it seemed to crackle at the ends of her hair. Even as she argued, however, a part of her felt guilty. She should not be contradicting the cazarro of one of Cassaforte's oldest and most esteemed families. Not her own father. Yet some vicious part of her could not resist dealing a final blow. "You may believe it, but I *don't*. The gods have set me adrift. I am at your mercy, Cazarro—I will waste no more time on a craft no one will purchase. If you have some other plan for the hours I spend under your roof, tell me. I cannot make you proud, like your other sons and daughters. But I will make myself of use."

Ero stared at Risa for a moment. After what seemed an eternity, he returned her bowl. "I've a delivery of goods to go to Pascal's shop this afternoon," he finally said, his voice as level and cold as hers. "It would do you good to get away from the caza for a few hours."

Risa lifted the hem of her practical shift and curtseyed. "Fine, Cazarro."

"Daughter." The word made Risa stop, mid-turn, to face her father once more. "I am proud of *all* my children." There was a stiffness to Ero's jaw as he ground out the words. "Believe me. Or not, as you choose."

If she was the girl she had been a week ago, Risa would have believed him. Instead, she bowed without words, turned her back on the man who had sired her, and stalked from the workshop. She wasn't the girl she had been. She wasn't sure what kind of girl she was, now. Nor was she certain she cared.

7

The Cassafortean lawes of succession, by lawe resting squarely upon the whims of the current ruler, were sorely tested during the fifth centurie after the citie's founding, when a dying and feverish King Molo declared his young seamstresse to be his heir. Though the decision was quicklie retracted, for two centuries following, loyalists to the self-declared Queene Poppy, mostlie friends and descendants, fought bitterlie for her line to be instated to the throne.

—ANONYMOUS, A BRIEFE AND COMPLEAT HISTORIE
OF THE CASSAFORT CITIE

The shop of brownstones was simply called Pascal's. No other name was necessary. Everyone who was anyone in the city knew that the finest Cassafortean glass from Caza Divetri and the insulas could be found there. The shopkeeper scorned displaying his stock, preferring instead to keep the fragile glassware packed inside snug cases. His showroom often surprised new customers, for it was merely a cramped and dusty space in which wooden boxes seemed stacked at random. But Pascal could, upon request, produce without hesitation any item a person might desire.

"It is indeed a pleasure," Pascal repeated for the third or

fourth time. "A distinct pleasure to have you in my humble establishment."

Via Dioro stretched west, from the Palace Square to the isle of Caza Dioro. There were many mercantile districts within Cassaforte, but none so exclusive or expensive as Via Dioro. Pascal's shop sat just a bit away from the noise and bustle of the square itself. Still, when Risa looked to the north and the east, she could easily see the hulk of King Alessandro's impressive domed residence.

This section of the street was the place to see and be seen. Outside the shop windows bustled members of the Seven and Thirty, some dressed in their finery, others in the robes of their insula. Risa had dressed herself in one of her better, lighter gowns, and spent more than a few moments tying her hair with cords so that it hung in a plait resembling her mother's. The finery made her itch. Resisting the urge to tug at her tight-wristed sleeves, she smiled at the old shopkeeper. "I trust my father's workmanship meets your high standards," she said.

Pascal's eyes were milky with the clouds that sometimes grow over the eyes of the very old. He took another look at her goods through a thick glass lens. "No question there, my dear. Your father is the most remarkable craftsman I've seen. Even more remarkable than his father before him. Fidelity goblets?" He lifted a pair of slender blue glasses up and rotated them in opposition to each other. Risa nodded. They were popular and expensive wedding gifts among the Seven and Thirty. "A perfect set," said Pascal, placing them in a velvet-lined box. "An admirable feat. They'll be snapped up immediately, you'll see. I'll give you thirty lundri for them."

"Fifty," Risa said automatically, knowing that Pascal would sell them for seventy-five lundri.

"Forty," said Pascal.

"Forty-five," she countered. It had been a test, she realized after he accepted, but she had been taught to bargain aggressively from a young age. They went through the entire cargo in a similar manner, piece by piece, pricing the stock until at last Risa's purse was full of gold coins and Pascal had a considerable number of much-used wooden cases filled with Divetri glass.

"Your father will be a happy man," Pascal said as he removed the lens from his eye. "And I will have a number of very happy customers."

"If you have a spare moment, there's one more thing—"

The front door creaked open, bringing the smells of the street into the musty room. "Shopkeeper, please..." a voice rasped out, barely comprehensible. Risa turned in mid-sentence to see an old man leaning on the door's handle for dear life, as if he might crumple to the ground without its support. What hair he had was thin and long and clumped with grime. A bruise was fading to yellow on his cheek, and shreds of clothing hung from his skeletal frame. His free hand trembled as he stretched it out, as if begging for alms. "P-please," he repeated.

"Out!" shouted Pascal, his wrinkled old face twisting into a scowl. "Out with you!" He made shooing motions with his hands, then raised his voice to a roar. "Via Dioro is no place for the likes of scum! If I see your face again, I'll have the city guards clap you in irons!" The old man cringed away from the door as Pascal kicked it shut. Risa, her ears still ringing, could see him out the window, his head hanging low as he made his way down the street.

"That beggar has been bothering merchants all day," Pascal explained, his voice returning to normal as his temper ebbed. "I hope he did not upset you, Cazarrina."

"No, not at all," Risa said, vaguely disturbed. The beggar had not offended her—Pascal's behavior had. She too was to blame, however. Not until the old man had been forced from the door had she even realized that a single lundri from the hundreds in her purse would have let him live comfortably for a month.

She might live as a beggar herself someday, dependent forever on the charity of others. Certainly, she would always have a home at Caza Divetri should she want it. Yet without any credentials from an insula or any skills beyond the ordinary to contribute to the Divetri workshops, could she ever be independent? She had to know. "I merely wanted your opinion, shopkeeper, on another piece."

Pascal crept forward eagerly, his lens at the ready. "Something special, Cazarrina?" From a separate padded sack, Risa produced her own bowl, the one plucked from the furnace shelf just that morning. Though she kept her expression impassive, Risa's heart beat quickly as she watched the shopkeeper run his hands over its surfaces. The sparse hairs of his eyebrow crunched in a question. "This is painted?"

"No," she said. "It is cut and layered glass, fused by heat and slumped into a bowl shape by gravity."

"Very curious," he said, returning to his appraisal. "Is it your work?" When she nodded, he gave her a quick glance.

"Pretty, but not extraordinary. You could sell it at the open air markets for ten or twelve luni."

"A few luni!" she exclaimed, outraged. Her bowl was not even worth a full lundri? She would have to craft hundreds to earn as much as a pair of Divetri wedding goblets!

"The workmanship is solid, if unusual," Pascal said briskly, but not unkindly. "It is free of container enchantments—am I correct?" He clucked, not surprised, when Risa nodded her head. "My customers are looking for enchanted blown glass, the finest I can find. Sell your bowl and collect a few luni for pocket money, child," he advised, handing back the bowl.

Risa nodded, bowed her head, and stalked out of the shop.

Had Pascal's eyes been sharper and unclouded, he might have noticed the tears beginning to stream down Risa's face as he followed her into the street. Nor was he aware, as he helped her into the cart and handed her reins made warm by the perfumed hides of the mule team, that she drove away with a face streaked red and white, and a head hung low.

One person saw, however. He stood at the foot of the Bridge of Allyria, watching her cart's slow approach. Risa noticed him as the mules pulled the cart up the bridge's gentle slant over the River Canal. The boy was staring at her—gaping at her, really. He looked no more than sixteen or seventeen. His sun-browned skin seemed all the more tan against his city guard's uniform—a crimson tunic, trimmed with gold braid, that reached to his thighs; dark red leggings; and a round red cap pulled over his head. From its sides spilled wavy blond hair. Unlike the palace guards with their long, heavy capes, the boy's cape was short and more functional.

His nose wrinkled slightly as she passed. She felt resentment at his bold stare, quickly followed by mortification at how awful she must look in his green eyes. He was going to have quite a story to take back to his comrades that night, she realized. The story of how one of the Seven and Thirty was sobbing on the streets would be all over the city by tomorrow.

Determined not to reveal how badly he embarrassed her, Risa straightened her back and neck and turned her head away from the young guard. Sniffing down the last of her self-pity, she snapped the reins and urged the mules forward.

Only when the cart had reached the bridge's peak did she look back, her eyes dazzled from the slantwise rays of the early evening sun. The guard still watched her. His eyes caught hers; he grinned and saluted. He was mocking her, obviously. Probably he was already making up the lies he'd be telling the other guards over supper that night. She pressed her lips together in annoyance and once more snapped the reins.

The Bridge of Allyria was one of Cassaforte's oldest, built by the first cazarro of Caza Portello. Like all of Portello's bridges, it spanned the broad canal with a graceful swoop. By this time of day, the traditional dinner hour for most, a good many people in Cassaforte had already made their way home to house and family. The bridge was nearly empty of traffic. A single gondola sliced through the water as its owner punted south, leaving the canal waters bobbing in its wake. Gulls croaked in the reddening sky above.

It had been near this spot, Risa remembered, that her

parents had seen each other for the first time. Her mother's sister had been staying for an extended visit with the Allecaris, a family of the Thirty who lived here, and had decided to lengthen her stay by another few days. As was the custom among Cassaforte's best families, Giulia had brought a hospitality offering of food and wine to the Allecari housekeeper so that the family would not be put out by the expense of a long visit. While at the house, Giulia had looked out from an upstairs window and glimpsed Ero for the first time. So very handsome she found him, she would say as she told the tale, that she felt an odd desire to attract his attention. She obeyed the compulsion and opened the window to call out a greeting before he passed. Ero had looked up, smiled, and greeted her. They were united within six months, as if fated to meet and marry.

Had Giulia never said a word, Risa considered with a shiver, there would be no Petro, no Romeldo. No Vesta or Mira. No Risa. Then again, the last would have been least missed.

Her cart clattered off the bridge. Then, over the sound of the wheels against pavement, Risa heard a muffled cry to her left. When she turned her head, she saw three youths clustered around a single figure, an elderly man. One youth lifted his knee abruptly into the man's stomach. When he returned his foot to the ground, he stomped hard on the man's toes. Another boy struck the man on the back of the head. Even from a distance, Risa could hear their victim's anguish. It was the old man she had seen just a few minutes before at Pascal's—the beggar.

Drive on, said a voice inside her head. *There's danger*

here. She instantly thought of the hundreds of lundri hidden in the floorboards of the wagon. Fear prompted her to spur the mules on, lest the treasure be risked. It was only an old beggar, part of her reasoned. If he belonged to anyone, he wouldn't have to wander and ask for luni. No one would care if he were injured. It would be easy just to pretend she hadn't seen, and take the cart over the bridge.

Yet there was a piteousness to the man's wordless cry that tugged at her heart. As badly off as he might be, no one deserved to be beaten by idle boys looking to harass someone weaker than themselves. Earlier, hadn't she wished she'd helped him when she had the opportunity? It seemed that she was being given a second chance—she would not so easily forgive her own inaction this time.

Risa abruptly banked the cart to the left. When the mules refused to move any faster, she brought them to a halt by the canal wall and hopped down. *"Help!"* she bellowed as loudly as possible, hoping the canal waters would carry her cry to the far end of the bridge, where people still lingered. "Help me, please!"

The youths startled at her approach. They might not have recognized her face, but they recognized her as a member of the Seven and Thirty by her fine manner of dress. She continued yelling as she ran, growing confident as she frightened them. One of the boys immediately broke into flight, sprinting down the canal street as fast as his legs could take him. The other two seemed to panic at his desertion. The taller quickly followed the first. The third was left holding the beggar. With a mighty shove, he pushed the elderly man away as he ran.

The vagabond fell backward against the low canal wall. As Risa watched, he lost his footing and toppled over. A moment later, she heard a loud splash.

When she reached the spot where the man had stood, she peered over the edge, horrified. In the waters of the River Canal below, she saw hands clawing at the surface, looking for something to clutch onto. Wildly she looked around. Near where she had left the cart she spotted identical sets of footholds built into opposite sides of the canal wall—the nearest ladder down, and it was too far away. There was no help for it. She lifted her skirts, bent her knees, and jumped down into the canal, more than twenty feet below.

Dark water flooded her mouth and nose, its mossy, foul taste causing her to choke. Risa blinked rapidly to clear her eyes. A hand, weak and listless, still flailed above the water not six feet away from her. Her skirts were hopelessly tangled around her legs, making it difficult for her to swim, but she thrashed toward it.

When her hand captured his, the beggar's strength seemed to return. He clutched her wrist with such force that it seemed as if her bones might break. In his desperation, he suddenly yanked her down under the water. She was caught by surprise. Her lungs burned as they breathed in water.

With force, she yanked her wrist free of the man's grasp and surfaced, coughing so deeply that her body wracked in pain. As the water drained from her eyes, she felt someone jump into the water quite close to her. A mighty splash soaked her face, and she bobbed up and down in the wake of the impact.

"Don't struggle," she heard someone yelling. She was

about to protest that she wasn't struggling at all when the water drained from her eyes once more. The boy who'd just dived in with her was already grappling with the beggar, addressing him while his red-clad arms attempted to keep the old man's head above the surface. "Grab his other hand," he told her.

She seized it as it flailed, nearly clouting the boy in the head. "Calm down!" she sputtered in the beggar's ear. "We're not going to hurt you."

There must have been something soothing about her voice, raspy with canal water as it was, for the old man's struggles lessened. "We've got to get him out," the boy said, shaking a length of his own hair from his face. His green eyes blinked open. "Can you swim? I don't have to save you, too?"

"I can manage. Take him toward the bridge," Risa suggested, beginning to kick out as best she could in that direction. "There's a foothold there."

Their progress was slow, thanks to the beggar's protestations and Risa's heavy, waterlogged gown. She was utterly exhausted by the time they reached the canal wall.

"I'll drag, you push," suggested the boy. He did not seem in the least winded. As Risa watched him pull himself out of the water with one of the handholds, she realized she hadn't even considered how, by herself, she would have gotten the old man up the stone ladder. It would have been simply too difficult to do on her own.

The boy in the red uniform managed to grab hold of the beggar's coarse coverings and haul him up to the first stone projection. Instinct took over. The old man's legs struggled for a hold, and his hands scrabbled against the notched gaps between the wall stones. Risa helped his feet move upward from step to step as the boy provided support from above. It was awkward work. Risa was nearly as wet from two sets of clothing dripping down on her as she had been in the canal itself. Eventually she felt a pair of hands helping her over the canal wall. She stumbled onto the street. The mule cart still stood only a few feet away, she noted with relief.

"Watch him for a minute," the boy instructed. He climbed back up on the canal wall and crouched.

"Where are you going?" she sputtered. The beggar sat down hard on the street and leaned against the wall.

"Back down," said the boy with a grin. He disappeared into the water with a leap and a splash. Risa ran to watch him as he swam out into the middle of the canal, where a red hat bobbed like a toy boat atop the water. He snatched it and once more paddled his way back to the ladder. "I don't suppose I can wear this now," he said mournfully, when once again he'd climbed up to the street. He turned the hat upside down. A cup or two of water spilled from it.

Risa couldn't help but laugh, both from sheer relief and at the boy's mock-sorrowful expression. As she studied his uniform and his long blond hair turned dark from the water, she realized where she'd seen him before. "You're the city guard who was staring at me in the Via Dioro."

"My name is Milo Sorranto, Cazarrina," he said, bowing slightly. "I heard your cry for help."

"How do you know who I am?" she asked, troubled.

"Surely you know the pride Cassaforte has for its Seven and Thirty," he said, grinning at her.

As she'd suspected earlier, she was merely a curiosity for

him. *You'll never guess who I saw sobbing her eyes out today ... the Cazarrina of Divetri!* "I see," she said, not at all pleased. "And what story will you be telling your mates tonight? That you rescued a helpless cazarrina from the canals because she was stupid enough to fall in after a beggar?"

He reached up and pulled his hair into a ponytail, wringing water from it before letting it fall loose again. "Stupid? Helpless? Gods, trust me, you're neither of those, Cazarrina!" He shook his head. Risa studied him closely. She didn't see a single sign of deception in his expression. Somehow, his utter lack of guile put her at ease. "It seems to me you're plenty able to rescue yourself," he continued. "If I tell anyone anything ... and I suppose I'll have to give some kind of report, if I'm to have a replacement uniform ... " He looked down at his ruined clothes, his mouth quirked.

"You'll tell them what?" Risa asked, curious despite being very much drenched. His lips were almost too thin, she decided. It was the only thing that kept him from being handsome.

"That you're so pretty," he blurted out. After the words tumbled, unbidden, from his mouth, he colored deeply and coughed. Risa felt as if she turned equally red. She'd never had a compliment like that from a stranger. "Or—that you were."

With his gesture, she realized instantly what he meant. Her hair had once more come untaped and hung like seaweed about her face. Her gown, utterly ruined, clung to her like a wet sheath. One of her sleeves was missing entirely. She almost laughed—both the truth of his statement and the shocked expression on his face at actually making it. She looked nearly as awful as the beggar himself.

Turning quickly back toward the old man, Risa saw that he was racked with shivers as he folded in on himself in a huddle. In a flash of inspiration, she remembered that the cart held a mule blanket. It smelled of animal hide and of the perfumes with which the Seven and Thirty disguised the odors of their beasts, but at least it seemed to give the old man comfort when she wrapped it around his shoulders.

"Poor man. What will happen to him?" she asked, kneeling beside the beggar.

"I'll have to take him to the jails for vagrancy, unless someone takes him into their home," the guard replied.

Risa was instantly outraged. "To the jails! The man was a *victim* of a crime. Those boys were beating him!"

"Unless someone takes him into their home, that's what the law requires," the guard repeated. She met his glance, and observed the tips of his mouth curve upward. "Cassaforte's Seven are reputed to be unstinting in their generosity, I've always heard."

Was he needling her? It was impossible to tell. Risa couldn't imagine explaining to her father how she'd managed to bring home a vagrant. However, there was no way she could allow the old beggar to be taken to jail. She could just imagine how the guard's story would end: *Just walked away, she did, nose up in the air. You know how they do, the Seven. Thought a mule blanket was good enough for the likes of him.*

He had bitten at her pride. Did he really think he had to shame her into behaving honorably? "If you'll help me put him into my cart," Risa said stiffly, "I would greatly appreciate it. What are you called again?"

The guard smiled, obviously pleased with her decision. "Milo, Cazarrina."

"A common enough name," she said, kneeling down to put the beggar's arm around her shoulder.

Milo swept wet hair away from his face, bowed low, then pulled the cap back onto his head as he knelt down to help her. "Surely you mean for an uncommon young man, Cazarrina?" he murmured, shooting her a wink. Together they began to lift the shivering beggar to his feet.

Risa had to smirk. A common enough name for an impertinent young man, at the very least.

8

It seems cruel that they are of the Seven and we only of the Thirty, does it not? Were it not for the random choice of an ancient king, it could have so easily gone another, more favorable way. Yet, my dear, I have heard that the winds of change are blowing. Who knows what good fortune they might tumble into our laps?

—RULIETTE VINCINZI OF THE THIRTY,
IN A PRIVATE LETTER TO HER SISTER

🕉

It was impossible not to notice the colors of each caza rising around her as the sun slid below the horizon. The poles upon which the cazas' banners flew were set on the highest point of each of the seven islands. At the sound of the palace horn, the beggar stirred beside her. Risa was already traveling slowly, for the old man's head bobbed alarmingly with each jolt in the road.

"So much has gone wrong," he murmured, opening his eyes to a slit. "So much ... wrong."

"You're safe," she assured him. Where in the world would he sleep? She couldn't just leave him in the Divetri courtyard.

Perhaps there was an empty servant's room where he could stay. It might be that he could even perform light servant duties until he was once again able to take care of himself. "Do you have a name?" she asked.

He was drifting off to sleep again. "Dom..." he murmured. "Dom."

For a while there were no sounds save for the caza horns pealing their fealty to the heavens, Dom's labored breathing, and the steady clop-clop-clop of the mules as they pulled their burden forward. It was strange to think that only a week ago, the musical sounds had thrilled Risa to her very core. Tonight, sitting nearly alone in the cart as it moved through the quiet and darkening streets, she felt nothing. Cry after cry of loyalty flew over the city rooftops, until at last all seven had been heard. The palace trumpet issued its benediction. Night began to settle over Cassaforte.

Legend had it that only once, in all the city's history, had a caza failed to complete the rite of fealty—Caza Legnoli, three hundred years ago. A family of wood workers. So fine was their craft that the carved Legnoli screens in Lena's Temple were still a popular destination for pilgrims from across the country. Its cazarro, however, had been quarrelsome and disruptive. He regularly argued with the other six cazarri and the crown—just to hear his own voice, said most people.

Risa had heard several variations of what happened to Caza Legnoli; it had happened so long ago that those who witnessed the event were long in the arms of the gods. What was certain was that the cazarro disagreed strongly with the king, and declared his intention to remain in his caza yet ignore the rite of fealty. Some people said that when his colors failed to rise and when he left the house's horn untouched, a great demon descended from the clouds and destroyed the caza and all within. Still others claimed that a great bolt of lightning struck the caza and decimated its contents and all those foolish enough to remain inside. Whatever the outcome, what Legnolis remained abandoned the caza. From among the Thirty, the king elevated the Dioro to the Seven, and chose an aspiring family from the common populace to replace Dioro among the Thirty. The chances to advance the fortunes of a family were exceedingly rare; should such an opportunity arise again, there would be no shortage of people vying to replace the dishonored.

Risa cast an eye toward Caza Dioro as the cart turned from the piazza onto the low bridge leading to Caza Divetri. Dioro, proud family of weapon makers. Their caza still stood proudly against the deepening horizon, its stone walls looking older than a mere three centuries. It was impossible to believe Caza Legnoli had been reduced to rubble by lightning, much less by a demon. It was all myth. Just as Muro and Lena, the gods she thought had abandoned her, were nothing more than pretty stories based on the two moons in the sky. Two cold and distant chunks of rock, their stables mere clusters of stars that surrounded them in a random pattern.

"Birds," muttered the vagrant. For a moment it did sound as if distant wings fluttered above. As the noise grew louder, however, Risa realized that what they heard was a carriage's rattle as it flew toward the city on the upper bridge. When the two vehicles passed each other, high and low, with a clatter of wheel rims upon stones, Risa heard the familiar jingle of the bells worn by her parents' best horses.

Where could they be going at this time of the evening?

9

Blessed Lena, grant us your peace, so that our lands may be harmonious. Grant us your wisdom, that we might prosper. Above all, grant your penitents mercy to others, so that we may have the serenity to be merciful to ourselves.

—FROM THE PRAYER BOOK OF THE INSULA OF THE
PENITENTS OF LENA

W hat?" Risa hated being awakened by cold. She had been warm, despite the city's chilly night, beneath her quilt. "What is it? Stop shaking me." For a moment, through her waking fog, she thought that Petro might be teasing her. As she reached consciousness, she remembered that her younger brother had been at the Insula of the Penitents of Lena for over a week.

Fita stood over her. The old servant had brought a breakfast tray laden with hot rolls and fruit. It was unusual enough that Fita bore the tray herself; more remarkable still was the fact that she was actually shaking Risa awake, something she had only done once before, on the dawn of Prince Berto's so-called blessing. When finally Risa sat up, Fita crossed her hands primly. "I've brought you a tray," she said unnecessarily.

Risa stared at her breakfast for a moment, her stomach grumbling lightly at the aroma of the fresh sweet bread and the jug of squeezed juice. "You *never* bring me a tray. You've told me trays are for children."

It might have been her imagination, but Risa thought she saw the corners of the housekeeper's lips twitch. "You're obviously not a child any longer," she said. "Going off and doing what you please without your father's say-so."

Breaking open one of the rolls seemed a wise course. Fita might change her mind and snatch them away, given her current mood. "What's this about? You've obviously something on your mind."

"It's about that beggar you brought home, that's what." Fita's tone was gruff and offended. "The smell! Honestly, Cazarrina, how could you!"

It was Risa's turn to draw up her shoulders and show offense. "His name is Dom. He was thrown in the canals by vandals. The guards would have arrested him if I'd not brought him home. What would you have me do? Send him to prison? Let him sleep outside another night?" When Fita did not answer, she grew suspicious. "Where is he now?"

"In the stable yard, I believe," Fita said, her manner stiff and formal.

"Still? Don't tell me he *slept* there!" Risa stood up and rapidly began to dress, anger making her actions swift and bold. "I told Allandro last night to ask you to find a place for him among the staff."

"It is not the *stable boy's* place to tell the *housekeeper* her business." When Risa looked as if she was about to protest, the woman added, "Only the Cazarro or Cazarra can instruct me to hire someone."

"You are not usually so unfeeling!" Risa commented. When the housekeeper shrugged, Risa pulled on her slippers. "Where is the Cazarro?"

"Your mother and father have not returned from the palace," murmured Fita. Risa made a noise of astonishment at the news—it was extremely rare that her parents spent the night away from the caza. "Will they be staying past the midday meal, Cazarrina? If so, it will be necessary for the kitchen staff to prepare a hospitality offering. Your mother is always careful to adhere to custom," she added at Risa's astonished stare.

"Why are they at the palace?" Risa demanded, finally assimilating all of Fita's news.

Fita threw up her palms. "I do not know, Cazarrina. They were summoned last night, after the rite of fealty."

"Did they know they were staying so long?" Another shrug. Frustrated beyond belief, Risa tied a shawl around her shoulders. "You don't know why my parents are at the palace, or why they've stayed overnight. You don't know why my friend Dom spent the night in the stable yard."

"That I do know. He was not allowed in the house because I did not receive an order from the Cazarro or the—"

"My order should be enough!"

"And if I might say, Cazarrina," said the housekeeper with some temper. "To call such a figure a *friend*, even loosely, when you are of the Seven—"

"You may *not* say!" Risa's voice rose above the house-keeper's. Ignoring the woman's prim silence, she gathered the tray and stalked from the room.

She found Dom huddled beneath the blanket still, smelling strongly of mule and perfume, canal water and offal, and a certain rank sweetness she associated with his age. She tried to hide the emotions that warred within her as the man turned his face toward her, a face lined with wrinkles and speckled with age spots. "You went away," he said, his eyes pitiable.

"I'm sorry," she said, angry once more with Fita. Though the housekeeper could be generous when inclined, she was a frustrating woman when determined to get her own way.

"I slept out here."

"That won't happen again," Risa promised. "I've brought you breakfast." She placed the meal down on the bench next to him. "See? It's all right. We'll share." She took half of the roll she had already broken and took a bite. It was impossible not to see the hunger and longing in his eyes. He seemed to hesitate. Risa suspected he was too proud to eat while she watched. She turned her head and consumed her own portion. She heard him take one of the sweet rolls and begin to consume it ravenously.

His hands were still trembling a few minutes later when, with Risa's gentle insistence, he finished the last of the rolls and gulped down the last mouthful of fruit juice. "You'll have regular meals from now on," she told him. "We just have to find something for you to do."

She had not noticed how many red veins lined the old man's eyes until he turned them to her in fear. "I ... there's nothing ... "

"Have you ever worked with glass?" He shook his head. "Have you ever worked in the stables? Have you served at the table?" As she worked her way through the list of possible functions he might perform around the caza, he continued to shake his head.

Why was she trying so hard to help him? With every job at which Dom shook his head, she wondered more and more if she had not picked up some true good-for-nothing from the street. He might have idled away his entire life begging, for all she knew. There were no skills to which he would admit.

She remembered the first time she saw the beggar's face in Pascal's shop, and how she felt his helplessness mirror her own. Now she could aid him, if she could think how. "You can't think of anything you've done before that you might do here?"

He clasped his hands together in his lap in an attempt to hide their trembling. "I've never worked as … " His cracked voice lapsed into a feeble whisper.

"We'll find something," she said kindly, wildly casting about for inspiration.

"Guard," he whispered.

"What?" Dom had been a guard? Perhaps he could keep an eye on the furnaces, then, or some other task that required little action but much attention. Her musing ceased once he raised his hand and pointed through the arch to the road beyond.

Over the lower bridge washed a tide of dark red uniforms. A contingent of city guards approached. When Risa swung her head around in alarm, she could see the caps and spears of another set approaching the caza on the upper span above.

Her first thought was that something was wrong. Her parents had been hurt. Ero was dead, and palace guards had come bearing the bad news. Panic clutched at her chest, making it difficult to draw air into her lungs.

Rising to her feet proved an exercise of will. Her steps, leaden at first, took her closer and closer to the guards, but she could not force herself to run. Finally she stopped and waited for them at the mouth of the bridge. They trudged toward her, faces grim.

"What's wrong?" she asked the first of them, a young woman with a crossbow slung over her shoulder. She searched the faces of the rest as they gathered around her. "Is something wrong?"

"You'll have to ask Tolio, Cazarrina," said a young man. "We just follow orders."

"Who is Tolio? Where is he?"

The man pointed toward the upper bridge. "He'll be in the courtyard even now."

As if her feet had been released from shackles, Risa broke free from the spot to which she was rooted and ran for the caza.

10

Every knot begins as clean string.

—A COMMON CASSAFORTEAN SAYING

"Which of you is called Tolio?" Risa demanded as she broke into the formal courtyard. Over a score of the city guard already crowded its formal landscape, their weapons and crimson cloaks spread over the benches and topiaries. It was as if they were making themselves at home, she thought wildly.

Fredo and Mattio followed her into the courtyard, accompanied by a blinking Emil. In her flight through the caza, Risa had stopped briefly to beg Mattio to come with her—if there was bad news to be heard, she wanted him to be there. The other craftsmen had insisted on coming as well, and even a gaggle of servants trailed behind, their faces betraying their nervousness.

"Now, now, cousin," said Fredo. He stepped forward and folded one hand over the other. "Surely a cazarrina can show more courtesy to such illustrious visitors."

For a moment she hated him for that remark. Cousin or not, a man not of the Seven and Thirty had no right to instruct her in good manners. She would have issued some retort had not her eye, at that moment, caught a glimpse of a face that seemed familiar. The boy was standing slightly behind a young fair-haired woman, taller than himself, who was busily instructing other guards where to pile their provisions. It was Milo—the uncommon guard with the common name—from the afternoon before. He flashed her a quick grin, then made a show of looking up at the sky and whistling and pretending not to have seen her.

"Which of you is Tolio?" Risa repeated, in a tone no less firm although she was oddly conscious of Milo's presence.

"I am Tolio, Cazarrina," said the oldest of the crimson-clad guards. The braid on his tunic was thicker than the others. Like many Cassafortean men in their fifth or sixth decade, he bore scars on his face won in the savage war against the Azurite pirates. They almost suited his rough-hewn features and sour expression.

"Are my parents well? Has harm come to them?" Her haste to frame the inquiry made the words come haltingly.

"I am certain that our guest, Tolio—Captain Tolio, is it? What an honor!—would not bring so many of his men and women for so trivial a task, young cousin." Fredo's smile was oily enough to calm even the waves of a two-moon tide.

"The Cazarro and Cazarra Divetri are well and in good health," Tolio said, bowing toward Fredo. "I bear a message from the Cazarra." He brandished a folded page.

"Praise the gods," murmured Fredo.

Milo had been following the conversation closely, Risa could tell. Despite the fact that the young woman guard was having him restack a pile of pikes that had tumbled over, his head was cocked in her direction. When he caught Risa's eye once more, he began to whistle and attend to his task.

"Is it truly necessary for forty guards to hand-deliver a message?" Risa asked.

"We are acting on the orders of Prince Berto," Tolio commented.

Mattio stepped forward. "I was a guard in my youth. Guards act only on the orders of the king, not his kin."

"The king is dead." Tolio paused to let the news sink in. Though the guards seemed unsurprised, none of the caza had yet heard the news. There was a stunned murmur among the servants. Risa felt dazed and empty. King Alessandro—dead? It had been several years since he had been among the citizens, due to his ill health. They had all been expecting the worst for some time now, but it was a definite shock to hear the words said aloud.

"May Lena have mercy upon him." Fredo looked up to the heavens as he spoke the words. "Muro, grant him rest and peace."

Tolio stepped forward, unmoved by the speech. "Until the Seven have officially bestowed the Olive Crown and the Scepter of Thorn upon Prince Berto, we act according to the dictates of the heir presumptive to the throne. And his order is to occupy the cazas of the Seven until the transition is secure."

So that was why her parents had taken flight in their carriage the night before. Whenever a monarch died, the seven cazarri were required to join together at the palace to award the country's sacred relics to the heir. From her history lessons, Risa knew that the enchanted objects had to be bestowed upon him in a unanimous gesture. Prince Berto could not just seize the crown and scepter; they could not be even so much as touched by any save the rightful king approved by the Seven. The Seven were key to ensuring a smooth transition between rulers, she realized—they were the fulcrum upon which rested the delicate balance between the will of the crown and the will of the people. Here was history in the making.

"I'm very sorry about King Alessandro," she said quietly. "But may I have the message?"

Instantly Fredo stepped forward. "Perhaps I should take it, little cousin." To Tolio he added, "I am the only male of Divetri blood in the household, and I feel my cousin, the cazarro, would wish for me to be in charge of the caza in his absence."

Outrage roared like furnace fires in Risa's chest. It was dampened slightly by the sight of Milo, standing to the side, mimicking Fredo's sanctimonious expression with the addition of crossed eyes. To his misfortune, the blond guard supervising him caught the mockery as well. She snapped her fingers and ordered Milo back to work. "I am the only Divetri of *pure blood* in this caza," Risa retorted, not bothering to hide her bile.

For an instant she thought she saw a look of loathing

in Fredo's eyes, but it must have been her imagination. His countenance was as smug and self-satisfied as ever. "I really must insist—"

"Mattio," Risa said, ignoring him. "Dispatch a servant to the Insula of the Children of Muro. I wish my brother Romeldo to be here in my father's absence, so that we may avoid any future misunderstandings."

She was happy to see that her order startled Fredo from his complacency. "I'm not sure that's entirely necessary, cousin," he began.

"I believe it is."

"It would be a pleasure." Mattio looked grim as he ducked his head and disappeared through the caza doors. Though he was civil to all, Risa knew that Mattio had no love for her cousin.

Tolio looked at the folded missive. "It *is* addressed to the Cazarrina," he said mildly. As if that decided the matter, he handed it to Risa. She accepted it with an air of triumph. Milo's surreptitious wink buoyed her, for a moment. It was heartening to feel she had an ally.

She noticed immediately that the message had not been sealed. Anyone among the palace staff could have viewed it. Judging from the smudged fingerprints along its edge, at least a few had.

Dearest—
Know that I miss you with each
passing hour. Your father, Ero,
and I are being amply entertained by his
majesty, Prince Berto. I would appreciate it

if you were to bring to the palace a
hospitality offering. Are you enjoying
the weather? It is my sincere hope
that we continue to have fair days.
—Giulia

Sensing motion behind her, Risa turned. Fredo stood over her shoulder, his lips still moving as he read. "I would be honored to take a hospitality offering to the palace," he said, his voice humble. Fita, who had been repeatedly wiping her hands with her apron as she stood in the caza doors, murmured to herself. She clapped her hands, ordering the kitchen servants to follow her so they could begin preparations.

"I will take the offering," Risa snapped back. "The letter is addressed to *me*."

"Yes, perhaps that would be best," Fredo countered. "You attend to that modest errand. It is best that I look after the household in the cazarro's absence." Before Risa could interject, he added, "Until Cousin Romeldo arrives, of course."

She knew her father would disapprove, but she had to say something. "Do not try me, cousin." She was about to stalk off into the household when Tolio clapped his hands.

"A moment, Cazarrina. I must assign you a watch."

"A watch?" She turned and regarded the captain in disbelief. "Am I under guard? Am I not free to come and go as I please?"

"My orders state that guards are to be placed throughout the cazas and at their bridges, and that members of the seven families are to be assigned watches," Tolio replied with courtesy. "You are not under arrest. You are free to come and go as you please, during the daylight hours. At night you are not allowed into the city. For your safety," he explained.

"I am glad to know I'm not under arrest," she said dryly. The remark went unheard. Tolio was calling for a volunteer from among the guard to act as Risa's watch. After a moment in which no one responded, Milo's arm reached into the air lazily, as if almost reluctant. The blond female guard gave him a sharp look.

"Very good, Sorranto," said Tolio with a nod.

Risa sighed, unable to believe the impertinence of both being assigned a guard and having Milo volunteer. "Very well then. But *you*," she said to Milo, who had approached with a face that feigned boredom, "keep ten paces back."

"Very good, Cazarrina," he drawled. "As you wish, Cazarrina."

11

Yes, I have stood upon the Petitioner's Stair and laid my eyes upon the Olive Crown and the Scepter of Thorn. Humble in name, yes, but not in appearance, for they are of the purest gold. I dared not reach out an arm to test their weight, however, for I was warned that powerful magicks protect them from thievery. It is said that in previous days the burnt husk of a corpse who had tried to make away with them was put on public display in front of the palace. So effective was the display that none have attempted a similar feat since.

—Marcel Cloutier, Ambassador of Charlemance to the court of Cassaforte

There was something about the letter that bothered Risa, though she couldn't put her finger on what. It was just unusual for Giulia to write about the weather but not say a word about why they had tarried so long. There was no apology, no instructions. No word from her father.

"I don't understand." Risa hopped down from her perch on the balcony rail. Above her, in the late morning sea breezes, flapped the purple and brown banner of Cassaforte. She paced across the red and black tiles, reading her mother's letter for the dozenth time and trying to forget the stress and strain of the last twenty-four hours.

Ahead of her, Milo sidled away when she approached. As she paced back to the rail, he eased forward.

The only thing that seemed sincere about the entire note was the first sentence. Although they had not really spoken much since the Scrutiny, it was so like her gentle mother to say how much she missed her. Still, there was something *wrong* here. Was she the only one who could see it? Oh, where was Romeldo? Was he too ashamed to come, after her tantrum of the week before?

With determination, Risa began once more to stride across the balcony, only to have her thoughts interrupted by the sight of Milo edging away from her. "Why do you keep doing that?" she said, stopping and putting her hands upon her hips.

"Begging your pardon, but the cazarrina requested I keep ten paces away."

A puff of air escaped from her lips. "You," she announced, "are maddening."

Milo cracked a grin. "You need a good laugh."

"Why do you think that?"

His green eyes looked her up and down. "My mother would say that a day wasn't worth living that didn't have one good laugh in it." Risa had in her mind an instant picture of his mother—a fat, maternal sort who stayed at home and cooked stews and dispensed advice and washed his crimson tunics when he came home. "You're the type she would like," he added.

"What type is that?"

The boy abandoned his rigid guard's stance and leaned against the wall. "The type who jumps into canals after beggars. That was a right special thing you did there. I don't know many of the Seven or Thirty or even us common folk who'd do a fool thing like that."

Risa laughed abruptly, but it was without humor. "There's nothing special about me."

"My mother would say there's something special to everyone, if they take care to find it."

"If I ever meet your mother," she told him, "I'll prove to her how very unspecial I am."

"Might be a bit of a task," mused Milo. "Seeing how she's dead." After seeing her shocked expression, he smiled again. "Don't apologize. You didn't know. However." He waggled a finger at Risa and narrowed his eyes, obviously preparing to make a point. "Just because a person's dead doesn't mean she's wrong."

He was obviously trying to use humor to smooth over the gaffe. Still, she felt badly. "It's strange that I should see you twice in two days."

His reply was quite cheerful. "Oh, it's not strange at all. When they were assigning guards to the cazas, I pulled strings to come here."

"Why?" She couldn't believe anyone would pull strings on her account.

"Why? So I could see you again! We saved a man's life together. I think if we lived with the savages on the Azure Isles, that would make us married." Before Risa could protest at anything so outrageous, he grinned. "But I'll settle for friends."

Did he want something from her? Even having the suspicion made her flush. Perhaps he was setting her up as the punch line for one of his jokes. "But why?"

"Um, let's see." Milo tapped his forefinger on his chin

and pretended to think about the question, though he delivered the answer as if it were self-evident. "Because I like you?" Seeing that she wasn't going to accept such a simple answer without explanation, he cocked his head. "You're different. For starters, I don't know any other girl who'd risk life and limb for a beggar. Any girl who wasn't a guard, that is. They're usually too dainty. You can take care of yourself!"

Risa almost smiled at that. After feeling lately that she would forever be a black spot on the Divetri line, hearing someone laud her independence was a refreshing novelty. "Well. Thank you."

"You should see most of the Seven and Thirty." Milo strutted back and forth, rapidly mimicking the straight-laced gait of an old man looking down his nose, a cazarra offended by the smells in the street who covered her face with a fan, and a vapid young miss giggling and primping in an imaginary shop window. From behind her hand, Risa laughed at the replicas. "But you can put on the high-class airs yourself, can't you?" he added, grinning at her.

"Excuse me?" She heard her tone grow cold.

"Excuse me?" Milo said in exact imitation. He grabbed the letter from her hands. "Watch." After taking a few steps back, he squared his shoulders and tossed imaginary hair. "I am so *happy* to know I am not under *arrest.*" With a dramatic flourish of her mother's letter, he pointed toward the city. "Mattio! Dispatch a servant to the insula *immediately!*"

Risa's eyes went wide and she felt a hot flash sweep across her. For a moment she thought he was seriously mocking her, but the good humor in his eyes gave away his playful intentions. She even started to chuckle a little.

"You're really quite impressive when you do that," Milo concluded. "Is it put on, or does it come natural?"

Risa was smiling again, although the way he handled Giulia's letter made her nervous. "It's a little of both. I have to, sometimes, or no one takes me seriously!"

"Especially that cousin of yours." Milo whistled. "A taste of him would make lemon seem sweet."

He kept making her laugh. The last statement, however, made her remember her father's constant prohibitions against teasing Fredo. Involuntarily, she brought a hand to her mouth. "You're worse than Petro," she said.

"Who's he?"

"My younger brother."

"Where is he?"

"At the Insula of the Penitents of Lena."

His brow knitted in puzzlement. "Why aren't you with him?"

It was the first time anyone had asked her the question. It pierced like an arrow to her heart. She jutted out her jaw, took a deep breath, and said quite calmly, "They didn't want me. Nor did the Insula of the Children of Muro."

"Oh." He shrugged. "No great loss."

"It *is* a great loss!" she exclaimed. Ridiculous to think that a common city guard would understand. "I've waited my entire life to be admitted!"

"You've better things to do than waste your time there." Milo's tone implied that he meant what he said. "Everyone knows about the insulas."

"What do *they* know about them?" she cried, trying to choke down her distress.

"They're just private schools, aren't they, for the wealthy?

Oh, they teach the enchantments, that I'll grant you, but they're really just to keep the younger members of the Seven and Thirty out of the way. They keep them busy running workshops of their own, so that the eldest sons can eventually move their families into the caza and inherit them without competition from their brothers and sisters. It's a way of keeping peace in the family, isn't it, all dressed up in fancy robes and ceremonies to make it seem important, right? You don't need all that nonsense."

Risa blinked, not responding. It was true that siblings usually never lived in their cazas again after leaving for the insulas. They performed research there, or devoted themselves to the priesthood, or moved to workshops in smaller cities or in the countryside. The idea that such a grand tradition was a way of enforcing the proper succession of the caza, though, had never occurred to her.

"I don't need it?" she finally said.

Milo shook his head. "My sister and I had our own private little club once. You had to know the password to get in. It made us feel special. We sent messages to each other in code, and collected dues, and . . . "

"Oh!" He had said something that stunned her—her skin tingled and sparked as if she'd been struck by lightning. She could scarcely think what to do first. "Give me that letter!"

"Why?" he asked as he handed it over. "I didn't tear it."

"I know, I know!" She lay the paper flat. For a few moments she studied it closely. When she looked back up, it was with tears in her eyes.

"Milo," she said, scarcely able to force out the words. "My family's in terrible, terrible trouble."

12

Catarre's books make people wise.
Portello's towers scrape the skies.
Folks worldwide are smart to go
See paintings by Buonochio.
Piratimare makes its crafts
Sturdy from their fores to afts.
Divetri, glass, Dioro, swords.
And Cassamagi charms with words.

—AN OLD NURSERY RHYME

🕉

"Gently, little Risa. You are overwrought." The workshop was filled with the sharp scent of glass annealing in the furnaces. Cousin Fredo smiled at her. "We all are, of course, with the king's unfortunate death. Perhaps you should lie down."

"Mattio," she said in appeal. "You see what I mean!"

"There's no denying it." Mattio grumbled in his deep bass, reading the letter. He let his finger trail over the final letters of each word:

h o s t a g e s

"Hostages," breathed Risa. When Cousin Fredo drew his breath in with a start, she felt a curious satisfaction.

"She must have known that anything she wrote was going to be inspected, so she used Petro's code," Mattio said slowly.

"But why write at all?" Fredo asked. Emil and Mattio started at him.

"They had to write something so we wouldn't worry. It must be the prince detaining them," Risa reasoned. "The guards received their orders from him." She looked to Milo for confirmation, then remembered that he wasn't as convinced as she was of the danger. At her implied question, however, he bowed with affirmation.

"Cazarrina, this is a family matter," said Fredo, rubbing his hands. "I do not think it concerns anyone other than the four of us—and your brother, of course. Surely … ?" He made a motion with his head toward the guard.

"Come, Fredo, let us not be *inhospitable* to our guests," Risa murmured, despite her worry. She took a certain pleasure in the wry smile that quickly crossed Milo's lips. "You heard Captain Tolio. I am to have a watch over me. I have no choice in the matter." She turned back to Mattio. "Is there any word from my brother?"

"The servant has only recently departed," said the craftsman. "Your brother should be here by the afternoon."

"I certainly hope so," said a female voice from the doorway. It was Fita, once more looking dissatisfied. "Half the servants are sobbing in the corners over King Alessandro, even those too young to remember the last time he ventured outside the palace. The other half are frightened by the guards.

The cazarro would have set things right by now! Everyone respects the cazarro!"

"Since it will take time for Romeldo to arrive, Cazarrina," said Fredo, sighing, "I will take charge of this highly volatile situation."

"Good! At least some one is taking charge!" said Fita.

"No. You are not of the blood." Risa felt a flush rising to her face.

"Due to my father's unfortunate marriage, I am not of the Seven and Thirty, my girl, but I *am* most assuredly of the blood." He paused, daring her to challenge him. "You are but sixteen. And of the tender, weaker sex. Your father—your *father*," he emphasized, as her anger prompted her to attempt an interruption, "would surely be more comfortable if he knew Caza Divetri was being guarded by a man such as myself."

"I know I would!" The housekeeper looked smug as she offered her opinion.

Risa glared at Fita. When she turned back and met Mattio's eyes in appeal, he shook his head. He might agree with her privately, but he seemed to feel it was useless to argue with Fredo. Perhaps it was. Her father had always been adamant that no woman should oversee Caza Divetri. He might even feel that she had brought dishonor upon the caza, if she were to persist. Even Romeldo would probably laugh at her attempts to keep the caza running. If only they were not so inflexible and old-fashioned!

In a level voice she said to Fredo, "I do not plan to sit by idly while ... " she lowered her voice so that Fita would not hear " ... while my parents are in danger."

"There is no need for idleness, little cousin," said Fredo,

suddenly all gaiety. "You may oversee the kitchens and take the hospitality offering to the palace this very afternoon. Suitable work for a girl with time on her hands. I, in the meantime, will be in your father's office. You two—back to work."

Emil blinked at this sudden coup. Mattio gasped audibly. Their jaws went slack as Fredo swept from the room. Risa's ire nearly roused her to throw something after her smug, sanctimonious relative. "He has no right!" she growled at last through gritted teeth.

"Not with Romeldo coming!" Mattio agreed. "He's certainly making himself right at home!"

"I say we could *use* a man who can take charge when the master's away," Fita countered. "Though why he'd place a mere…no offense, child, but why he'd place you in charge of the kitchens is beyond me. Your mother was always too busy with her beautiful windows, Lena bless her, to teach you—"

"I order you to take Dom on as a kitchen servant, starting now," said Risa, suddenly very tired of the housekeeper's constant carping.

Fita let out a squawk. "That filthy vagabond? I won't, Cazarrina, and there's the end of it."

"You can't have it both ways," Risa snapped. "If you admire Cousin Fredo so much, you have no choice but to obey me. He's made me your boss. Get someone to wash Dom, if he offends your nose. Give him some old clothing. I know you *can*. You just *won't*."

"He's not suitable for anything!"

"Let him wash the fruits and vegetables," Risa cried, plucking something at random. "If I could do it when I was younger than Petro, it's a task Dom can do as well."

Fita's nostrils flared as Risa stalked past. "Well!" she said, obviously put out. "If you say so, Cazarrina."

"I do say so!" Risa shook her head, still angry. There were outcasts enough within Caza Divetri. If no one would help her, she would at least help another. When Romeldo finally came, he would set things aright—and Risa was already planning what she would say to him about her cousin.

13

My dear! It was the scandal of the summer when that violin-ist—remember, the handsome one?—was sent packing back to Pays d'Azur. Apparently his instrument was a Cassamagi, I believe they called it—some foreign name, anyway, and the point is that it was enchanted—and the violinist was supposed to have used it to charm his way all the way to the position of concert master. It's a pity, for he was so very handsome, and his playing was the only reason I could stomach chamber music.

—Dama Vanessa Innsbruck, in a letter to the
Most Honourable Monica Chubb

"You'll need a guard to go into the city," said Tolio. He stared at Risa with cold detachment.

"I have a guard. I've had a guard following me all morning," Risa replied, controlling her temper. It was absurd, being watched every moment of the day. Her parents were missing and in danger, and she was having to waste time arguing with this stubborn captain! She did not much mind that Milo had so far been the one keeping her company. His cheekiness reminded her of Petro. Yet even good-natured company could not make her forget the urgency of her mission.

"You'll need another," said Tolio, bored now. He went

back to whittling chips from a peg. They landed in a small pile on the courtyard tiles. "Who would you pick for the job, Sorranto?" he asked, narrowing an eye at Milo.

Milo had been leaning on the wall lazily, sucking on a long blade of grass, barely seeming to pay attention to the proceedings. "What? Me? Oh, definitely Eli, sir." He grinned at another boy his age, who was playing at dice in a corner. "Eli and I get along famously."

"Oh you do, do you?" Tolio smiled, though Risa could tell it was the smile of a man baiting a trap. "You two lads would keep a good watch over the Cazarrina?"

"Yes sir!" Milo leaned forward and lowered his voice. "Just don't send me with Camilla, sir. Anyone but her."

Tolio winked at him in a conspiratorial way, nodding toward the capable young woman Risa had first noticed earlier in the day. She was engaged in a bit of sword practice. At least, that's what Risa supposed it was. She seemed to be in a world of her own, the girl did. After making sure that no one was in the immediate vicinity, she began whipping the sword around her in a sort of dance. The blade dipped and swayed and swirled through the air in an almost hypnotic fashion, gleaming in the sun as she twirled it expertly. "Anyone but Camilla, eh? Why would that be?"

"You know how she is, sir. Little bit of a spoilsport."

The trap was sprung. Tolio leapt to his feet. "Camilla's the best young guard I've seen in many a year!" he roared. Behind him, the female guard ceased her swordplay and swung her head about, wary. "You'd do well to follow her example! There'll be no trip to the palace with Eli. Not now, not ever! I'm sending Camilla with you to keep you in line!"

"But sir!" Milo protested, apparently chagrined.

"That's enough, Sorranto. Camilla! You heard me. Leave your practice for later. Take *this one* into the city with the Cazarrina. If there's an ounce of mischief from him, I'll ... I'll ... I'll do *something*, that's what I'll do. In fact, stay with him for the rest of the day. No!" he said, when Milo protested. "Stay with him for the *rest of our time here!*"

Chips from his peg flew in every direction as Tolio returned to whittling. His anger was so concentrated that for a moment Risa forgot about her parents. Milo looked stunned. Fair-haired Camilla resheathed her sword and picked up a pair of gloves, obviously irritated. She scowled as she marched over. "Let's go then," she said. Risa could tell she was not at all happy.

Through the caza Risa led them until they reached the stable yard. She almost felt that she could not run quickly enough. In the back of the mule cart Fita had packed hampers full of foods and wines. Enough for a week, it looked like. Surely her parents would not be absent for so long a time. They simply couldn't be.

It was not until they were underway and the cart had trundled across the lower Divetri bridge that anyone spoke. "Do you *always* have to get your way?" From her position at the reins, Camilla turned her head and growled at Milo.

"Not *always*," Milo said, flashing his teeth in a grin. "Just when it suits me, that's all."

The cart's wheels rattled as they trundled into the piazza. Camilla nodded curtly at the crimson-coated guards flanking the bridge entrance. Out of earshot, she continued. "It suits you all the time. That's the problem."

"I didn't think you'd mind, Cam," Milo replied. "All those boring things he's making you do. You want a bit of scenery."

"Didn't you learn anything from Mother? All those boring tasks teach you how to manage. When you're a good manager, they promote you."

"I know, I know. But still, guarding can't be all about inventory."

"And it can't be all about swash-buckling, either," Camilla retorted.

Risa spoke up, astonished by the conversation. "She's your—?"

"Sister," said Milo. "Can't you tell? We have the Sorranto nose." From the back bench he leaned forward and stuck his head between the two girls, so that his face was parallel to his sister's. Risa did notice a distinct similarity in their profiles. Their noses, their green eyes, and their neck-length blond hair were so identical they might almost have been twins. Camilla was taller, however, and her expression was the sterner. With a single hand, she covered her brother's face and pushed him backward. He landed on the rear bench with a thump.

"Don't be so peevish," Milo complained. "You should be thanking me."

"Why in the world would I *thank* you?"

"We can stop and see Amo afterward, that's why." Camilla's mouth quirked in an unidentifiable expression, but she kept her eyes on the road ahead and said nothing. "Risa won't mind. Will you, Risa?"

Camilla's eyebrow raised slightly at that. "I'm sure the *cazarrina* would rather attend to business and return home."

The slight emphasis she placed on Risa's title implied her disapproval of Milo's familiarity.

"I don't mind him calling me Risa. Either of you. Really, I don't," Risa told Camilla.

"She's not stuffy, like most of them," Milo said, leaning forward. "You should have seen her yesterday in the canals, trying to pull an old beggar man out of the water. It was incredible!"

"Oh," said Camilla. "She's the one you ruined your uniform for?"

"It was worth it!"

Flushing slightly from Milo's effusions, Risa interrupted. "Please. We have to get to the palace." There had been scarcely a second that fear for her parents had not gnawed at her. Anxiety left her stomach feeling tense and bitter.

"Everything's going to be fine," Milo said for the dozenth time since she'd shown him the hidden message in Giulia's letter. "If some … I don't know … crazed Vereinigteländer had taken your parents hostage in the palace, the guards would know all about it, wouldn't they?" In response to the question, Camilla nodded. "And why would the prince be involved? Her parents are just there for the succession. Sometimes it takes time. Right?"

Camilla agreed silently once more, while Risa sighed. He made sense.

"I know you're worried, but I'm sure you'll find out that there's some logical explanation."

"I hope you're right," Risa admitted.

"Of course I am. You'll see. Then we'll visit Amo afterward."

Camilla shot him a withering look. "It wouldn't take long!" Milo muttered, but he sat back and kept his peace.

For a few silent minutes they drove on through the city. Camilla sat erect and stern, her uniform and cap immaculate. She was the very image of a proper city guard. Milo also sat quietly, his posture straight, but whenever Risa turned to look at him, there was an alertness in his eyes for the sights of the city. He seemed to drink in the shops and the street vendors and the passersby who stepped aside so that the Divetri wagon might pass. She recognized the look; she often wore it herself. It was love for Cassaforte—its sights, its smells, its people. She had often felt the same. From time to time, when she turned, his friendly eyes met hers.

As they came closer to the center of the city, she caught glimpses of the palace through the maze of buildings and bridges. At first she could see just the tops of its grand red pillars and the curve of its dome, several stories above ground. But when they pulled into the busy square at the city's center, the palace suddenly loomed before them. Caza Portello's architects had designed the structure to have only the narrowest of openings on the lowest floors; the arrangement had proved invaluable during the rare times Cassaforte had come under siege. Between these frequent, narrow windows were niches arranged with statuary, a favorite resting place for the sparrows that flocked the square looking for food. The uppermost stories had graceful casements that opened wide.

Although the palace appeared as serene and beautiful as ever, today it took on a more ominous aspect in Risa's eyes. It seemed to loom over the square as it cast afternoon shadows across the milling crowds. The great dome was blotting out the sun. Somewhere in that palace were her parents. Could they see her from the windows, or were they being held in a tiny cell? Either thought was scarcely tolerable.

"Why aren't we going to the entrance?" Risa asked, when Camilla yanked the reins to take them around the western wall.

"No one uses the grand entrance," Camilla said. "We'll unload at the rear."

For a moment Risa thought of pointing out that she had used the grand entrance every time she had accompanied her mother to the palace for the installation of a window. But she decided to keep her mouth shut. After Milo's compliment, she did not want the siblings to think she was pretentious.

The mule cart moved slowly from the square onto the bridge that ran over the canal spanning the palace's western facade. Milo hopped out of the cart and ran alongside it, so he could guide the mules to a shallow courtyard within the palace walls. He and Camilla both nodded at the single guard posted there.

Within a few moments, palace servants began to unload the hampers from the cart's bed. Risa watched from her perch in the cart as Milo gamely assisted, hauling down baskets of breads and fruits and rattling boxes of wine with great vigor. When he and the other servants reached the last of the baskets, Risa called out, "Be careful with that one. Please!" She turned to the kitchen servant. "This basket is to be delivered directly to my mother and father. Is that understood?"

"What's so special about it?" the servant demanded. Milo leapt onto the cart and brought it to her.

"It just has my mother's favorite grapes," Risa replied,

opening it. She had arranged the grapes, along with some pears and other choice fruit, in one of the bowls she'd made herself—a pretty bowl of deep blue with red roses around the edge. She had packed it in one of the thick baskets to keep it cool. "Please, you'll take it to her directly?"

The servant inspected the fruit and lifted the bowl slightly, as if he was looking for a concealed weapon. He opened the note that she had enclosed, and read it to himself:

Mama—
All is well. I am taking your sac-
rifice to the temple later, so
don't worry. I hope you
and papa enjoy your
visit to the palace. Fita
sends her love, too, and a big
hug from Mattio and me.
—Risa

Satisfied that there was nothing in the basket beyond fruit and glass, the servant replaced the bowl and nodded. Risa sighed with relief. At least the bowl would let her parents know she had packed the hampers herself and that she was thinking of them.

As the last of the servants disappeared, Risa's shoulders slumped. For over a week she had been feeling helpless and grim. The last time she had seen her father, they had argued—and badly. She knew that if anything ever happened to them, she would never forgive herself.

Milo leapt onto the cart's front bench next to his sister. As Camilla nudged the mules forward, he turned around and looked at Risa. "It's going to be all right," he said, his voice trying to give her the same courage she'd wished for her parents. "This will turn out to be one of those things that you'll laugh about when you realize how worried you were for nothing."

She nodded. "I hope."

"I think you really need a change of scenery. Let's give Cam a treat and take her to see that big strapping beau of hers." Risa was about to protest when Milo added, "Oh, don't say no. It won't take any more than twenty minutes. They'll moon at each other, he'll kiss her when she thinks we're not looking, then you and I will have a good laugh and we'll be on our way. You still want a laugh, I think. Ow!" He rubbed the spot on his shoulder where Camilla had punched him with her knuckles.

"I need to be home," she said, feeling urgency grip her like a vise.

"Why?" Milo said. "So you can watch that cousin of yours strut around like one of the king's peacocks? That would make you feel better, wouldn't it!" He pulled down his face and pushed up the tip of his nose with his finger-tip in imitation of Fredo. Though she could not laugh, Risa responded with a wry pucker of her mouth. "Or that house-keeper of yours! You'd feel better hearing that voice of hers shrilling in your ears, wouldn't you?" He turned to his sister. "She sounds like a cat with a stepped-on tail."

Risa snorted. "She does not."

"She does too!" Milo averred. "Made me want to pick out my ears with a dagger so I wouldn't have to listen." He swiveled in his seat once more, nearly catapulting off the side when the cart hit a rut. "So don't worry. I can see why you'd want to go home instead of taking Cam to see her big manly man with the enormous hands."

"Milo, don't drag me into this," said Camilla, not at all amused. "You just want to see Ricard and his crew. And Amo does not have enormous hands."

"They're like big... really big legs of mutton," Milo mock-whispered over the bench, measuring out a length an arm's span apart. Camilla attempted to push him from the cart. "You see how she treats me!"

Their antics were intended to liven her spirits. Risa wished that she knew her older siblings better; the Seven and Thirty never had the luxury of this kind of closeness. And Milo was right. There was no telling how long it would be before Romeldo arrived from the insula. Watching Fredo revel in triumph would be bitter medicine, indeed. "I don't mind a detour," she said. "A *short* detour."

Had they been afoot, Milo might have turned a cartwheel, so happy was he. "Thank the cazarrina, Camilla."

"Thank you, Cazarrina," repeated Camilla, not turning her head but bobbing it in a quick nod. "And no thanks to you," she said to Milo. "It's obvious she'd rather be home than out with the likes of *us*." She heard the girl add, in a quieter voice, "Though I don't know what all the worry is about with her parents. They're just there to bestow the crown to the new king. How bothersome can that be?"

Milo raised his eyebrows, asking Risa permission. She nodded and pretended to watch the gondolas passing below.

"That's not the whole story." Milo began to murmur in his sister's ear.

14

*I have just seen a play, written entirely in rhyming couplets,
called BARNACLE BARABBO: A NAUTICAL TRAGEDY IN SEVEN ACTS,
written (I use the term loosely) by someone claiming to be the
"Poet of the People." The only tragedy is that I shall never
have back that evening of my life again.*

—Amaretta Di Ponti, in a letter to Renalda Settecordi
of the Thirty

I don't think we should go inside when we're on duty," Camilla
said as they pulled to a stop in front of the antiquated building. "It wouldn't be right."

"I'll just nip in and see who's there," Milo suggested, leaping up from his seat and swinging to the ground with athletic
grace. "We won't have to go in at all. If any captains walk by,
tell them we're picking up a jug of cider for your cousin," he
said to Risa with a wink.

"He's only joking," Camilla said, turning around slightly.

"I know," Risa watched as Milo ducked under an arch
and disappeared down a narrow cobbled street. She had never

before ventured into this maze of tight roads and centuries-old canals with cracked walls where grew moss and grasses. The streets here were muddy, the buildings worn and crooked. Two children with dirty hands and faces stared at them from across the street. When Risa tried to smile at them, they turned their heads and ran away on bare feet.

Camilla cleared her throat and looked directly at Risa for the first time. "I'm sorry you're worried about your parents," she stammered. Risa nodded, both appeased and embarrassed by the sympathy. "If Milo gets too much—I think he—I know you're of the Seven and we're just—"

"I like Milo," Risa said simply.

"You *are* different," Camilla said, seeming surprised. "I can't imagine anyone else from the Seven and Thirty saying they *liked* a guard." She paused, looking for the right word. "We're not the usual kind your sort socializes with, you know."

Although she knew Camilla meant it as a compliment, Risa resented being held accountable for the bad behavior of others. Apparently the people of Cassaforte thought the Seven and Thirty to be arrogant and aloof. Many of them were. "My family … we don't participate in the social functions of the Thirty. Few of the Seven do," she said. "The Seven are families of craftsmen. We work. Many of the Thirty are different."

Camilla shot her a sideways glance and nodded awkwardly. For a moment Risa feared her flat statement of fact had been taken as a rebuff. Before she could clarify, a clatter of rapid footsteps echoed from the enclosed street, followed by Milo's laughter. He came barreling out from under the arch, breathing heavily. "Beat you," he said to the boy following.

"I *let* you win, fool!" said the boy. He was Milo's age or a little older, and wore a formal tunic of bright colors trimmed with bright yellow braid. It was a costume intended to catch the eye—the costume of street entertainers. He stopped short when he caught sight first of Camilla, and then of Risa, both still sitting in the cart. His eyes locked upon Risa, taking in her prim dress and the long red-brown hair hanging over her shoulder. "Fair lady," he breathed, his mouth open in rapture. He touched the shock of black hair hanging over his brow and stooped low. "I would die for thee."

"Oh no," groaned Camilla.

The boy shot her a quelling look before turning back to Risa. "Beautiful thou art, and fair. Like a perfumed poppy's fragrant air!" He moved closer to the cart, placing his hands on its rail and peering up at them in wonder. "My heart doth beat—nay, leaps and skips! To think of kisses from your lips!"

Appalled, Risa stared at the boy. He turned his head sideways. "Milo," he whispered. "You did not tell me your lady was so beautiful."

Risa looked at Milo in appeal. He had an expression on his face she had not seen before; she thought it was the first time she'd seen the young guard half-angry. She finally found words. "He didn't," she said. When she heard her voice tremble, she took a moment to breathe before continuing. "He didn't, because I am not."

"Oh lady, but you *are*," said the boy. "Were this another day, battles would be fought in your honor. Men would fight for even a snippet of your hair. Empires would be lost for the honor of kissing that fair-skinned hand!"

"Ricard," Camilla said, "Stow it. This is the Divetri cazarrina you're speaking to, not some giggly serving girl."

"Poor Ricard! He only falls for the unattainable ones now, Camilla," said another girl. She emerged from the street accompanied by a tall, scowling man. "The serving girls aren't much of a challenge."

The boy turned and frowned. "The Poet of the People begs thee desist, sister," he intoned frostily.

"Oh, desist yourself! I hate when you start in with the blank verse. It makes my teeth ache. Hello! I'm Tania. Ricard's twin, believe it or not." The girl leaned over Ricard's shoulder and extended her hand in greeting. "And you're the cazarrina. Milo told us about your adventure yesterday." Risa caught Milo looking at the ground, embarrassed. "Just ignore the Poet of the People," she advised. "He's easily smitten." Ricard mumbled something inaudible.

"Haven't I seen you somewhere?" Risa asked her. Ever since Tania had stepped out from under the arch, she thought she knew her. There was no mistaking that curly black hair cascading down her back, the full lips, or the laughing eyes.

"You may have," said Tania. "I'm an artist's model. And an actress."

"Oh, of course! Lena's handmaiden!" Dana Buonochio's oversized painting had been hung in the great anteroom of the goddess' temple the previous year. A study of a young woman prostrated before a statue of the moon goddess, it was widely acclaimed to be among the cazarra's finest work. And here was the handmaiden herself, looking not the perfect picture of mute adoration, but blossoming with life and vitality.

"Among others, yes. I'm so pleased you recognize me!

Hello there, Cam. You're looking well." As Camilla jumped down from the cart, Tania gave her a quick kiss on the cheek.

Ricard stuck out his hand, palm up, waiting for Risa. "Descend to earth, goddess divine. Take this poor hand, for I claim you mine!" Tania made a rude noise.

The poor hand in question had dirty fingernails, Risa noticed. "Ah ... I don't think so."

"Leave off, Ricard," Milo said gruffly, pushing him aside. "Let her alone. Pay him no mind," he added to Risa. When Milo held out his own hand to assist her down, she accepted, trying to ignore Ricard's unwavering stare. "That's Amo," Milo murmured, nodding in his sister's direction.

Camilla was standing close to the tall man, murmuring to him with a rare and shy smile upon her face. He could not seem to take his eyes from her, nor she from him. When Milo led Risa over to the pair, a sour look briefly crossed Amo's heavy features.

"Risa, allow me to present Amo Stilla. Amo is a glass maker too," he said. Judging from Milo's expression, she realized he intended the news to be a pleasant surprise.

"You're a Divetri?" he asked, his manner abrupt.

When she nodded, he said nothing. Obviously conversation was up to her. "Are you with a workshop?" she asked, looking down at his hands. They were indeed large and callused from hard work, but nowhere near the size of a mutton shank.

"I blow glass for the Anaplezzis," he said, almost defensively. "I do well enough."

She had not heard of them, and felt badly for it. There were many makers of glass for common use throughout the city, yet she knew little of the workshops beyond those of her family and of the insulas. "That's wonderful," she said with enthusiasm. Camilla glanced up at Amo with pride.

"You know all the proper enchantments, then," Amo said. "What they do to containers and windows?"

From behind, she heard Ricard's lilting voice. "She is an expert in enchanting men's hearts as well."

"No. I haven't learned any of that." Risa looked around at the astonished faces, flustered herself. They didn't know. Save Milo, none of them knew what a failure she really was. "I never will." Perhaps they would stop questioning her now.

"But you're a Divetri," said Amo, not comprehending.

Why didn't these people just leave her alone? She wanted to go home. "I was told by the gods that they did not need me. I am not insula-trained, nor will I ever be."

She expected looks of shock and dismay. All she saw were expressions of interest. "No big loss there, is it?" said Tania at last, her perfect teeth gleaming as she smiled. "I mean, everyone knows the insulas exist to keep the unimportant relatives occupied with a trade."

"The younger relatives," Milo corrected, one eye on Risa. "Not unimportant."

"The Poet of the People ne'er was trained by an insula-bred tutor," exclaimed Ricard.

"The Poet of the People ne'er has earned a luni, either," Milo retorted, making Tania trill with laughter.

Amo shook his head. "Never heard of a Divetri not insula-learned," he said. "But they're right. There's plenty of good craftsmen who never saw the inside of an insula or a fancy Divetri workshop, no offense. You're none the worse off."

She could not believe her ears. There had not been a day of her life she had not dreamed of entering one of the two insulas. She couldn't conceive of a life outside it. When Milo had told her that not everyone saw the insulas as the most desirable place in the world to be, she thought he'd been trying to make her feel better, in a ham-handed way. Yet here were all his friends, similarly shrugging away the setback as if it were nothing.

Could it be possible that a life in service to the gods was not what she had dreamed it was? She would have to think carefully on that, later.

"We don't mean any harm, love," Tania was saying to her. A number of bracelets studded with cheap and colorful stones clattered around her wrist as she briefly stroked Risa's hair. "I've known many good-hearted people from the insulas, especially among Caza Buonochio. I can tell that you wouldn't enjoy being among their number, though. Especially today!"

"What rhymes with Divetri?" asked Ricard suddenly, looking up from a folded paper on which he was busily scribbling notes with a piece of fine-pointed charcoal. Milo pressed his lips together and refused to answer.

"Why especially today?" Risa asked, trying her best to ignore the self-proclaimed Poet of the People.

Tania's bracelets jangled once more as she dropped her hands. "Haven't you heard? The insulas are under siege."

Three voices exclaimed as one, "What?" Risa, Milo, and Camilla looked at each other and then at Tania.

"No one's allowed in or out of either insula. It has something to do with Prince Berto's orders." Tania was obviously startled at their response. "I found out when I showed up to model for a Penitent's drawing tutorial and was turned away. City guards were posted there," she said to Camilla and Milo. "Don't you know what the other guards are doing?"

"I hadn't heard a thing about it!" exclaimed Camilla.

"The last two days have been nothing but confusion," Milo said. He looked at Risa. "Are you all right?"

Risa felt anything but all right. Her legs were trembling. Had her summons to Romeldo reached him before the siege started? Her father had always promised that if he were unable to complete the rite, Romeldo would be there. He was her last hope! Everything was spinning out of control too quickly.

"Why are the gods so set against me?" she cried, giving voice to all the dread and anguish that coursed through her. Milo's friends looked disturbed at her sudden outburst.

Tania once again placed her hand on Risa's arm, but comfort from a stranger was the last thing she wanted. Trying not to seem curt, Risa moved away from the model and got back into the cart, taking the reins in her own hands. "I've got to see for myself," she told Milo. "We have to leave now."

"I'll drive." Milo sprang into the cart without hesitation. It almost seemed as if he were anxious to atone for reassuring her earlier. "You have enough to worry about."

I have nothing to do but worry, Risa thought to herself. It was going to be a very long ride.

15

What are the sweet sounds of the horns at sunset but a daily reminder of the harmony upon which our city was built? The ceremony is living proof not of any deep magics—for they do not exist—but of the pact between monarch and working man, and the balance that must exist between them.

—Martolo the Sceptic, in Cassaforte's So-Called Enchantments Debunked: A Thinking Man's Rational Manifesto

When first erected hundreds of years before, the high-walled Insula of the Children of Muro had sat serene and alone in a wildflower field northwest of the city. Two canals had been built to provide it with access and supplies. In the centuries since, countless markets had sprung up along with pretty neighborhoods of respectable houses, many belonging to members of the Thirty. The two original canals had been lost among a complex of newer channels. Today, the western quarter of Cassaforte was indistinguishable from any other section of the city, save that the buildings were not

as wind-worn and the canal bridges were more lavishly orna-
mented, in the elaborate styles popular in recent decades.

Milo brought the cart to a halt just across the canal bridge
from the insula, and Camilla and Amo quickly crossed over
to talk to a few of the guards clustered before the closed main
gate. More guards stood at attention around the perimeter
of the massive structure, spaced twenty or so feet apart,
unmoving and alert.

"You shouldn't worry," Tania said, leaning forward to
murmur in Risa's ear. "I'm sure everything will be fine."

"To her I would pledge my trow, though worry's creased
her noble brow," Ricard was mumbling to himself, scribbling
on paper once more. "That's quite good, isn't it?"

"No," snapped Milo, while Tania simultaneously said,
"Do keep quiet, Ricard."

Without really hearing either of them, Ricard went back
to mumbling and composing his verses. Risa watched tensely
as Camilla continued to talk to the guards. "You shouldn't fret
about your family," Milo told her. "The insulas were designed
to stand up to siege. During the Azurite invasion the people
inside the Insula of the Penitents of Lena managed to survive
for two years without supplies from the outside, remember."

"I know," she said, only slightly comforted. The win-
dowless wall that protected buildings within the insula was
intended to withstand the most brutal of attacks. "I just can't
help it. Every time I think the day can't get worse, it does!"

"Will you try something?" For a moment she thought
it was another of his jests, but when she looked into Milo's
eyes, she saw that he was entirely earnest. "It's nothing bad.
Sometimes when I'm nervous, it helps."

"You, nervous?" said Tania, listening in. She seemed surprised. "You've always been the coolest character I've ever seen, Milo. I didn't think there was anything you couldn't do."

Milo narrowed his eyes slightly. "I can think of one thing I can't bring myself to do, actually. And it's none of your business," he added quickly when Tania opened her mouth to ask. When he looked at Risa again, it was with a shy slant to his eyes and mouth. "My mother taught this technique to me. Now, close your eyes. Go on."

His voice, warm and soft, encouraged her. She lowered her eyelids to block out the late afternoon sun. "I know it won't be easy," he said, "but you need to imagine yourself in a place where you're totally confident and comfortable. Someplace you feel most yourself. All right? Where are you?"

Risa thought hard for a moment, then realized what Milo meant. Trying to ignore the sun's heat and the noise of the crowds was difficult, but she focused on a single image: a picture of herself standing before the caza kilns, using the poles to retrieve one of her works. It had been gradually moved away from the heat of the flames to the very edges of the furnaces, and although it was hot to the touch, it was not so hot that it would instantly shatter from room-temperature air. In her imagination she envisioned removing the large platter. Thick gloves protected her hands. She placed the glass disc on a table, knowing that although she should be modest about her skills, she had created a thing of beauty—and more importantly, she had the talent to do it again. "Where are you?" Milo repeated.

"In the workshop," she murmured, concentrating on the image.

Beside her, as if from a distance, she heard Tania whisper, "On the stage."

"Take that feeling you have of absolute confidence. Capture it. Now imagine it's something physical. Something you can touch. What does it look like?"

"A butterfly," breathed Tania.

"A marble." Just like the marbles Petro played with. Beautiful marbles worked in an open flame were Mattio's hobby, when he was not blowing vessels with her father. She saw her favorite of them all, a perfect globe of clear glass with scarlet streaks. When younger, she had always wondered how those ribbons of flame came to be trapped in the glass.

"I want you to take that object and put it in a box," Milo continued. "Somewhere safe, where you can find it again when you want. Close the box. When you're frightened or worried, you can take it out, open it up, and look at the marble. You'll remember the feeling, I promise. Open your eyes."

When Risa opened her eyes, the image of her marble seemed to linger for a moment. Milo regarded her with his head cocked forward, his face wearing a question. "Well?" he finally said.

Risa shook her head. She still felt apprehension, but its edge had dulled. The nervous excitement that had made her stomach twitch and her palms sweat seemed to have ebbed away. She could not truthfully say she was completely free of anxiety. Her mind, however, did not race around in the crazy circles that had distressed her all afternoon. "Does it really work?" she asked him.

"If you let it."

For the first time in several minutes, Ricard spoke from

the back of the cart. "When in repose sweet Risa sleeps, my heart, it aches, it droops, it weeps..."

"She was *not* sleeping," Tania snapped. "Honestly, Ricard. If you have to write your terrible poetry, write it about someone else. Risa will think we're all lunatics because of you."

Privately, Risa already thought that Milo and Camilla's friends, with the possible exception of Ricard, were among the nicest people she had ever met. Aside from Petro and her older sister Vesta, Risa had never known many people near her own age. These people had been working, planning out what they wanted to do with their lives for years now. She had been merely sitting by, waiting for hers to begin. It amazed her how competent and self-assured they all seemed to be.

Camilla nodded at the guards and started back across the canal bridge toward the cart. Amo trudged a few steps behind her. Anxiety flared up inside Risa like flames; they must have news. To quell her panic, she thought of the marble. She remembered the marvelous feeling of proficiency she'd felt when Milo was murmuring to her. Her breathing returned to normal just as Camilla reached them.

"They're under the prince's orders to keep both insulas under guard," Camilla announced without a hint of emotion. "No one's allowed to come out."

"Or go in," added Amo. "No messages, no deliveries. It's supposed to be for their protection, until the crown and scepter have been bestowed upon Prince Berto."

"That's ridiculous," said Risa.

"There's nothing we can do about it," Camilla told her.

"You city guards are holding people *hostage*," Risa

retorted. Camilla's flat acceptance angered her. "Just like you've invaded my caza. There's no reason for it. No one's in danger but my parents!"

"We're just following orders," Milo said to her.

"I wager there are guards outside my parents' dungeon saying the same thing."

"What?" said Tania, alarmed. "Dungeon?"

"Camilla, what's going on?" Amo asked, obviously alarmed.

"Later," said Milo. "And there aren't any dungeons in the palace. Don't imagine such things."

The argument did not fill Risa with despair, as it might have an hour ago. She felt recharged and energetic and full of righteous anger. "It doesn't take a dungeon to make a prison. I know that better than anyone. Even Tolio said that you guards shouldn't be taking orders from anyone but the crowned king. But look what you're doing!"

Camilla had the decency to seem a little ashamed. "You're right about that, but Prince Berto is the heir. He'll be king soon. None of the captains wants to be in a position of disobeying someone who'll be king any moment now."

"*Soon* doesn't make him king *yet*," Risa pointed out. "No king in history has ever given such orders! It's as if—"

Realization stung her like a bucket of ice water poured over her head. She reeled at the enormity of her notion— for a moment all she could hear was the thud of her heart and the heavy coursing of blood through her veins. "No. It's evil!"

"Will someone explain to me what's going on?" Tania complained. "It's very intriguing and I must say it's all miles ahead of the last play I was in, but I haven't a clue what's happening."

"Prince Berto *wants* the cazas to fall," Risa murmured, remembering the possessive look she'd seen in his eyes that morning of the blessing. "He does. He wants them to be destroyed by demons, one by one."

"That's impossible," Camilla said quickly. Her face, however, had turned white. Milo hushed her, listening intently.

"Not impossible. He's kidnapped the cazarri."

"What?" exclaimed Amo and Tania and even Ricard, almost in unison.

"He's shut up the insulas. Almost all the caza heirs live in the insulas. Even the ones who work in the cazas daily live here." Milo's eyes widened at her words. She knew her logic was persuading him. "Romeldo never received my summons this morning. He probably doesn't even *know* Divetri's cazarro is gone and he's needed."

"But that's crazy," said Camilla.

"I don't know why, but Prince Berto wants the cazas to fail."

They were quiet for a moment. "I never liked the prince," Tania said softly. "I've seen him—he looks at people like he's a snake and they're his dinner."

"But that's outrageous!" Ricard said, for once not rhyming. "It would take a monster to do such a thing."

"Mother didn't like him, either," said Camilla. "But I can't believe … "

Risa looked over her shoulder with panic. "It will be sunset in less than an hour." Her throat rasped as she voiced the words. "We have to get back to the caza. Now."

She thought she would have to argue more strenuously, but Milo was already collecting the reins.

16

To trust is wonderful. Not to trust is sometimes wiser.

—A COMMON CASSAFORTEAN SAYING

Ⰾ

"How pleasant you could join us, cousin." Cousin Fredo stood on the balcony arrayed in a set of formal houppe-landes that belonged to her father. They were much too large for him and nearly swallowed his feet and hands whole. If she had not been so thoroughly out of breath from running, Risa would have gasped at his audacity. "In honor of your father's absence, I think we will have none of the usual waywardness from you this evening? Or from your ... little friends?"

Milo had burst onto the balcony side by side with Risa; they had hopped from the mule cart when it had pulled close to the upper bridge and run as quickly as they could.

Camilla, Ricard, and Tania had followed, their eyes drinking in the spacious expanse of the caza and its furnishings. They now stood in the doorway to the caza, panting.

"Fredo, this is serious!" Risa yelled at him.

"Gently … gently!" Fredo replied, touching his fingers to his temples. His fingers twitched in the direction of his metal box of *tabbaco da fiuto.* "My nerves … "

"Curse your nerves!" Risa cried, just as the palace horn blew from the domed roof.

With fingers that felt like steel knives, Fredo grabbed Risa's shoulder and leaned his face close to hers. "Do not presume to use an insolent tone with *me*, girl," he hissed. "I am Cazarro in your father's absence. He would not be pleased at your impertinence, and you know it. You will *obey* me or suffer the consequences."

"Release her," Milo barked out, his voice resonating more deeply and more maturely than she had previously heard. Her cousin's talons slackened, but their tips still dug into her flesh.

"There's no call for that," Fredo said in a quiet tone. "I'll inform your captain."

"And he'll inform you that we were ordered to protect the cazarrina," Milo proclaimed.

"Even from her cousin," Camilla added with authority.

The silvery cry of Cassamagi's horn seemed to cut through the air between herself and her cousin. Risa stumbled back as he released his grip, and Camilla kept her from tripping. When she looked around, she saw that the brother and sister guards had drawn daggers from the sheaths in their belts. Both still regarded Fredo with hostility.

The confrontation had clearly shocked those who witnessed it. Several of the servants were murmuring nervously at the perimeter of the balcony. Mattio looked as if he wanted to brandish a dagger of his own. Even Fita, who had been smug at Risa's tardy appearance, looked drawn and wan. "Let us speak of this later," intoned Fredo, trying to calm everyone through gestures and a soothing voice. "We must first conduct the rite. It has been a stressful day for us all, but would that my cousin Ero could see how well you all have carried on in his absence. It warms my heart to belong to this family. It truly does." He tugged to adjust the shoulders of his robe, which were far too broad for his own narrow frame.

"In my profession," Tania murmured in Risa's ear, "we have a name for your cousin's acting style. Pure ham."

A rumble sounded in the east, as of distant thunder. Risa looked up in surprise, for it was a cloudless night. The colors of the western sky were the pure reds and pinks of the finest glass.

"I accept it as my humble duty to act as cazarro in my cousin's absence." Fredo unfurled the blue and green silks of the Divetri banner. He attached it to the rope that in mere moments would take it into the heavens. "For years have I labored in the Divetri workshops without thought of personal gain. This moment, brief as it is, will be reward enough."

Risa agreed with Tania. Fredo's speech sounded practiced and insincere. If her parents returned—*when* her parents returned—she felt certain he would never let any of the family forget how he got to blow the Divetri horn this night.

For a moment, she thought it was her anger that produced the rumbling sound that once again echoed to the east, but with a start she realized it was a much more ominous noise. It rattled them all to the bone.

"Something's happening at Portello," said Milo, leaning in behind her. He pointed east, at the next caza.

"Why haven't they sounded their horn?" Risa asked. She had heard Cassamagi's several minutes ago.

Tania gasped; Ricard and Amo ran forward to the rail. Something indeed was happening at Portello—the entire caza seemed to be rumbling, producing the thunder-like shaking that Risa had heard just moments before. The first two tremors she'd heard had been low and quiet; Caza Portello now seemed possessed by the force of an earthquake.

"Good gods," she heard Fredo say.

Several of the female servants watching the sight clapped their hands to their mouths, smothering cries of horror. From Mattio's direction, Risa heard a shout. A moan swelled and died in her own throat. No one said a word, however. The iron loops of the Divetri banners, forgotten, rapped metallically against the hollow pole.

The delicate stone spires that distinguished Portello from the other cazas were rocking as if fashioned from playing cards. Often during the rite of fealty, Risa had felt as if she sensed an invisible tie connecting each caza with the palace; now, as the tremors grew stronger, she felt an invisible rope snap, disconnecting Caza Portello from the center of the city.

A covered portico, which extended beyond Caza Portello's southern extremities and over its rocky beach, buckled. Like twigs, its graceful pillars splintered one by one. The supports that held it over the waters crumbled to dust, dashing the entire walkway into the sea. Portello's great stone gates, which had faced the city for centuries, now toppled forward, crashing onto the bridge that connected the caza to the city.

A number of servants and craftsmen were running from the Portello residence, barely escaping the great stones as they fell. Risa bit her lip as she watched a man sweep a tiny girl into his arms, his legs trying to propel them both to safety as the first section of the bridge crumbled into the canal. A second section followed, and still the man ran on, not looking behind him. *Run!* Risa thought. *Run!*

One of the spires slid from the caza's roof into its courtyard just as the third section of the bridge disintegrated and fell, smashing onto empty gondolas below. A woman standing at the bridge's end screamed at the man as he ran on; her shriek was audible even over the earth's terrible roar. A moment later and the man and girl were in the woman's arms, safe in the piazza in the city. The last section of the bridge disintegrated into pebbles. The traces slowly disappeared under water.

The rumbling stopped. There was a moment of silence.

Screams and crying began to echo through the streets and canals of Cassaforte. In the Piazza Divetri, women and men wailed. A flickering light leapt ablaze at the southern end of Caza Portello, where the portico had been, licking flames along the tinder. Risa gaped in horror at the shell of Portello—a ragged silhouette of rock and fissure against the twilight sky. Architects, the Portello family had been. They were left with little to show for their centuries of labor.

Beneath her own feet, Risa felt a rumble. She looked down to see a pebble dancing across the red and black tiles of the balcony. She stared at it, her mind scarcely comprehending what was happening.

Caza Divetri was beginning to shake. They had not raised the silks. The horn had not been blown.

Mattio spoke first. "Fredo—the banners!"

For a moment Risa thought her cousin might be ill. He had witnessed the destruction of Caza Portello as silently as the rest. She saw that he was trembling.

The tremor subsided. It had been a warning, Risa realized through her fear. They had to act.

"Raise the banners!" several of the household cried out in alarm. Fredo sprang for the flagpole. With shaking hands, he yanked furiously at the rope. It clanked and jerked to a stop as the Divetri silks reached their summit. With the rest of those assembled, Risa looked up into the slate blue sky as their flag flapped in the sea wind.

A second tremor struck the house, much stronger than the first. Its buckling was so intense that Risa's knees threatened to give out from under her.

A number of the household members began yelling and running for the door, trying to escape. From the lower bridge, Risa heard the shout of the guards and a number of the stable men as they began frantically running from the caza's outbuildings.

"The horn, you fool!" Mattio shouted in Fredo's ear.

Her cousin looked nearly as panicked as the most frightened kitchen servant. "I—I don't know … " he stammered, the words audible only as the rumble once again began to subside. Below them, on the bridges, servants and craftsmen yelled in terror as they began to stream from the doorways, fleeing the caza.

"Blow the bloody horn!" Mattio roared. He took four long steps to the pedestal and removed the copper lid. "Blow it before we're all killed!"

"It will be the glass," Risa said, suddenly sure of herself. She turned to Milo and Camilla, who regarded her with alert eyes. "For Portello it was their buildings that failed. They're architects. For us it will be the glass. All of it."

Though she did not know from where it came, she had a sure instinct of how their doom would unfold. First the Divetri windows—centuries of metal and glass undamaged by even the strongest of storms—would explode and collapse. Every item of glass in the household would burst and shatter, sending shards of glass everywhere. The great dome over the family's hallway would disintegrate, splintering and falling in a deadly rain of slivers that would pierce flesh and bone alike. Mirrors, bowls, goblets, the tiny menagerie of hand-blown animals in Petro's old room, every object in her father's workroom and the hundreds upon hundreds of sheets of glass waiting to be cut and used in the storehouses—each would become a deadly weapon. Loosed of their enchantments, they would fracture and fly in every direction, destroying the caza and all those who could not escape its deadly trap.

"Get away!" Milo yelled to Amo and Ricard, who were only an arm-span away from a stained glass window, the very window Petro had almost broken a week before. "Stand back!" he yelled to Emil, who stood in shock, unable to move.

Camilla also seemed to understand Risa's warning, for

just as the third rumble began to shake the caza's foundation, she ran to herd the remaining servants to the farthest end of the balcony. "Lie down!" she commanded. "Cover your heads! And keep your eyes closed!"

The windows began to rattle in their frames. Risa felt as if she could hear every individual piece of glass shaking in the lead channels that held them. Near the pedestal, she saw Fredo struggling with the horn. He held it to his lips as had her father, every night for year upon year. No sound came from its bell.

From the bridges, the shouting increased in volume. The earth began to shudder in anger. Tania and Ricard huddled against the balcony edge in each other's arms. Once more, Fredo placed his lips against the horn's narrow mouthpiece. It was a struggle for him even to stand upright, much less muster enough breath to blow.

Risa watched in astonishment and anger as he crumpled to the ground, folded over the horn. From below she heard the sound of a single pane of glass shattering. Fredo could not complete the rite.

She felt Milo grab her by the shoulders. "You're a Divetri!" he yelled at her. "You're more Divetri than your cousin!"

"It's too late!" she shouted back, choking down the lump in her throat.

"Not yet!"

She saw something in her mind, then: a glass marble streaked with red. The terrible din of the island's mad roar diminished as cool determination flooded through her limbs. "Not yet," she repeated, feeling the confidence stir her to action. "Not ever!" Vaulting over to Fredo, she attempted to take the horn from his terrified grasp.

"We're all going to die!" He struggled against her, shouting the words over and over again.

"Not if I have anything to say about it!" With a mighty twist, she wrenched the instrument from his hands. Fredo protested, then crumpled into a ball and squirmed to get away.

There was not much time left. Planting her legs firmly against the angry earth, she lifted the instrument to her lips.

She blew.

A single pure tone floated into the night air, soothing the ground's savage temper. The note grew louder, pealing through the pandemonium. With barely a hesitation, the tremors came to a standstill. Risa heard the shouting cease from the bridge and piazza below.

Yet again she felt an imperceptible cord fly from the caza to the center of the city, anchoring her to the palace. It stretched taut between them, holding the household in its grip.

She blew until her trembling arms could no longer hold the horn and its musical tone faded into memory. In the distance, atop the palace, she thought she could sense displeasure, as if the prince had been willing her caza to fall and raged when it did not. But as her father had often told her, the palace was too far away. It was probably just her imagination.

She had done it. She had completed the rite. A moment later she heard the answering cry from Catarre, but it was all but drowned out by a sudden roar from the bridges below. Risa looked down to find the Divetri servants cheering and applauding madly. It took another moment before she realized that they were celebrating none other than her.

Ricard was standing, helping Tania to unsteady feet. Once up, he was the first to speak. "That was the most marvelous feat I have ever witnessed. You are a wonder, Cazarrina!" he breathed, his voice astonished.

"Cazarra," corrected Mattio. He turned to the balcony rail and with his mighty voice cried into the night. "Risa, Cazarra of Divetri!"

"Risa! Cazarra of Divetri!" echoed Milo. He was grinning from ear to ear. Soon Camilla joined him in the cry. "Risa! Cazarra of Divetri!"

From the bridges it echoed. *"Cazarra! Cazarra of Divetri!"*

"I knew you could do it," Milo said under his breath. "I think you could do anything." She turned in surprise, unexpectedly touched, but Milo was looking at the crowd below. For a moment it flashed through her mind that perhaps she had overheard something not intended for her ears. He was joining in the cheering, bellowing her name at the top of his voice.

Amidst the cheering and the commotion, a steely hand clasped her on the shoulder. "Nicely done, cousin," said Fredo. His white face was wreathed in the most funereal of smiles as he leaned in close. "But I doubt your father would be well pleased. You know how he feels about girls performing a man's job. If I were you, I would hope he will overlook the dishonor when he returns." He stalked away, whipping Ero's robes angrily about him.

His speech was like a slap. She watched as he vanished through the doorway, and shivered once he was gone.

At that moment, Mattio grabbed Risa around the waist. She gasped in surprise when he hoisted her to his broad and comfortable shoulder. *"Cazarra of Divetri!"* he shouted once more to the crowds below. He deposited Risa upon the balcony rail, where she stood illuminated by the lamps burning on both sides of the canals and the bridge below. Directly above her head flew the banners of her household. Above them shone the two moons, already marking their course across the night sky.

Face after face beamed at her for as far as she could see. The cheering sounded as if it would never stop. *"Risa! Cazarra!"* She should have been enormously happy.

Why then, could she only imagine her father's face turning from her in disappointment?

BOOK

—

TWO:

—

THE GLASS

—

BOWL

17

I will not dissemble. It frightens me, Nivolo, that I am grown so old and yet have never found an apprentice to whom I can pass on the arts that only I can practice. But no matter. You once told me I was the answer to a prayer you made. Let us hope the gods are willing to answer all such prayers in the future.

—Allyria Cassamagi to King Nivolo of Cassaforte,
from a private letter in the Cassamagi historical archives

D on't cry. You must sleep." The man's whisper cut through the darkness. "Please don't cry, my darling. She'll be fine."

"She's only a baby," said the other voice, tantalizingly familiar. "She's all alone."

"She's not all al—"

The man's voice was interrupted by a sound, and then the intrusion of another speaker, his voice dark and sharp. She had heard it before, too. "Have you reconsidered? Or do you really want to endure another sunset like tonight's?" She heard a slight, unamused laugh. "The others are ready to talk."

What others? The question, formed in her dreams, pulled her from the depths of sleep. She woke and found herself surrounded by silence.

"Who's there?" she whispered back into the night. The voices faded. The only sound was a symphony of crickets from the canal banks.

Risa listened carefully, but the voices were gone. With weariness, she thought of rising from bed to see if anyone might be conducting a conversation on the waters below. Her limbs, however, were too heavy and tired to move. It must be several hours until dawn yet. Already her mind was drifting back to sleep … She didn't even remember the dream the next morning.

"Good morning, Cazarra," a servant murmured as she walked toward the outdoor garden room her family used for the morning meal. Her entrance caused a stir. At the sideboard, a number of the staff were busily folding cloths and sweeping away crumbs, but they instantly set down whatever they held and dropped into deep curtseys and bows.

"Good morning, Cazarra," they all said in low voices, staring at the ground.

"Have I missed breakfast? I'm sorry. I slept late." Risa's stomach rumbled just then, making her wince in embarrassment. They must have heard it. "I'll just get something from the kitchens, then."

"If you please," said the first servant, curtseying once more, "it is not fitting for the Cazarra to eat there. I will fetch the housekeeper for you." With another dip, she vanished indoors.

At the head of the table, a male servant pulled out the

139

carved, elaborate chair belonging to her father. "No, thank you, I'll just sit there," Risa said, shuffling in the direction of her usual seat near the foot.

"If you please, Cazarra." The servant's entreaty halted her progress. He gestured to the chair and gave her a pointed look. At last she sighed and walked the length of the table to take her father's seat. The half dozen attendants bowed in unison and left the garden room. Risa felt stunned. Never before in her life had she received such deference; she was used to politeness, but not awe. The servants were treating her as they would her father or mother.

"Cazarra." The housekeeper entered the room with her head low. "I apologize that a tray was not sent to your room. We are short-staffed after last night's events. It will not happen again."

"Oh no, I overslept." Risa yawned and blinked. "Why are we short-staffed?"

"After what happened to Cazas Portello and Dioro—"

All her sleepiness vanished. Risa lurched erect. "Not Dioro too!"

Fita nodded gravely. "And Piratimare."

It was true, then. The prince wanted the cazas to fall. Three of the seven, destroyed in one night. It was unthinkable. The only thing worse was knowing how close to the precipice Caza Divetri had staggered. Thinking of it only frightened her, though. She instantly reminded herself that they had not failed to complete the rite of fealty. They would not fail tonight, nor the next. When her parents returned, they would find the caza just as they had left it.

"We've lost several servants," Fita continued. "They're

afraid to work here. But I shall find one to bring your meal, Cazarra." She nodded and glided from the room. Normally the old servant loved nothing more than to gossip and scold, but today she was curiously abrupt.

It was because of last night, Risa realized. Everyone was treating her differently now. Before, she was just Risa. Plain, unwanted Risa. Risa the nuisance whose experiments in the furnaces were a waste of glass and time. Risa the helpless little girl, the daughter who had disappointed them all. Now she was Risa the Cazarra, head of household. Protector of Divetri and bearer of its horn.

"Breakfast, Cazarra," said the voice of an old man, a few moments later. Dom stumbled in, his steps shuffling and tentative. In his trembling hands he carried a bowl stuffed with fruit and bread. For a moment Risa nearly jumped up and took it from him, but she noticed another servant in the doorway, observing Dom's performance—most likely so he could report back to the eagle-eyed Fita. She remained seated, holding her breath in the hope he would pass whatever test he was undergoing.

He tottered forward and set the bowl on the table in front of her. It landed a little unsteadily and without any of the invisible grace she had taken for granted with the other servants. His glance caught hers briefly as he bowed low. She smiled encouragingly at him just before the servant snapped his fingers. Dom's head inclined toward the ground as he backed away, then he turned and hobbled from the room.

When the servants had thought her of little importance, they'd treated her like a normal human being, if not quite an equal. Today, now that they respected her, the distance between herself and them had increased. She was not certain if she liked the new arrangement better.

Footsteps sounded in the garden beyond the pillars. She turned to find Milo in his crimson uniform. "Cazarra," he said in a formal, bored tone. "You have a visitor awaiting you at the far end of your upper bridge."

Still clutching half of a sweet bun in her hand, Risa rose from her chair. Why was Milo sounding so stiff and reserved? He did not offer smile for smile when she stepped in his direction. Surely he, of all people, would not treat her differently.

His eyes flicked back over his shoulder. "Captain Tolio," Risa said carefully, understanding her friend's sudden formality. "Good morning."

"Good morning, Cazarra," said the captain. He was civil, but only just. "I trust you slept well after last night's ... distressing events?"

"Oh yes, quite well, thank you," she said.

His smile was so slight that she wondered why he even exerted the effort to feign it. "I do not intend to keep you from your visitor," he murmured, stepping in front of Milo. "I only wished to verify that our guards were not intruding upon your ... good will. Certain guards, that is." Milo assumed a look of bland rigidity.

"The Sorranto boy?" She shrugged. "Oh no. He's been very ... businesslike." On instinct, she affected the bored, snobbish tone used among many families of the Thirty. "Someone of his class would scarcely bother someone of mine, would he?"

The captain relaxed somewhat. "I just wanted to hear it from you, Cazarra."

She shooed Tolio away with her hands. "Leave me. I would see my visitor." She sounded so much like the social leaders she mocked that she nearly laughed.

With a quick, respectful bow and a dark look at Milo, the captain stepped from the garden room. Scarcely had he left when Milo let out a deep breath and grinned. "You *can* lay it on thick!" he whistled.

"Don't underestimate me," she said.

Milo laughed abruptly. "Oh, believe me, I'm learning not to."

18

History claims that it was the enchantments of the so-called Piratimare ship builders that enabled a minor principality such as Cassaforte to turn back the Azurite invasion after two years. The Piratimare crafts are said never to sink, or take on too much water in a storm. I have seen the ship builders at work, however, and save for a few prayers made at regular intervals, their techniques are no different from our own.

—Comte William DeVane, **Travels Sundry & Wide Beyond the Azurite Channel**

The interior of the carriage reeked with the nose-tickling scent of must and the sweet, heavy decay of old velvet. There was another odor as well—a sharp and faded perfume that lingered in the low ceilinged space like a whisper. With the door closed, every breath of air seemed hot in her lungs. Risa shifted uncomfortably on the backward-facing seat, hoping that in the dim light the old man could not see her perspire. He did not seem to be warm at all; if anything, beneath his old-fashioned cloak and layers of thick clothing, he gave the appearance of shivering.

His spectacles had spectacles. In front of each of the

thick lenses held upon his nose with twisted wire sat another, smaller circle of glass. He was peering through both sets of lenses now, regarding her from the other carriage seat. His overgrown gray eyebrows furrowed in concentration for several moments until, at last, he moistened his lips and began to work words from his mouth.

"But you are a child!" he exclaimed. His voice made him seem even older than his withered and frail appearance would indicate. To Risa it sounded like leaves rustling in the breeze, come autumn's end.

There was no possible polite reply to this. "You're Ferrer, Cazarro of Cassamagi," she said at last. He seemed surprised that she recognized him. "You've come to the caza before, to see my parents. Not for a long while, though."

"Ero is your father?" He seemed to be puzzling out the relationship. "You must forgive me, my dear. It is easier to remember children when one is young. When one reaches my age, everyone seems like a child." He peered at her through the curious spectacles once more. "And you blew the Divetri horn, last night?" When she nodded, he said gently, "It is indeed fortunate that you did. I admit to being frightened, however. Seven houses—once so strong—diminished to four, kept alive last night only by children and old men."

Through the glass of the carriage's window, beyond the deep crimson of Camilla's cap where she stood guard outside, Risa could see past the canal to the distant ruins of Caza Portello. Smoke still poured from sections of the rubble. At the center of the residence, visible now in the daylight, the great dome over the caza's center had collapsed. Only a few ribs still arched skyward. Ferrer leaned forward and followed her gaze. "My people tell me that only the caza itself suffered. The other works, by generations of Portello craftsmen, have endured—half the city would be lying in dust if all their enchantments were destroyed. Still…it is a pity so much of their property was fortified with enchantments. The caza would not have suffered so much, otherwise, when the pact was broken. Piratimare suffered comparatively little."

"What pact?" Risa asked. For a moment, in her curiosity, she forgot the fetid closeness of the carriage.

"The rite of fealty is a pact, child. Have you never heard the story? No? It is an agreement between the crown and the people, established eight centuries ago by one of my ancestors. She was fierce as a lioness, and just as brave. Allyria Cassamagi, her name was." He said the name in much the way he might have whispered the name of a girl he loved in his youth.

"Tell me about the pact," Risa prompted, a little afraid to break his reverie.

He startled slightly. "Your mother never told you this story? She is half Cassamagi. Charming girl. Well, there were none like Allyria before, and there has never been another since. She had power—the true power of enchantment—not the mere trifling talismans we have left to us. You see, there was a time when the kings of Cassaforte were not as benevolent as those we have known. They were proud, cruel men who murdered their enemies, even those who were part of their family. These tyrants were constantly declaring war, hoping to increase their own coffers of gold. There came a time, however, when a gentler man took the throne. King Nivolo. He looked at the poverty of his people and at his savage, warring forefathers and decided that if Cassaforte were to prosper, all its abuses had to stop."

"Allyria? Like the Bridge of Allyria?"

"It was named after her." He paused, looking out the window in the direction of Portello once more. Risa, fascinated by his story, gave him a moment to breathe before he began again. "Nivolo prayed to Muro and Lena. They heard his pleas and sent Allyria to help him. She took the two badges of the king's office, the Olive Crown and the Scepter of Thorn. With them she created a great magic—an enchantment so massive in construction that it dwarfs any other we know. She transformed them from mere symbols of power into items that could protect and unite the city—for as long as there lived just men and women to defend it."

"How?" Risa could scarcely contain her impatience to hear the rest of the story, though she could not have expressed why.

With a shaking hand, Ferrer removed the spectacles from his face and blinked at her. "Do you really think Cassamagi exists solely to enchant flints and toys and household objects? The *how* of it is what my caza has studied, has striven to relearn for the better part of eight centuries. We simply do not know the *how*. Yet we know *what* she did. She enchanted the crown and scepter so that they granted the king long life and health—on the condition that the ruler was not separated from them for an extended period of time. Most importantly, they granted him a right to reign, a right that could only be bestowed upon him by seven families from Cassaforte."

"The Seven," breathed Risa.

"They became the Seven, yes." The old Cazarro sighed

and put on his spectacles once more. "At the time they were the families of six reputable craftsmen. And my family too, of course, known for scholarship. Their responsibility was to remain loyal first to Cassaforte, and then to their king. Only they were allowed to bestow the crown and scepter upon the chosen heir. A ruler could not even so much as touch them without their unanimous consent. And if the families all agreed that the king was overstepping his powers, they would also have the power to remove him from the office."

Risa was so entranced that she utterly forgot her surroundings. "And the rite of fealty was Allyria's doing?"

"She crafted the seven horns herself, and invested them with great magic. The rite is part of the scheme's great balance," the old man explained. "You see, the seven families were given a grave and heavy responsibility. In return, however, they were granted two rewards. The first was the seven islands—upon them they built their cazas. The city began to grow between the palace and the cazas, and beyond."

"What was the second reward?"

"As long as the seven families completed the rite of fealty every night, they would find themselves able to perform certain small enchantments in their craftsmanship—such as the protection enchantments of Portello's buildings, or your mother's windows, or the learning enchantments of Catarre, or the novelties of my own caza. When the Thirty were established among their grandsons and granddaughters, the privilege was granted to them as well."

"But the enchantments aren't small at all," Risa protested. "They're marvelous."

Ferrer shook his head. "Many share your opinion, yet

they are mere tricks. Your father keeps furnaces, child. Think of Allyria's grasp of magic as the roaring fires within them, bright and hot as the sun itself. She could do amazing things. She could see and speak to people from afar, and rise in the air like a phoenix. She could craft horns that could peer into the hearts of those who attempted to play them, so that only the right man or woman or the king himself could make them sound. Compared to her burning glory, the enchantments you think so marvelous are but tiny sparks from a campfire. Despite what you may have learned at your insula, they are insignificant in scope."

Risa sat still for a moment. The heavily padded interior of the Cassamagi coach reduced the bustle of the city streets beyond to a muffled hum. "I have not learned any such thing from the insula, Cazarro."

To her surprise, the old man smiled. "Ah, yes. You are the one who went unchosen, am I correct?"

She nodded and said stiffly, "The gods said I was not needed there."

"It may be that you are not," he replied. She stared at him with such unveiled hostility that he was at last moved to rusty laughter. "Do not be offended, young Cazara. The insulas are good for many things, but they were not able to save Portello or Dioro last night."

Immediately she felt ashamed. Ferrer had not meant any harm, that much was obvious. "I have friends," she said tentatively, "who say the insulas exist merely to keep the children of the Seven and Thirty occupied."

The corners of Ferrer's mouth crooked into a smile. "Between us, your friends are not far from wrong. The insulas have their place—they educate, they inculcate ethics, they foster independence away from the homes of the Seven and Thirty so that their children will not develop rivalries for house control. And I have lost too many wagers over the years over their bocce tournaments. But not everything important is learned within their walls." Risa was thoughtful for a moment at that news. "We have a more serious matter to discuss, I am afraid. Your parents are at the palace. My heir, who went in my stead, is there as well. All the cazarri are at the palace. I do not wish to alarm you, little one, but I suspect they are being held there against their will."

"They're hostages," Risa confirmed, feeling oddly relieved to be able to say the words to someone. "I've known since yesterday." At Ferrer's astonished inhalation of breath, she nodded and told him about the coded message sent by her mother.

"Clever woman, to have sent such word in her note," he breathed. After a moment, he added, "Clever girl, to have noticed it."

"The prince wants the cazas to fall. But why?" Risa lowered her voice instinctively, though she knew no one would hear them outside the stuffy enclosure of the carriage.

"Because the cazarri, or some portion of them, do not wish to award him the Olive Crown," Ferrer said in a rasp. "They must be unanimous in their assent. They are not, and it angers the prince. He will wait for the seven cazas to be loosed from Allyria's pact, one by one. Then he will be free to appoint seven more families in their place—seven families from the Thirty who, out of gratitude, will award him the crown and do his bidding."

"He's evil!"

"His actions are obscene. They are an abuse of the rite of fealty and all it was meant to prevent." Spittle flew across the old man's lips with the accusation. The carriage was quiet for a moment. "And we are all in danger, for the prince will move to destroy those of us who can defend the cazas. That, child, is why you must keep your profile low. Does anyone outside the caza know your father trained you to blow the horn?"

The laugh that escaped Risa's lungs was scarcely more than a breath. "My father would never allow a woman to complete the rite," she said. "It's inconceivable to him."

"And to many others. An antiquated notion, true. Yet one that will work to your advantage. We must all keep out of the prince's clutch. Buonochio's new acting cazarro, Baso, is a mere boy who happened to be staying the night in his caza rather than his insula. Catarre has one old man to blow its horn, the cazarro's infirm uncle. And my house... I am no protector, child. I am too old."

Risa's instinct was to protest otherwise. But as she looked at the frail old man sitting with dignity across from her, wrapped against any possible draft, she realized that he spoke nothing more than the unadorned truth. "We are all very fragile, then," she said.

"We are," he agreed. "Like glass." Impulsively he reached out and placed his hand over hers. "There are many who wish to see us fail. Thirty houses, hungry for advancement. Not all of them will be disloyal," he added. "No. Not even most. But it will only take seven. Be careful, child. You must be careful!"

19

*Every object has its natural and primary purpose. The blessings of
the gods can only enhance that one natural purpose.*

—FROM AN INTRODUCTION TO SUPPLICATION:
A FIRST-YEAR PRIMER FOR THE INSULA INITIATE

After the stifling heat of the carriage, the sea-blown breeze
felt like a cool bath. Smells from the streets assaulted
Risa's nose while the crowd's noises attacked her ears. Flowers and fruit from the vendors in the piazza, stones baking
in the sun, the damp canal waters—all the scents erased the
carriage's sharp and acrid aroma. She had scarcely set foot
in the piazza when Ferrer's vehicle began to ease away, his
team trotting across the bricks toward the east. It was with
genuine regret that she watched the old man go—he seemed
one of her few true allies.

"Cazarra," murmured a voice in her ear. Surprised, Risa

realized that Camilla's hand was upon her wrist. Milo stood on her other side, silent and alert. She had forgotten her guards were so close at hand. "If I might beg a favor."

Camilla looked so uncharacteristically nervous that the hairs on Risa's neck prickled in alarm. "Is something wrong?"

"No, not at all. My—Amo, that is, is here, and he wonders if he might…"

While Camilla struggled for words, Risa looked past her. The girl's enormous suitor stood a few feet away. "Oh, does he want to visit our workshops? Mattio won't mind."

Camilla flushed and looked embarrassed. "It is a little more than that, Cazarra. Amo was dismissed when he did not return to his master, last night. We were so frantic to return you here—"

"Oh no!" Risa suddenly understood. His firing had been her fault. Amo looked at the ground.

"I cannot ask you for anything, Cazarra, but if you might…" Camilla bit her lip.

Milo spoke up. "A cazarra has the right to employ whom she chooses, you see."

Risa felt a momentary twinge of annoyance. She knew the rights of the cazarri without being reminded. She put her own hand atop Camilla's. "I owe Amo, after his assistance yesterday. Present him to Mattio. If Mattio thinks he may be of assistance, he may stay. With my father gone, they will appreciate a skilled craftsman."

Amo bowed low before her. "I will not disappoint you or your father's men, Cazarra," he said to her. "I ask for nothing more than a chance to prove myself." To her surprise, he smiled.

Camilla appeared relieved as well. "Milo, keep by her side. I will not be long." Her step was light as she beckoned to Amo and led him down the sloping street to the lower Divetri bridge.

"You have a knack for solving people's problems," Milo commented once they were out of sight.

"Me?" Risa was surprised that he should say such a thing.

"Take Amo. His work is his life. It was his choice to come with us yesterday instead of returning to his workshop. You really didn't owe him anything."

"He'll have a chance to show his skills. I did it for Camilla, just as much as for Amo," Risa admitted. "She'll be happy, knowing he's nearby."

"The day goes by faster when you're close to the one who makes you happy."

"Who else do I make happy?" she asked him, suddenly curious.

The question made him startle; his eyes rapidly flicked away from hers, then back. "Why, Dom, of course," he said. "And your caza. It's happy to be here still." Then he signaled in the direction of a small crowd milling in the center of the piazza. "You've made Ricard very happy."

"Ricard?" Some part of Risa's mind had noticed the crowd, earlier, but she had failed to notice the Poet of the People at its center. He was again dressed in a tunic of brightly colored patches, with braid at the hems. Fringe dangled around his wrists. It was a marvel the long strings of yellow did not interfere with his lute. The bells on his multi-colored cap tinkled in time to the tune he played on the stringed instrument.

The crowd had left some space for Ricard to perform. Risa noticed Tania, her curly hair tied with ribbons, dancing at the crowd's margin, keeping occasional time on a shallow tambour. The crowd had thrown a number of coins into her little drum, and continued to do so as Ricard sang and Tania danced. The coins rattled and jingled as Tania added to the noise by beating the stretched skin from its underside. "What are they doing?" Risa asked, the fun distracting her from her conversation with Ferrer Cassamagi.

"He's written a new song," Milo said. As usual, a grin was broadly splayed across his face. "People actually seem to like it, for once. This is the third time in a row they've had him play it."

This Ricard was quite a different figure from the Ricard who had mooned around her the day before. Wild expressions animated his face as he sang. His eyes seemed alight with the sheer joy of performing. She drew closer to the perimeter of the crowd. "He's so *alive*," she marveled to Milo.

"That's Ricard," he murmured to her. "He just loves an audience."

Ricard drew a deep breath and launched into the next verse of his song.

"The caza's so empty, my brothers are gone.
No sisters I have I can turn to!"
Tears fell down her cheek, so pale, soft, and fair.
To stroke them away, men would burn to.

The rhythm of the song was irresistible. Risa found herself grinning at it. Several of the spectators were already humming along with the simple melody. "He's good!" she told Milo in surprise.

"There's more."

She stood 'neath the moons. They cast down soft rays.
A goddess in white, yes, I thought her.
"Yet no harm will come here. Oh gods, hear my vow!"
Cried Risa, the glass maker's daughter.

Her toe stopped tapping at the sound of her own name. Never before had she heard it used in public, much less in song. Even in the late morning sun, she could feel a prickle of chilly premonition across her shoulders. When she turned her head to look at Milo, he was smiling at his friend and bobbing along with the music. It took a few moments before the confused jumble of bells and coins and tambour and singing and lute resolved again into a more comprehensible muddle:

A rumbling shook poor Portello that eve.
Foundations were rocking like thunder.
And Risa's poor cousin and servants took fright:
The girl spoke as they looked on with wonder.

"I'll not let my caza see such dire fate!"
And just as her father had taught her,
She took up the horn. Everyone marveled
At the brave, fearless glass maker's daughter.

A blossoming tone deafened all who stood round
As she blew in the marvelous horn.
"Cazarra am I!" she cried loud, without fear,
And she looked at her cousin with scorn.

The caza she saved, that night of dark fate—
Every brick stayed firm in its mortar.
And the masses sang loud, round the beautiful maid,
This tale of the glass maker's daughter!

There could have been no more perfect a setting for his performance than the background of ruined Portello. The crowd burst into rapturous applause at the end of the song. Ricard bowed several times with a flourish, then placed his lute on the ground and leapt to help Tania retrieve the coins that were still being tossed from the back of the crowd. Milo let out a whistle that pierced through the clamor.

"Milo! Risa!" Tania jumped into the air at the sight of them. When she turned to point them out to Ricard, however, Risa froze, horrified. She did not want to see Ricard, nor him to see her. It was *her* life he'd been singing about—and it was not his for the plundering.

It was too late. Ricard's face lit up; he began to push through the crowd in their direction. He held up his hands. "Quiet! Quiet!" he said. "I, Ricard, the Poet of the People, am but a simple recorder of events. It is my great pleasure to introduce to you all my muse, my goddess upon earth ... "

"Oh, gods," Risa breathed.

" ... and oh, I would wish her to be more than that, if I dared court her." The crowd rippled with amused laughter. Milo's lips pressed together tightly; for a moment Risa thought she was looking in a mirror, as his expression seemed to reflect the impotent anger she herself felt. "It is my great honor to present the glass maker's daughter, Risa, Cazarra of Divetri!"

For a moment, the small crowd looked wildly about to find the song's heroine. When Ricard reached her, he knelt down at her feet. Applause gave way to silence. "Aid me to rise, fair Cazarra," he said, in a voice intended to carry to the edge of the crowd, "and I shall perceive if my chronicle of your triumph meets with your pleasure." He extended his hand in her direction, obviously waiting for her to clasp it and pull him to his feet.

If she did, the crowd would coo and clap their hands. She would be mortified. At that moment, she felt no generosity toward the would-be bard. The sight of him prostrating himself as would a lover only made her chest tighter and her breathing more furious. Before she knew what she was doing, she placed her foot on his shoulder. With a mighty heave, she propelled the brightly clad poet backward. He sprawled on the stones with a grunt.

"It does *not* please me!" she barked.

The people assembled around her fell silent. Ricard looked up from the ground, utter surprise written on his face. There was a chuckle from one of the onlookers. Then another. Soon others joined in, until finally the whole crowd roared with laughter. For a moment Risa felt a savage stab of satisfaction.

Ricard glanced around the crowd, seeming embarrassed as he struggled to his feet. Then he began to laugh, himself, as if the joke had been his. "I always fall for ladies with spirit!" He twirled and lifted his hands up to the heavens, once more making for Risa.

Milo leapt to Ricard's side to move him away, but the twirling made it difficult for him to approach. When Ricard came to a stop in front of her, leaning forward for a kiss, Risa completely lost her temper and slapped him. The crowd burst into laughter again, but Risa knew better this time. They were not laughing at Ricard. They were laughing at the both of them, and at the illusion they were a quarreling couple. Any denial she made would only make it worse.

So while Milo grappled with the troublesome rhymer, she turned and walked across the upper bridge as fast as her feet could take her. She tried to maintain a semblance of dignity, though her face burned like fire.

20

The street performer is a sort of vermin, in a way.
They spring up in the most damp and squalid of conditions,
feed hungrily, and when they are squashed,
another dozen scamper to take their place.

—CHARLOCO DA SPERANZA,
A HISTORY OF THEATRICAL TRADITIONS

G o *away!*" she said for the third time. Her image danced
in the plates and bowls displayed around her room. She
noticed for the first time that her hair had once more come
undone.

"It's me—Milo," she heard through the door.

She could imagine him on the other side, his face knotted with worry. She bore Milo no grudge, but she couldn't
bear to let him see her in a fit of temper.

And temper was exactly what she felt at that moment.
Only the fact that the glass objects at hand were of her own
making prevented her from seizing and throwing them, just

for the satisfaction of the noise and the confusion. "Go away."

"I'm not leaving. You may as well let me in." Her fury did not abate during the moment of silence after his plea. "There's nothing wrong with crying, if you're worried about that."

"I'm not crying!" she yelled. Her anger was too hot and her emotions too confused to weep. Her face was flushed and scarlet, but so far she had not shed tears. "I just want to be left alone!"

"I have to explain about Ricard," he said. "Please let me in."

It was vain to pretend she was angry with Milo as well, when he had only minutes before tried to defend her against Ricard's excesses. "I can't let you in my room unchaperoned," she told him, searching for any excuse to send him away. "It wouldn't be seemly."

"Camilla is with me."

Risa heard his sister's voice scolding in the hallway. "I only walked away for ten minutes. Ten minutes! I don't know how you could let that happen. Honestly!"

Apparently they were determined to come in. It took but a moment to unlatch the door. "Before you ask again," Risa warned them, "I'm not crying. I'm just angry."

"And I don't blame you!" Camilla followed her into the room and shut the door behind her. Her expression was cross. "Ricard's been bothering her since yesterday, Milo. Why do you encourage him?"

"I didn't encourage him! You know how he is!"

"Regardless." Camilla sat down on the settee next to Risa. Obviously annoyed though she was, her voice was surprisingly gentle—much more so than usual. "Ricard's a little *intense* for most people."

"He was singing that new song of his and it upset her," Milo explained.

Camilla appeared confused for a moment. "The bad one about the female pirate?"

"It was a bad one about *me*," Risa said with heat. "About the brave and fearless glass maker's daughter, a goddess in white."

Camilla had the courtesy to look dismayed. "No. Really? Oh gods. Milo! That's enough to upset anyone."

"He came along with Amo! I didn't invite him here!" Milo sounded defensive. "You were right there with us when he started writing it!"

"I don't pay attention to that boy or his songs." It was the most peevish opinion Risa had heard from Camilla. "Neither should you," she said more gently. "He really is a fool."

"I hate the way he looks at me. He acts as if he's in love!"

"It *is* only acting," Camilla assured her.

"What's wrong with him looking at you?" Milo's voice was on edge. "Is someone outside the precious Seven and Thirty not allowed to look upon a Divetri?"

"That's not it at all. You know what I mean," Risa retorted, angry he could think such a thing.

"I just don't think that a cazarra should act so … stand-offish."

"Milo," Camilla said in warning.

"I'm sorry Ricard upset Risa, honestly I am. But he just admires her for the hero she is."

"I am *not* a hero!" For a moment Risa nearly wished

162

to strike Milo. Again she felt frustration at him telling her how the Seven should behave. "Three cazas were ruined last night. People were hurt! My parents were kidnapped! This is real life. It's awful and ugly, and all Ricard can do is make bad rhymes about it—bad rhymes about *me!*" She pounded her chest for emphasis. "He's using *me* to collect coins. It's not right!"

"You *are* a hero," Milo protested, his own voice raised. "You saved this caza last night. Whether you like it or not, the gods favor you!"

"They do *not!* The gods did not want me at the insulas. My glass is worthless. My father turned his face from me— and now he's gone and I'm here…coping. There is nothing about me that is remotely in favor."

Milo was shouting now. "If you just stopped acting like a child with her feelings hurt, and began to think like a cazarra, you would *see*. The priests said you were not needed at the insulas. It was because the gods knew you would be needed *here*." His normally friendly face had gone red with frustration. "You *are* needed, Risa. Everyone in this caza needed you last night! Do you think the brother and sister moons didn't know what Prince Berto would do? Only you could have blown your family's horn last night. *Only you!* Your cousin was worse than useless. If you had been chosen during the festival, you would have been imprisoned at one of the insulas last night and this caza wouldn't be here. Your family would no longer have a place among the Seven!"

His speech hit her like a savage blow. She staggered and sat down in a chair as tears sprang to her eyes. As she breathed, something fluttered in her chest. It was the barest glimmer of hope, alive for the first time. Scarcely without realizing it, she took one of her bowls from the table beside her and began to stroke its surface, letting the smoothness of the glass soothe her. He had no right to lecture her—and yet she wanted desperately to believe him.

"Milo." Camilla's voice was low, as if warning him of something.

"I'll have my say with her."

"We discussed this last night."

Milo stood erect in challenge. "I know the limits here, sister," he said. Risa felt as if she was listening to a conversation she was not supposed to hear. Camilla took a step back and crossed her arms while he continued. "Risa, I'm sorry to be blunt, but you know I'm right. I have never known a girl so blessed by the gods as you. You might have convinced yourself that you are unneeded, but every person alive in this caza today would testify otherwise. I wish you would believe them. Gods, I wish you would believe in yourself! That's all I have to say."

During the last portion of his speech Milo's voice had returned to its softer, normal tone. Emotion had made him slightly hoarse. He looked away from Risa at his sister, apology written plainly on his face. His shoulders sagged.

I can't take much more of this.

Though a heavy silence hung over the room after Milo's appeal, the woman's whisper was barely audible. Risa saw Milo's head whip around. Camilla looked just as surprised as he.

When will it be over?

"Who is that?" Milo asked. He strode in the direction

of the balcony. Camilla put a hand on the dagger she kept sheathed at her waist and moved for the door.

A deeper voice answered the first, equally faint: *... as long as it takes.* It was her father's voice.

I know I must be strong. I know it, my dearest, but I worry so—

"Where are they?" Risa cried in anguish. For a moment she thought she had imagined the voices, but when both Milo and Camilla also heard them, she knew they were real. "It's my mother and father! Where are they?"

"Shush," said Camilla, cutting off Risa's cries with a gesture.

—fine. She's fine, said Ero's voice again. *Don't raise your voice. The others might hear.*

I cannot believe those Dioros, urging us to grant Berto the Olive Crown on the prince's promise to return their caza!

You know I will never agree, said Ero. *At least Urbano Portello is on our side, even after last night. He won't give in.*

"It's there!" Milo pointed at Risa. For a shocked moment she thought he was accusing her of producing the voices herself. He was pointing to the item in her lap, however—Risa's most recent bowl, the one she had shown to Pascal the shopkeeper only days before.

"Careful," warned Camilla, as he raced across the room to retrieve the fragile object.

I'm sorry. Giulia sounded distant and far away, but her words were clear. *But I'm suspicious that the king was interred so quickly. Never before in our country's history has a royal burial taken place without ceremony.*

I praise Muro for Fredo, said her father. *If he had not been present last night to complete the rite—*

Hairs raised on Risa's neck at the words, but she was distracted as Milo knelt before her. "This is definitely it." With Risa, he peered into the bowl of blue glass, tipping it backward and forward to catch the light. "Look!"

Frustrated that his voice was obscuring the barely audible voices of her parents, Risa for an instant just wished that Milo would keep silent. The room's light was puddling at the bottom of the bowl, shifting around its sloped edges as Milo adjusted it. *—can survive within the insula walls. But what of Risa?* When she took the bowl from his hands, the shadows took on sharp edges. In the pools of light she saw not her own reflection, but those of her parents. She was looking up at them from below, as if they were hovering over her. Giulia's fine nostrils flared as she asked her question.

Beside her, his arm around her shoulder and his mouth near her ear, Ero sighed. *You worry too much. Our little lion-kit will be fine, my love.*

Giulia's hand reached toward them, causing Risa to catch her breath. Milo and Camilla continued to observe the shadows over her shoulder. "Do you see it too?" Risa breathed.

"It's amazing," whispered Camilla.

But I worry about her, all alone. Giulia's fingers obscured most of the image as she traced a circle in the middle of the bowl.

Fredo will look after her, just as he is looking after the rest of the caza.

"How are you doing this?" Milo asked. "Is this Divetri enchantment?"

We don't know that it was Fredo who completed the rite last night, Risa heard Giulia murmur.

"It must be one of my parents doing it," said Risa. "It's not me."

Who else could?

The image flickered and died. Nothing but a splash of white light and their own reflections remained. "Come back!" she cried, shaking the bowl. Despair rose in her chest. It was too late.

"What happened?" Camilla also took hold of the bowl's edge. "How did we see them, from so far away?"

"I don't know," said Risa. Two emotions held her in their grip. The joy of seeing her parents, hearing their voices, and knowing they were together and alive, grappled with the anguish of having them so suddenly vanish. "I just don't know. Ferrer Cassamagi said that his ancestress used to work such enchantments, but my parents cannot."

"It is a wonderful thing," said Milo. "You saw the Cazarra and Cazarro. And you still believe that you do not walk in the gods' favor?"

"The gods must be fickle," said Risa with some bitterness. "They show me that my mother and father do not believe I can care for myself, much less the caza."

Camilla's voice was reprimanding. "They said no such thing."

Did Camilla, too, think she was a child to rebuke? The sour taste on Risa's tongue did not diminish. "My father would rather die than have a female put her lips to the Divetri horn. I wish that *he* would hear Ricard's ... oh no." Risa held a hand to her mouth. "Ricard."

"What about him?" asked Milo.

"His song! Ferrer Cassamagi warned me to be careful and to keep a low profile—if any of the Thirty who took the prince's side were to hear that blasted song, I would be a target!"

Milo whistled. "Gods forbid the prince himself hear it!" Risa looked at him with widened eyes.

Camilla wasted no time in speculation. With quick strides across the room she crossed the hall to stick her head out an open window with a view north. In mere seconds she returned, shaking her head. "There's no sign of Tania and Ricard in the piazza. You must have frightened him away, Cazarra."

"I'll look for him," said Milo. "He's probably searching for a midday meal."

"Or sleeping away the hottest hours of the day," Camilla replied. "Tolio would never let you out on your own. I don't have to ask permission, with my rank. I'll go." She touched her dagger lightly, as if to make certain it was still at her side. To Risa she said in a soft voice, "Don't worry. Stay here and do *not* leave the caza. And you," she said more sharply to Milo. "See that you stay by her side at every moment."

"Tell Ricard that he's got to stop singing that song." There was urgency in Milo's voice.

"Believe me," said Camilla with a grim smile. "I have quite a list of things I plan to tell Ricard."

21

*For centuries it was thought that the citie-state of Cassafort
was poised to aim its speares at the Azure Islandes,
so firm was its hold on the northernmoste coast of the Azure Sea.
Either their feare of our noble armies or their lacke of ambition,
however, has kept them at bay.*

—Anonymous, **A Briefe and Compleat
Historie of the Cassafort Citie**

"You've taken him down a few pegs. He's been quiet all afternoon." Mattio leaned his large frame close and nodded in Fredo's direction. "But your cousin's been acting like *he's* the chief craftsman here, lately."

Risa pretended to check over her father's inventory notes, written in spiky italic. It had been just days since she'd last witnessed his hand dancing across the page. The last line ended in a scrawl; Ero had hastily aborted his record-keeping in the middle of a word. Had he abandoned his quill at the news of the king's death? What was he doing now? Her sea-blue bowl sat on the old desk beside her. Look as she might in its reflective surface, his visage had not once appeared since she'd seen it in her chambers. She had intended to ask Mattio if he had ever seen her father work such an enchantment into glass, but she knew that his answer would be a surprised negative. So she asked instead, "How is Amo doing?"

"He's a good and hard worker," Mattio admitted. It was his highest praise, Risa knew. "Technically I'd say he's better than Emil, and he's not too high and mighty to get his hands dirty, the way your cousin sometimes can be."

"Can he stay here?"

"Until your father gets home, that's up to you," said Mattio. "I wouldn't mind an extra craftsman about the place in Ero's absence." Risa cast a smile in Milo's direction. Sitting by the side of the desk on a stool, he was listening to every word they said—though for once he refrained from offering his own opinions. "But when your father is cazarro once more, the decision will be his. That reminds me," he added, his face blank. He had followed the direction of Risa's glance. "Let me show you something." With one of his arms around her shoulder, Mattio began to escort Risa across the room toward the bins where they stored sheets of glass in an upright position. "We'll be right back, lad. No need to worry," he assured Milo. The guard relaxed slightly, though he still sat alertly on the stool.

"Is something wrong?" Risa asked.

"That's what I mean to ask *you*." Mattio gestured to a collection of clear glass sheets. "Pretend we're talking about the inventory. Is everything all right with you and that boy?"

A hot flush began to creep into Risa's face. "What do you mean, all right?"

"He seems a little more worried about you than a guard ought to be in the line of duty." Mattio's grumbly voice lowered so that no one would overhear. "Like he's taking an interest in you, that's what I mean."

"He's a friend," Risa immediately rejoined. "That's all. Boys don't think of me in that way." Her face once again reddened as she remembered Ricard's earnest protestations of infatuation just a few hours before. If that was love, she wanted none of it.

It was different with Milo. Her presence did not inspire him to poetry, or make him rapturous with song. He did not live his life as if he was on the stage of some imaginary drama. The words that came out of his mouth were sometimes playful, sometimes annoyingly blunt, yet always honest. He had no misgivings about pointing out her errors, but he did not embarrass her in public. He didn't tease, like a brother. He was just … comfortable to be with. It was as if she had known and liked him long before they had actually met.

Across the room, Milo was looking about with obvious interest, as if full of curiosity about the workroom and its equipment. It was with respect that he watched Amo shape a rotating white-hot gobbet of glass with a heavy pair of metal tongs. Milo enjoyed learning about things. He was not content merely to make them up, like Ricard.

"You're at an age, love. Boys will start liking you soon enough, if they haven't begun already."

"You sound like Papa. You'll be saying I'm only good for bewitching men's hearts, next."

"Your father's a bit blind when it comes to all the things a woman can do," Mattio said. "You've years to go and plenty to learn here before you start a family of your own. You're a Divetri. Glass is in your blood."

If what Milo had suggested was true, the gods had foreseen that Risa would be needed in Caza Divetri during this time of crisis. But when it was over—if it ever ended—of what good would she be then? By the time of the next Feast of the Two Moons, she would be twenty-two. Far too old to be scrutinized and enter an insula for the first time. Would saving the caza mean having to forego learning the enchantments of her family's trade?

Though Ferrer Cassamagi had called those enchantments insignificant, part of her railed against the unfairness of being left without their use. She was the first Divetri to be denied, without choice or say—and she had been burdened, unasked, with doing the work of a cazarra without any of the benefits.

She could choose to leave the caza. She could walk out that very moment and hide until it was all over. The caza would fall and her family would lose its small magics, but she would be no worse off than before. For a moment she felt vengeful. Let the others see how it felt to do without!

In her heart, however, Risa knew she could never do any such thing. As best as she could, she would defend Caza Divetri and raise its flags high every night. Her family's horn would sound at her lips. Sacrificing the training of the insulas was the price she must pay so that her family could continue in its craft and responsibilities.

"Sometimes I think I'm being punished," she told Mattio in slow, measured words. "Why does everything have to be so hard for me?"

He hugged her until she could not breathe, as he had countless times since she was a baby. "I think you're walking a different road from the rest of us right now," he said. "A rockier one, to be sure. But sometimes the gods give us rough traveling so we can enjoy the destination more when we get there. You just keep moving ahead, girl, no matter how tough it gets. You hear?"

From across the room sounded a roar of voices. "What in the name of Muro d'you think you're doing, you *fool!*" Amo bellowed.

Both Risa and Mattio turned and rushed across the room. "You're the fool!" Fredo was saying, in tones no less heated. In his hands he still held the long metal rod upon which was suspended the glass they were working. Already the white-hot semi-solid at its end drooped out of shape. "A real craftsman wouldn't overreact."

"A real craftsman! You call yourself a real craftsman? If I hadn't moved, you would have burned off my face!" Amo was plainly angry. His fists clenched into balls at his side. "Where I worked, my masters would have you skinned alive for such an idiot trick!"

Seething with anger, Fredo's thin nostrils flared. "This is *my* workshop. *My* family's! Not *yours*, you low-born, unknown…"

"Fredo!" Mattio raised his voice in warning.

Amo carefully felt the reddening spot on his forehead, where it looked as if he had sunburned. It was not blistering, but it still appeared painful. "I am disappointed to find that in the famed Divetri workshops a craftsman would be so careless as to—"

"You do not belong here!" Fredo's voice cracked as it spit out the venomous words. He brandished the hot glass at Amo. The man backed away, hands up, plainly ready to defend himself. Milo had leapt to his feet. Behind Fredo, Emil stood motionless.

Silence fell. In a low, angry voice, Risa spoke first. "Cousin. My father would never treat a guest with such disrespect."

It was with wild eyes that Fredo turned to face her. The lump of glass sagging from the end of the rod deepened in color as it cooled, but it was still hot enough to disfigure any object or flesh it touched. "Yes, Cazarra," he said at last, unmoving. The words struggled out, as if he begrudged them both. "Of course, Cazarra."

It took only three strides for Mattio to overcome his rage and reach Fredo's side. "That's enough," he said, plainly upset at the antics in his workshop. He pulled on a pair of gloves and seized the iron rod. He handed it to Emil, who scurried to return it to the hole in the furnace wall in which the molten glass simmered. "Take off your apron and cool down. We'll do without you until tomorrow."

The reprimand caused Fredo's eyes to open wide. He looked at Risa in appeal, but she merely nodded. For a moment she feared he might burst into tears; the thought of someone as self-contained and remote as her cousin blubbering like a baby made her uncomfortable. "Just take the afternoon off, cousin," she said at last, trying to feign a smile. "Try to relax. We're all upset today."

"My apologies, Cazarra," Fredo said at last. His voice was low and quivered with emotion. "This workshop is everything to me. I would not know what to do if it were lost."

Everyone drew a collective sigh of relief when Fredo removed his protective clothing and hung it on the hook by the door. Without a word more or even so much as a look over his shoulder, he stalked from the room. Emil and Milo immediately began to talk over each other, trying to win Mattio's attention.

Emil was apologizing. "I'm sure it must have been an accident. Fredo would never, ever ... "

"I saw him!" Milo was saying. "He *deliberately*—"

Mattio, however, had his eye upon Amo. "What are you doing, lad?" he asked as the craftsman removed his gloves and heavy apron.

"Going home."

"Why?" It was a question Risa wondered as well.

"I'll not be wanted here, after all that." Amo's large, broad face was wreathed with disappointment as he lifted a neck strap over his head.

"That's for the cazarra and me to decide, lad. Get your gear back on. There's work to be done."

Milo seemed relieved that his friend was not being dismissed. Any further defense of Amo vanished from his lips. Mattio gave him a wink.

Emil scuttled to Risa's side. "I really don't think Fredo meant to burn him, Cazarrina," he said. Then hastily he added, "I mean, Cazarra."

"I'm sure it was an accident," Risa said. She had her own doubts. Fredo had been acting as cazarro of the household, and she had taken that position away. Who knew how he might react if only a few short hours later he felt his place in the workshop to be on equally shaky ground?

"It must have been accidental. It simply *must* have been. He has been very upset, you know."

"I know," said Risa. *Upset* was too mild a word to describe the look on her cousin's face, short moments ago. "Don't worry."

"He should have been cazarro," Emil blurted out. Risa let out a gasp of astonishment that made Emil hastily backtrack. "He thinks that, I mean. No offense, Cazarra, but your father would have thought so as well."

"I see." Risa did not think Emil was being deliberately malicious in his statement, but she felt as if she had been slapped in the face. It was perfectly true that her father would have much preferred a man. How many more people would agree with him?

"Quiet your tongue!" Mattio barked at the nervous young man. The master craftsman scowled. His glance at Risa was meant to apologize for the incident, but already she had turned her back to hide the grim expression disfiguring her mouth.

22

When all else is dark, let work be our solace.
In the daily work of the hands, in the bend of the back
and the sweat of the brow, there is salvation.

—FROM THE PRAYER BOOK OF THE
INSULA OF THE PENITENTS OF LENA

🜚

"Cazarra?"

The whisper was tentative and barely audible. Risa stopped at the sound of it, her heart pounding. Her back was hurting from shifting large boxes of glass sheets all afternoon; even with Milo's assistance, they had been heavy and awkward. Until that moment, steeped with sweat and weariness, she had wanted nothing more than to return to her chambers and immerse herself in a tub of cool water.

"Who's there?" she asked. Behind her, she heard Milo tense.

A figure hobbled slowly out of a shadowed niche. He was

a frail man, with wrinkled skin that clung to his bones. In the stippled light cast by the arbor vines above, he seemed nearly skeletal.

"Dom?" Risa asked. Her pulse still raced. The old beggar had startled her.

His hand trembled as he held out fists clenched together. For a moment she was struck by how his posture, in profile, resembled a script capital *S*. His knees were bent forward, as if he staggered under the weight they carried, and his head projected out. He looked as if he were stooping under a low-hanging ledge. Dom's eyes were fixed upon Risa like a hungry man's upon a feast.

"What is it, Dom?"

"Cazarra," said Milo, his voice polite and businesslike. "You should return to your chambers."

"It's just Dom," she said to him, slightly out of sorts at his intervention. Then in a lower voice she added, "What's wrong?"

He shook his head and whispered back, "Something just doesn't seem right, here. I've been feeling it all afternoon."

"You were the one who suggested I take the poor man in," Risa reminded him.

"I know." Milo nodded. "But—"

"He's harmless," she told him, almost laughing. After all she had been through in the last twenty-four hours, the sudden appearance of an aged servant should have been the least frightening event of the day. "What is in your hands?" she said to Dom, kindness in her voice. The man's hand trembled as he once more held out his upturned fists. "Is it for me?"

Dom nodded, then opened his lips. Breath issued from

between them. "For you." A light breeze from over the sea wall ruffled wisps of white hair around his head like a cloud.

His fingers unfurled from around a round object. In his withered hands lay a fruit with a wine-red rind. "Oh, a pomegranate. How lovely! Thank you, Dom. It's just what I wanted."

A spark of static electricity passed from his hand to her fingers when Risa took the ripe fruit. The sensation startled her for a moment, but then she smiled again. From behind her, Milo cleared his throat. "Cazarra…"

It was not until she had watched the old man disappear back into the shadows and they had walked into the residence that she spoke again. "Milo, what's wrong?"

"I just don't like people lurking in dark places around you," he said. From the way he blurted out the words, she could tell his usual good humor had been replaced by anxiety.

"It's only Dom," she repeated. "No one is going to harm me within my own caza."

"We don't know that," he said, then placed a hand on her shoulder to stop her. "This is serious business, Risa. We guards don't have any orders to keep people out of the caza except at night. Anyone could pretend to be a friend or tradesman and cross those bridges if they wanted to see harm come to you."

"You're being ridiculous." She resumed the trek to her chambers.

"I don't want any 'accidents' like the one in the workshop. That could have been you with a burned face. It's my duty to protect you."

"You're overreacting." Even as she rebuked him, though, Risa felt a chill in her bones. He was right. She was at risk.

"Perhaps I am. Perhaps not. Just promise me you'll not go haring off on your own, Risa. It's best you not stray from my sight for the next few days."

"Mattio will think you're just saying that because you like me, you know," she joked.

His face was utterly absent of expression at her remark. For a moment, she panicked at the thought she might have offended or repelled him.

"I'm sorry. I promise," she said at last. She had reached her chambers on the upper story, and she took the latch in her hand and pushed open the door. "Would you care to inspect my room for assassins?"

Milo remained silent. He seemed to take her question seriously, and it frightened her a little. She watched as he entered her chambers with his hand at his sword sheath. He looked into the tiny tiled room where she washed. He then peeked under her bed and investigated the large wardrobe that contained her dresses. He inspected a number of small objects laid out upon a table. Even when he found nothing out of the ordinary, he still looked wary.

"Am I safe?" she finally asked, impatient to sit down after several hours of standing and stooping. She tossed the pomegranate into the air and caught it again. "I don't mean to rush you, but I am tired."

"I suppose," Milo said with genuine reluctance. "Should I have them bring you a dinner tray? You look starved."

Shaking her head wearied her muscles too much. "I'll eat this for now," she said, holding up the fruit. "After the rite tonight I'll have something else. Just now I want a rest. Please?"

"I'm not moving from this hallway," he warned her. "If you need anything just call." Wordlessly he took the pomegranate from her, scored its thick rind with his knife, and then handed it back.

"I'm sorry for what I said. About you liking—"

"Don't be," he said abruptly, pulling the door closed. "Rest well, Cazarra."

Slowly crossing the room, Risa dug her nails into the pomegranate's scored rind and began to tear apart the fruit's inner membrane. Juice from the fleshy seeds within spilled onto her hands, soaking them with their sticky fluid. She plucked some of the juice-laden sacs from the fruit and thrust them into her mouth, sucking the sweet pulp. The fruit's astringent aftertaste refreshed her. For a few moments, she felt almost revived.

Near her balcony, upon a low table set before the reclining sofa, she noticed a quantity of little gifts set out. Many were bedecked with ribbons or bright paper. There was a bundle of oranges tied with a ribbon, and a satchel of ground cioccolato beans that could be steeped into a bitter and aromatic hot drink. A small pot, when opened, revealed a spicy mixture of olives, garlic, and oils. There were small sugary raisins and a pot of stuffed figs. Some of the delicacies had small tags attached. *Thank you so very much, from Natella,* read a small scrap of paper attached to a compote of berries, donated by one of the kitchen servants. Had she been hungrier, she could have indulged in quite a feast without leaving her room.

You saved us all. Blessings upon you. Marcello, read a note from one of the gardeners. It was rolled between the legs of an adorable tiny dog whittled from a block of wood. A lovely music box sat beside it; when Risa opened the lid, its delicate mechanics began to tinkle forth a folk tune from the hill country. She knew it well, and smiled at the sound.

As she sank deep into the sofa's cushions, her muscles relaxing against its downy softness, she listened to the melody chiming from the music box. The little gifts touched her. From the handmade wooden dog to the extravagance of the ground cioccolato—a concoction so rare that she had only once before tasted it in her life—to the simple pomegranate given her by Dom, the display of little gifts truly moved her heart.

She lay back lazily on the sofa and enjoyed another cluster of juicy sacs from the pomegranate, and then another. The sweet song from the hill country lulled her eyelids lower, and lower. With a start, she realized she must not sleep ... she was tired enough to slumber the night through, if she closed her eyes.

No, she would just relax and enjoy the breezes that blew in from the balcony, and think about ... She wondered what Milo was doing, out there in the hallway. And where was Camilla? Had she found Ricard? She had been gone since before noon.

A yawn stretched Risa's jaw out as far as it could go. Tears formed as her eyes squeezed shut tightly. She blinked several times to clear them, but found it difficult to keep them open. The music was so sweet and calming ...

Her face was burning with pain, as if set afire. "Stop it!"

she found herself screaming. A hand dug into her shoulder, while another shook her roughly. When she pried apart her eyelids, they felt heavy and crusted over. Risa cried out in protest once more, not even able to comprehend what was happening.

Milo stood above her, Camilla over his shoulder. His hand was raised to strike her once more. "Get off me!" she insisted. It seemed as if her voice was weak and unused.

"She's awake, finally," said Camilla. "Give her some space."

On the floor beside her lay the crushed remains of the pomegranate, its ruby red juice staining the matting. Her hands, face, and dress were all bloodied with its dried and sticky sap. "Is she all right?" asked another voice.

"Mattio? Is she—?" Amo was there, too, hovering in the doorway, as well as a number of the servants. Even Fita stood off to the side, her hands wringing her apron into sweaty creases.

"What happened?" It felt as if her throat had been soldered shut. She coughed, wincing at how it pained her chest.

She had never seen Milo's fair skin so red nor his expression so furious. "You wouldn't wake." He spat the words out grudgingly. "We tried and tried, but you wouldn't wake up."

"Did I fall asleep? I'm sorry, I was so tired ... "

Milo knelt down beside her. "Are you all right?"

Mattio pointed with disgust at the music box parts scattered across the matting. "You didn't open your eyes until we knocked *that* onto the floor and it broke into bits. I think it's Cassamagi-made. Never seen one like it before. Blasted thing nearly cost us the caza!"

Camilla was gathering its pieces together. "Who gave it to you?"

"I don't know …" she breathed. "It was just there, on the table."

"We've been trying to wake you for nearly an hour. Can you stand?" Milo still seemed grim, but his anger was fading.

"Do I have to?" From the side of the room one of the maids burst into tears. Fita instantly began to shush her. Startled at the fuss, Risa asked, "How long was I asleep?"

"Long enough," said Mattio. His voice also sounded hoarse and tense. "You have to perform the rite. *Now.*"

Ice water suddenly seemed to flow through her veins. With wild eyes, she looked out the balcony doors. Beyond Caza Catarre, the western sky was darkening. The sun hovered just above the horizon. She couldn't have been asleep that long!

In the distance, from the center of the city, she heard the unmistakable cry of the palace horn.

"Help me," she cried, suddenly fearful.

The staircase to the residence's uppermost balcony was just down the hall, but as heavy as her limbs felt, it might have been a mile. Milo and Camilla heaved her to her feet and carried her the entire distance. Her arms clung to their necks, and her feet barely touched the floor.

Though she still felt weak and strangely dreamy from her unusual slumber, the sound of Cassamagi's horn pealing from the easternmost point of the city revived her. There was no time for reflection or delay. Mattio was already attaching the caza's green and blue banner to the pole's hooks. It was with his assistance that she hauled it into the sky, the rope flying so quickly that it threatened to burn her hands.

Milo and Camilla removed the weathered copper lid from the pedestal, exposing the Divetri horn. A fading glint of sun caught the flare of its bell. For a moment Risa feared that she would not have the strength in her limbs to raise the heavy instrument.

She need not have worried. When she placed a hand on the handpiece, a strange surge of power rushed through her. It felt like an invigorating rain shower on a summer afternoon; it felt like laughter, like joy in a moment of solemnity. The horn almost seemed to recognize her. Risa gasped as its resonance tingled throughout her entire body. Was this what her father felt every night when he grasped the brass instrument?

Above her, the banner's metal eyelets rattled against the pole in the sea's gentle winds. She raised the horn and blew.

It was the first time she was truly able to relish the sensation as the horn reverberated across the rooftops of Cassaforte. Pure enchantment was in that sound—she sensed it now in a way she never had in her childhood. Though created centuries ago, it sparkled as brightly as new. She could not see its traces, but some part of her could discern its presence in the periphery of her vision. So delicate was it that it would vanish if regarded directly. Yet it was so durable that an entire city had been built upon its foundation. It fed her strength.

For a moment, she felt that she would live forever.

The entire family of craftsmen and servants remained silent. The horn's cry faded into the gathering darkness.

There were none of the previous night's cheers; a somber mood hung over the Divetri balcony. They were safe for another night. For how many more to come could they withstand the prince's threat?

It was not until she heard the sound of low thunder that Risa realized how long she had been standing still. Like enormous drums it rumbled, jarring her every bone.

"No," she whispered, clutching the Divetri horn for strength. She stumbled to the edge of the balcony, where she could hear the screams and shouts from the caza to the west. Every jolt and tremor it suffered was silhouetted by the setting sun. "Not Catarre!"

23

Why is speaking to you, my friend—my King—
easier than talking to my own kin? I fear they think me odd.

—ALLYRIA CASSAMAGI TO KING NIVOLO OF CASSAFORTE,
FROM A PRIVATE LETTER IN THE CASSAMAGI HISTORICAL ARCHIVES

🜚

"This uniform is tight."

"It fit Camilla well enough. It's her spare." Milo peered around them into the shadows. Lanterns lit the streets above, but precious little of that light spilled into the canal as they floated northward.

"She has muscle in places I don't." Judging from a certain slackness in the chest, Camilla had certain other qualities Risa lacked as well.

Milo punted the gondola under a bridge and into a wide area where several of the city's channels intersected. River lights, their poles anchored deep into the canal mud, cast

Milo's features into sharp silhouette. He seemed grim, and worried.

They had to find Ricard. They had to stop him from spreading that song. Risa had already had a close-enough call with the enchanted music box and could not afford another. But it had been difficult to talk Milo into this plan. When she'd finally allowed him to tear her away from the sight of ruined Catarre—littered with paper and book leather and the wood and glass that once contained them—Camilla had told them that she hadn't been able to find the Poet of the People at any of his usual haunts. They had found her sitting alone, nursing the broken, oozing blisters she'd accumulated during her day's trek around the city.

"I really hope Ricard hasn't been singing that song everywhere," Milo had said with a groan. "But he's sure to be at Mina's tonight. We'll just have to catch up with him there."

Though Camilla had merely rubbed her sore soles and nodded, Risa noted a flash of pain and weariness cross her face, and spoke quickly. "No, she's bone tired. I'll go."

"I'm not tired," Camilla had protested, but weakly.

"Risa, it's not safe for you to go out into the city," Milo had warned.

"It's not safe for me to stay in my chambers, either!" she'd replied. "You said yourself that it would be best for me to stay with you."

Milo had stood still, stubborn and unyielding. "Tolio will never let you out of the caza after dark."

In the end, it had been Camilla who devised the plan to dress Risa in an extra guard's uniform. In the dark of night, no one would think to look closely at two guards leaving the caza for an evening meal after a long shift on duty. Camilla would rest in Risa's chambers with the door locked; she could tend to her feet and soak them in water with salts.

As Risa now looked across the glittering waters, she saw that they were littered with wet paper—pages from books. "So much learning enchantment, wasted." She leaned out and fished a sheet from the canal, peering at its running ink. Whatever had once indelibly marked this page was now illegible. "Did you ever read a Catarre book?"

Milo nodded. "It could have been worse. It could have been as bad as Portello, or as bad as ... "

The rest of his words went unspoken, but she knew what he was thinking. *Or as bad as Caza Divetri would be.* Again she had a premonition of glass exploding throughout their island. The workshops, the kitchens, the residence windows—all of it piercing wood and bone and flesh alike.

When Milo remained silent, Risa spoke again. "You're worried that Tolio will find out what we're doing. That Camilla will get in trouble if we're caught."

Milo continued to punt the gondola up the canal. "We won't be caught. That's all there is to it."

Running footsteps sounded in the streets above. Risa turned, apprehensive at the sudden flurry of noise. When the boots faded into the distance, she relaxed. Milo did not seem at all unsettled. He slowed down as they approached another junction, and began to maneuver the craft around the corner to take them eastward.

"I did see a Catarre book, once. On swordcraft. It was my mother's." He sounded almost lost in a dream. Risa had another vision of his late mother, white-haired, fat, and maternal, occupying young Milo with a book on swordsmanship while she trimmed his fair curls. "I never forgot a page of it."

"That's the beauty of the Catarre enchantments," Risa said. "That *was* the beauty, anyway." She could not keep dwelling on loss, for it only frightened her. She changed the topic. "What is this Mina's we're going to?"

"Oh, you'll love Mina's," said Milo, relaxing. "It's a taverna on the artist's spit. We eat there almost every night."

"You don't have meals at home?" Save for the rare dinner at another caza or home of the Thirty, Risa had almost never eaten a meal prepared outside Caza Divetri. She certainly had never visited a public house.

Milo laughed. "Camilla and I don't have a kitchen like the Divetris. No servants, either. Although we used to, when we lived on the Via Dioro." At Risa's gasp of surprise, he quickly added, "It wasn't one of the big homes! Just a small cluster of rooms over one of the shops. We had a servant, though. That was before Mama died. Now we just eat our dinners at Mina's." He shrugged. "It's easier."

As they punted farther past the center of the city, the canals widened and became broader and lower. Entire banks of tall and grimy buildings directly fronted the waters, their doorways bordered with stone staircases that descended directly into the waters. In the wealthier sections of Cassaforte, the homes had long ago been built with berths and small docks where the families and servants could tie their gondolas. Here, the canal was littered with long boats along its sides, clustered heavily around the doorways. They sometimes collected five to six boat-widths deep. In the dim light of the gondola's lantern, Risa watched as someone crawled over boat after rocking boat to reach one of the entrances.

"Who lives in these places?" she asked as Milo carefully navigated the waterway. The abundance of boats moored haphazardly along the low-banked canal walls left only a narrow sliver of water to navigate. From the balconies above came the sounds of entire families arguing over their dinners, squalling babies, laughter and shouting. From one garret she heard a flute, its song melancholy in the dark. Overhead, long ropes were strung with shirts. Smells of boiling laundry and human waste mingled with fish and cabbage, making her clutch her nose.

Milo shrugged. "Families live here. Workmen. Servants." There was something odd about the nonchalance with which he spoke. Only too late did Risa realize that he and Camilla probably lived in one of these crumbling structures, cramped into a room together. It would be quite a set-back for anyone who once held rooms over the Via Dioro.

"They look cozy," she said, trying to be cheerful. He did not reply. She felt awful; despite the smell and squalor, she had arrogantly forgotten that good people lived in these homes. She did not want to seem like many of the Thirty, full of conceit and entitlement. And yet, she had managed to offend him.

They completed their journey in silence. Speaking would have been nearly impossible anyway, in some areas through which they passed, for they were often noisy and crowded with people. On a fire-lit bridge above them, children and adults alike sat on the ledge of a brick wall, yelling out as a pair of men in short tunics engaged in a wrestling match;

the cheering could be heard two streets away. From the public houses came sounds of singing and dancing, while in the upper stories, women in fancy clothing leaned from windows and flirted with men in the boats below.

Milo continued to steer the boat north and east through this old, dilapidated section of the city until they came to an area where the water's current would have carried the boat south had he not been pushing all his weight against the pole. "The river gates are just ahead," he explained, nodding to the north. Then, the east-west canal broadened as Milo pushed the boat out from the closeness of the cramped buildings. Light from the brother and sister moons shone brightly across the rippling waters. "It's a bit trickier here."

He seemed to be steering toward an isle in the canal—or a peninsula, which projected from the Portello-engineered river wall that controlled the flow of water into Cassaforte's intricate complex of canals. Every inch of land on the peninsula was covered with the same timeworn buildings, but she saw that the southernmost structure boasted a long pier that jutted into the canal. Warm yellow lamps shone from its windows, mingling with the pure white light of the moons on the waters. "That's Mina's," Milo told her.

From the taverna's front door came the sounds of men and women singing to the strains of a lap harp and drums. Climbing up to the pier, Risa smoothed down her borrowed guard's uniform as Milo tethered the gondola. Anxiety leapt in her stomach. Would she be able to convince anyone that she was a guard? She checked her posture to ensure it was erect as possible.

"Don't worry," Milo said as he climbed the ladder to

join her. "You're with me. We're just two city guards here for dinner. You'll be fine." She stared at him for a moment, wanting to relax but finding the clamor intimidating.

It was over his shoulder that she first glimpsed the taverna's interior. Light spilled from fireplaces at either end of the room, and oil lanterns hung from the broad-beamed rafters. Smells of smoke and burning wood and fish stew and wine filled her nose, as well as perfumes and sweat and the dank smell of the canal water seeping through the doors. Everyone seemed to be happy and smiling, which comforted her. The harpist finished her performance to a round of raucous applause that drowned out shouts and laughter from the groups of men and women playing a complicated game with tiles upon several of the wooden tables.

"Milo!" Scarcely had they begun to cross the room when a gray-haired man clasped the guard's shoulders and shook him. "Good to see you, boy!"

"It's Milo!" exclaimed one of the taverna servers as she walked by with a tray of mugs and stuffed olives. Risa looked around in bewilderment. Everyone seemed to know her friend. Most greeted him by name, turning from their dinners or their mammoth mugs of wine to cuff him on the back or reach out to pat him on the shoulders. Many of the men and women were genuinely affectionate; one matronly looking woman stood and hugged him tightly and commented that he was looking too thin, which generated a laugh from the rest of the table.

Milo did not introduce her to anyone, nor call attention to her. Risa was glad of it. If anyone were to question her about her uniform she would have precious little to tell them. A good number of people nodded at her while they pushed their way through the rows of tables. It had been quite some time since she'd last seen so many smiles. As she began to relax, so did the tense feeling in her mid-section.

"Milo!" A large woman of several decades of age put down a tray so that she could squeeze the guard's head between her hands. With her painted lips she imprinted a kiss on his forehead, and then immediately licked the heel of her hand and began to wipe the mark away. "Edmundo's been worried sick about you," she said, dragging him away while talking and wiping at his forehead. "You know how he is. He thinks of you as one of his own sons. You shouldn't stay away for so long without sending word! Naughty boy! Go say hello!" She laughed giddily and with great good humor.

"Milo Sorranto!" cried an older man sitting at one of the back tables near the stage. He gulped down the last of his wine before he stood. Risa began to wonder if everyone in Mina's knew Milo's name.

"Edmundo!" Milo replied, waving. His face had been jovial the entire time they had been weaving their way back to this edge of the room, but now it seemed genuinely affectionate at the sight of the man.

"I was just telling him how you were fretting," said the large woman, brushing imaginary dust from her skirts.

"Sit! Sit! We saved seats for you and Camilla, although you haven't been here the last two nights to use them … ah, and that's not your sister, is it?" Though puzzled, Edmundo bowed politely in her direction.

"This is Muriella," said Milo, using the false name they had agreed upon. "And this is Edmundo, with his daughters

Charla and Missa." The girls had to be Milo's own age; they fluttered their eyelashes and giggled at the sight of him, but barely looked Risa's way.

"Mina, meet my friend Muriella." Milo put his hand on the large woman's back. She was busily talking to one of the other men at the table, but stopped her conversation to look up. "Why, hello…hmmm. Muriella, did you say?" She looked straight into Risa's eyes, winked, and laid a hand on hers. "Well then. Muriella!" Risa feared that she had not fooled the taverna owner for even a moment, but the woman broke out in a smile and squeezed her hand fondly. "Always glad to have the king's guards at Mina's. Mind you come back often!"

Milo continued introducing people around the table, who all seemed to be members of Edmundo's large family. At last he reached a large man utterly engrossed in his stew. Risa's blood froze to ice her in veins. Here was one person who would recognize her instantly. "And this is Amo," he said neutrally. "Camilla's friend."

The glass worker automatically reached out one of his colossal hands in greeting while using the other to rip a bite from a heel of bread. It was not until their flesh touched that he actually looked at her. Ceasing to chew, Amo blinked at Risa and her borrowed uniform, then looked at Milo with a scowl on his face, as if about to ask what joke he was trying to play. "Muriella," Milo repeated. "Of the guard."

Amo hesitated. After a long pause he nodded, moved over on the bench, and gestured for Risa to sit. Edmundo also rose and issued gentle commands to his daughters; they parted so that Milo could take a place between them.

Though they kept their faces turned toward the stage, from across the table Risa caught them both peeking slantwise in his direction. *Silly fools*, she thought to herself. She looked at their carefully coiled curls harnessed in the back in matching retas; their pale, porcelain complexions; and their jeweled ears. They were not of the Thirty, these girls, yet they aped their fashions.

She startled from her absorbed thoughts, apologizing when she realized Edmundo had spoken to her. "I said, I don't believe I've seen you on duty in the city," he repeated.

"I—"

"She's new," said Milo.

"I've seen her," said Amo at the same time. He and Milo looked at each other, horrified at their contradiction. Amo continued, still chewing his stew. "Stationed in one of the piazzas near the sea wall. Right?" Risa nodded gratefully at him.

"So you've seen every guard in the city now, 'Mundo?" Mina wanted to know. "You must have more time on your hands than I!"

Edmundo tut-tutted and shook his head. "These are dreadful times indeed. They're saying the prince is a madman," he told Milo, including Risa in the conversation with a nod. "It's a terrible time to be a guard, lad, I keep telling you. What happens if the prince tells you to start murdering the innocent, like the bad kings of the old times?" While he talked, Edmundo ladled out servings of stew for both of them from a communal container in the center of the table. He tore off portions of bread from a loaf and then pushed the provisions toward the two newcomers.

"We don't take orders from the prince," Milo said, gratefully accepting the stew. He began to spoon it into his mouth. "Guards only answer to the man or woman who bears the Olive Crown. The captains only take the prince's suggestions under advisement."

"That's what you say now, but there's ways of installing new captains who would gladly dance to the beat set by the prince." Edmundo nodded at the raised platform in the corner near them, where a woman in full skirts pranced to the rhythm of a tall, deep-voiced drum. "Best get out before you're asked to do something against your nature."

"Being a guard *is* my nature," Milo said. One of the girls—Charla, Risa thought it was—tittered and held several dainty fingers before of her mouth. Milo turned and winked at her as he chewed.

For a moment Risa wrestled with an irrational urge to slap the chit. For the life of her she did not know why, save that she had no patience for useless, frilly, simpering *girls* who practiced no craft and did nothing more than rehearse their wiggles and giggles in the sole hope of making a good marriage. Instead, she turned her attention to the stew. Though the splintery bowl in which it lay in no way resembled the caza's fine plates, it smelled delicious. She tasted it eagerly.

"His mother was a guard, you know," Mina told Risa. "And her mother and father before that. Oh, we all loved Tara. She was like a daughter to me. A real daughter!" Tears glittered in her eyes as she spoke. From her capacious bosom she withdrew a handkerchief and blew her nose into it.

Before she could stop herself, Risa turned from the spectacle of emotion and blurted to Milo, "Your mother was a *guard?*" She closed her mouth, aware that she was gawking.

"Didn't you know? Not just any guard," said Amo, his cheeks bulging with chunks of meat. "She was of the king's own flank. Bodyguard to the king."

Risa looked from Amo to Milo, astounded. For days she had envisioned Milo's mother as a jolly old lady who puttered around her family's kitchens. That she was of the king's own flank meant that she had been one of the most deadly and powerful fighters in all Cassaforte—small wonder she had been gifted with a Catarrean book on swordcraft! "But..."

"Oh, Tara was the best of the best," Edmundo told her. "Moved like a mountain cat on the prowl when she had to, and pounced just as sweetly. Four times decorated with awards for bravery! Four times! More than any other of the king's flank."

Milo was refusing to meet her eyes. He steadily consumed his meal as she stared at him. "You'll be decorated one day, Milo," said Charla, tittering once more. "I'm sure you're just as brave."

"I'm sure you're braver!" said Missa, crowding in more closely and grasping Milo's upper arm. "You're *ever* so strong." She gave his bicep a squeeze.

Risa stared at the girls with loathing.

Just then, applause broke out among the crowd. In the flurry of raised and clapping hands, Risa for a moment lost sight of Milo's face. When she saw it again, he was looking at her as he took a drink from his flagon. Did she think differently of him, she wondered, now that she knew more about him? How could she say he seemed more important, now that she knew his mother had been one of the most respected guards in the country? He was just Milo. Sometimes funny, sometimes serious, sometimes smiling Milo. He was impossible not to like, no matter who had given him birth.

"It's Ricard you'll be after, isn't it?" murmured Amo in her ear as the applause began to die. She nodded, and he pointed in the direction of the stage. Ricard was already on it, holding out his hand to help up Tania up beside him. His costume was considerably more refined than the scrapbag he had worn the past two days. Although just as colorful, the fabrics seemed to be richer and the cut more fashionable. Tania also seemed to be wearing new clothes, which flattered her shining, curly hair. "He'll be up next," Amo continued. "You'd best stop him before he starts. The crowds here get ugly if the entertainers don't follow through."

Risa looked across the table. Milo had already gotten to his feet. As he began to shift toward the stage, both Charla and Missa grabbed him by his hands. "You've only just come!" said one.

"Oh Milo, you can't leave *now!*" said the other.

The tinny sound of Ricard's lute quieted the crowd. Risa watched as he inclined in a slight bow, his fingers never leaving his instrument. Behind him, Tania tapped out a beat on the tambour as he began to sing.

A shrill cry of woe sounds into the still night.
The city lies quiet in dread.
And high in the palace, a king in his robes
Lies quiet and still: He is dead.

"Missa, I can't stay," Milo told her. He tried to disentangle his arm from the girl's clutch, but she held him in an iron clasp.

Risa stood up and walked around the table. She had noticed that some of the people in the taverna were already humming along to the tune. Although she had only just heard it herself that morning, it was so simple and memorable that she cursed to realize she could have sung it herself.

A thunder as hoofbeats pound over the bridge—
Its echoes sound over the water.

"Let go of him. We've city business to attend to," she snapped at Missa. She was very surprised at how the girl instantly obeyed her, even seeming slightly contrite. At that moment she would have admitted that there was a certain seductive power to the uniform of a city guard. Milo, in the meantime, had sprinted away from the table to the stage.

"Oh father, don't leave me!" resounds a soft cry—
The cry of the glass maker's—

Whatever cry the glass maker's daughter had planned to make thereafter went unheard, for—in one athletic motion—Milo covered Ricard's mouth with one hand and pulled him off the stage in another. The poet's lute strings jangled in alarm.

Tania turned to find herself alone on the stage; she continued to beat her tambour absently as she watched the guard haul Ricard through the taverna. The poet's feet barely touched the floor. When Tania finally leapt down to follow, Risa grabbed her arm and pulled. Tania's eyes widened in alarm at the sight of Risa's uniform, but when she saw who was hauling her away, they nearly popped out of their sockets.

The crowd was already protesting. Some people yelled and shook their fists. Others had risen to their feet, yelling loudly in her direction. "This is official business!" Risa cried loudly, but she knew she could barely be heard over the ruckus. "This is official business of the crown!"

A loud laugh cut through the clamor. It was the proprietress, standing up on one of the benches around Edmundo's table. "And that's what happens," she cried out, "if you dare sing out of tune at Mina's!"

Everyone laughed. Like a double-moon low tide, the room's tension ebbed away. The bosomy taverna owner snapped her fingers and the harpist climbed back onto the stage and began to play.

Ricard and Milo were already arguing outside. In the light pouring from the taverna's open front door, it was plain to see their flushed and furious faces. "You're asking the impossible!" Ricard shouted. Spit flew from his mouth.

"What in the world is going on?" Tania wanted to know. "Honestly, Milo. I am the last person to deny anyone a fit of drama, but usually I prefer to know the script in advance!" She stood with her hands on her hips in an attitude of confrontation.

"He wants us to stop singing the new ballad!" Ricard told her in a passion.

"What? I love that song! It's wonderful!"

"It's my pinnacle!" Ricard agreed.

"It's dangerous," Milo said. "Every time you sing it, you're putting Risa in peril."

They looked at Risa. "You know," Tania said at last, "crimson really suits you. It brings out your eyes."

"You aren't getting it," Milo said, frustration coloring his voice.

"What Milo means," said a quiet and friendly voice, "is that that precious song of yours, love, brings quite a lot of attention to someone who very likely doesn't need the publicity at the moment." Mina had appeared from nowhere. She stood with her arms around both Tania and Ricard, smiling from one to the other. "She's probably an ordinary girl—like Muriella, here—who just wants to go about her work without having her name sung around the city. You'd hate that if you were in her place, wouldn't you, my dear?"

The plump woman was looking right at her. Risa nodded and caught Mina's conspiratorial smile. She knew. She had known all along, somehow. Risa nodded in agreement and gratitude. "There. You see?" said Mina.

"It's my best song! People actually *like* it!" Ricard was still arguing.

Risa felt compelled to speak. "It's a good song. If you can write a song that good, the next one will be even better. Please, Ricard."

"It's dangerous to sing it," Milo said in a gentler tone, inspired by Risa's own. "The prince might be trying to find out who blows the horn at the remaining cazas. Anyone out there with an eye to advancing their families might try to harm them. Someone has already attacked Risa." Tania gasped as the meaning of Milo's words sunk in.

"The gods know, there are enough people in this taverna

who'd sell their mother's wigs for a luni!" said Mina with a mock shudder. "Listen to Milo, lad."

Ricard looked from Milo to Risa and back again, his bottom lip pouting outward. Even Tania looked grim. "Do you really think I can write an even better song?" he said at last.

Risa reached out and took Ricard's free hand. "I know you could. But please. Until this is all over … just stop. I beg of you."

"How many places did you perform it today?" Milo wanted to know.

Ricard and Tania looked guiltily at each other. "It's hard to say," Tania said at last. "We started at Caza Divetri and just worked our way from square to square."

"And all the tavernas," Ricard said. He looked slightly ill.

Tania nodded slowly, looking equally disturbed. "We performed it maybe forty—"

"Maybe fifty times?"

The little group stood there in silence at the news. "That's not so bad," Mina said at last. "Is it? Small groups of people at each one … "

"Not small groups." Tania had a pained look on her face. "Some of them were largish."

"Well, at least it's not as if it's being sold as a broadside!" Mina said cheerfully. Then, at the sight of Ricard's panicked face, she shook her head. "Ricard, lad, you didn't!"

Ricard nodded. "Dimarco the printer bought it. He's using the same woodcut he used for 'The Pirate's Lass' and had begun typesetting it when we left."

"Well stop him!" said Mina.

"He'll want money. I can't just ask him not to. He paid me a whole lundri for it! A whole lundri, Milo!"

Abandoning any pretense that she was Muriella of the guard, Risa said urgently, "I've a bag of lundri from the glass I sold for my father. I'll give you as many as you need to buy every copy of that broadside back from this printer." Her mind was filled with a nightmarish vision of how many long sheets of paper that might be. Broadsides of the most popular songs and ballads circulated widely throughout the city. Thousands of people collected them; even Giulia had a score of pretty verses pressed between two boards in her chambers. If even one of those broadsides made its way into the hands of one of the Thirty, they could easily show it to the prince.

"And a lundri for the effort," said the poet with such haste that Risa suspected he had been calculating the request while she spoke.

"Ricard!" Tania appeared disgusted with her mercenary brother.

"Done," said Risa before he could change his mind. She fumbled for the sack of coins hidden inside her tunic.

Ricard grinned as he bit into one of the coins to test its purity. Satisfied, he pocketed them. "All right then, Cazarra. Your every wish shall be obeyed! Come, sister, and let us away on our mission of mercy!" Strumming his lute as he sauntered into the shadows, Ricard beckoned for his sister to follow.

Tania lingered for a moment, and took Risa's hands. "I'm sorry," she said, and then kissed both of her cheeks. "I'll make certain he takes care of it, though."

"That's all right," Risa said in reassurance, and then let her go.

"Mission of mercy," Milo said with a grumble. "The only *mercy* is that he didn't ask for more than a single lundri for all the trouble he's caused."

"You children," clucked Mina. She brushed off her apron and turned to return to her den of light and music. "Don't underestimate the power of gold. Some men will do anything for it!"

24

When the house is on fire, why not warm your hands?

—A COMMON CASSAFORTEAN SAYING

The candles that illuminated the upper hallway of the residence had guttered long before. The only lights came from the moons' reflection off the canals and from the distant torches burning in Piazza Divetri. At first Risa was surprised how quiet the hallway seemed. Then she remembered that she was the only inhabitant of this wing of the house, which was reserved for Divetri children.

"Do you think Camilla is asleep?" she asked Milo, who crept along the stone floor ahead of her.

"If I know Camilla, no. Not while she's on duty," he whispered back. "Not even as tired as she is." It must have been three hours past midnight. Risa could not even imagine remaining awake so late after tramping over the city all day.

"You watch," Milo whispered as he turned the door handle to her chambers. "She'll still be awake." He stepped into the room.

Several things happened at once, it seemed. First came a rushing noise, followed by a massive grunt in a female register. Risa felt bodies tumble by her and slam into the hallway wall opposite her door. In the near-dark she saw shadows twisting against each other and heard the rumbles as Milo and his unknown assailant struggled. Snarling like wild animals, the bodies tumbled back into her chambers.

There were tinder stones in one of the niches, Risa remembered through her panic. The darkness felt like a blanket, masking her tentative movements away from the melee. She had to find them, to create some light—the thought of an assailant in the dark was nearly unbearable to her. She had thought the tinders were in the candle alcove nearest to her own room, but when her fingers fumbled along the shallow shelf, she found nothing save a stub of wax.

From within her room came a clatter, the sound of something wooden falling and skittering across the floor. She caught her breath at the noise. Her glass bowl was in that room, sitting on a table. One jolt would be all it took to send it crashing. It was the only connection she had, no matter how shaky, to her parents.

With desperate hands she felt along the wall. The glass edges and corners of the rough mosaic nipped at her skin. But the tinders were there, in the next niche, two flat Cassamagi-honed flints. She heard something else fall to the floor of her room—not glass. But there was no guarantee her bowl would not be next.

She rushed back to the room. "*Illuminisi!*" she commanded as she struck the flints. Light flared from the rounder of the stones; a single flame burned around one edge. The two figures grappled with each other near her balcony, too far away for her to see what was happening. The stone's enchantment flared, then died. "*Illuminisi!*" she commanded, striking them again as she moved closer.

The brother and sister guards had each other in tight chokeholds, desperation straining their faces. In the tinder's light, their eyes flared in surprise at the unexpected sight of the other. As the enchantment sputtered and faded, she saw them both dropping their grips and scrambling to regain their balance. Camilla reached up a hand just as the light vanished.

"Don't move!" Risa commanded, suddenly finding her voice. She once more struck the stones together. "*Illuminisi!*" In the flame's dim light, they all looked at where Risa pointed—Camilla's hand was only an inch away from toppling the glass bowl.

"I thought it was him again," Camilla explained, minutes later. Even though she was calmed down, her eyes seemed wide and frightened in the candlelight. "I had an attacker earlier."

"You look terrible," said Milo. "Honestly, I'm so sorry…" Risa noted the narrow gash splitting Camilla's lip, around which blood caked as it dried. Her cheek was a dark purple, as if it had been bruised by a blow.

"Don't flatter yourself, brother. You didn't do this," she said, pointing to her face. "He did."

"Who?"

Camilla sighed in exasperation. "I didn't see his face. After you two left, I spent a long time just sitting here in the dark. You've no idea how tired I was! I did the things we learned from Mama to keep awake. I sang songs in my head, counted stars, did sums." Her voice grew quiet. "I still fell asleep."

"Oh, Cam."

"I couldn't help it!"

"I'm not blaming you. I know you've got to feel terrible."

"I still shouldn't have. Anyway, I was on the bed when it happened. I woke up and there was a hand on my face, Milo." Camilla's voice sounded frozen with fear at the memory. The iciness in her voice chilled Risa. "Someone had come into the room." They gave her a moment to recover. "He had me pinned down on the bed and he was trying to stuff a cloth in my mouth. So I kicked him between the legs."

Milo winced slightly at that, but the word that came from his mouth was "Good!"

"I didn't quite connect, but it was enough to make him stagger back. So I kneed him in the stomach. When he bent over, I smashed his nose with the heel of my hand. I think I broke it."

"Did you see him?"

"No! It was too dark. All I know is that he smelled awful. It was disgusting." Camilla touched her cheek and winced. "I was trying to figure out where in the room I was when he jumped over the balcony. I heard a splash in the canal. When I finally got over there, he'd swum away." Ice gave way to heat. "I'd have done worse to him if I'd had half a chance."

"Why didn't you follow? You should have called for help!"

"Milo! How could I! And let people know that you were off with the cazarra? We'd all be tried for insubordination. She's not supposed to be out after dark! I was trying to decide what to do when you opened the door. I thought you were him again, or one of his friends."

As she listened to the list of injuries Camilla had inflicted upon her assailant, Risa gazed around the room. Save for the path along which Camilla and Milo had grappled their way across the floor, most of the room was untouched. Creases on the bedclothes betrayed where Camilla had curled up. The glass bowl now sat in one of the display cases for safety, its surface dark and unmoving as the pair bickered.

"He came for me," Risa finally interrupted. The guards stopped their conversation and looked at each other warily, plainly unwilling to admit the right of Risa's claim. "You're both being very good about not saying it, but he expected to find me in that bed."

"I don't think—" Camilla started to say.

Milo shushed her and nodded. "You're probably right."

At the sound of Milo's quiet affirmation, Risa's jaw began to quiver. It was too much for her to take. "Who would be desperate enough to harm me?"

"Anyone who wanted to see your caza fall," said Camilla.

"An aspiring family of the Thirty, an enemy of the Divetris, the prince—you know the suspects." Milo sat down beside her.

"I didn't ask for any of this! Two attacks in one day! And because of me, Camilla—" Risa gestured at the guard's bruised cheekbone, for which she felt profoundly guilty. "Please forgive me."

Camilla smiled, but before she could speak, Milo interrupted. "A cazarra should not ask forgiveness of a guard who was doing her duty." Risa protested, but Milo spoke over her. "That's what guards do. That's what guards *do!*"

"I can apologize!"

"You've got to stop thinking like a child, Risa! A cazarra sees a larger picture. She thinks ahead. She plans for her house and for her position. If Divetri had no cazarra, what would happen on the morrow? What would it mean for Cassaforte?" He seemed unnaturally tense and edgy after the fight in the darkness.

"Stop lecturing me! I do think of those things!"

"Then what, after tonight, are you going to do to protect yourself?"

She considered before speaking. "It's too late for me to learn to fight like you two. I want you both by me all day, and guards posted outside my room and at all the entrances to the residence, tomorrow night. That will keep out anyone who doesn't live here."

He nodded at that. "Now you speak like a true cazarra." She should have been pleased with the praise, but once again she felt a flash of annoyance. Why did he lately seem to irritate as well as gratify her?

It was not until they had left her alone in the room that the thought came to her, lending the gravity of the darkness even more weight. The caza's main residence had three floors. The top was reserved for the Divetris. Their isolation in the building's uppermost story made it too easy to forget that others lived in the house as well. The first story consisted mostly of rooms reserved for family use, but at the far end of the wings were suites for the craftsmen and their families. In the canal-level story below dwelled scores of servants like Fita, who were without homes of their own in the city.

What if her attacker had not come from outside the residence?

25

There are more canals than buildings in Cassaforte,
or so it seems. It is a city of water, its buildings suspended
by bridges lighter than air. Of all the wonders of the world,
none is more of a testament to its peoples.

—The artist Moissophant, in his personal journal

🜂

"That's absurd. You can't quit." Arms crossed, Risa stared at Emil without blinking once. It was a technique her father used in his sternest moods.

At least the craftsman had the decency to look abashed. "I'm sorry, Cazarrina…"

"Cazarra," prompted Milo, alert.

Risa repressed her sigh of exasperation at the both of them. "I refuse to accept your resignation." She hoped she sounded firm, yet calm.

Her temper had been rising all morning. The caza was in a state of disarray. Burnt candles had not been replaced. The daytime banners atop the residence were wrapped and wind-tangled. Some of the hearths had not been cleaned since the arrival of the guard. Weeds were appearing in the gardens. Someone had left the annealing furnaces unattended so that they had cooled nearly to a critical level. Servants were abandoning the house in droves, it seemed. Fita had been near tears when Risa encountered her, and would not take any form of consolation.

"The caza's safety is so uncertain," Emil said, twisting his hands nervously. "I don't *want* to take a post elsewhere—I could come back when your father returns."

"Who says I'll let you?" Mattio's face was dark with anger. He spat out words like projectiles of hot glass. "I'll have no fair-weather workers here. You leave, and I guarantee you'll not be coming back!"

Risa tried a more reasonable approach. "If you leave, Mattio will only have Cousin Fredo. Amo's barely gotten his feet wet!" Amo stood in the corner of the workroom arranging materials for the day. At the sound of his name, he looked up and shook his head at her, as if to ask that she leave him out of the discussion.

"There's no Fredo." Mattio continued to scowl at the junior craftsman. "He's gone too."

"What?" said Risa. As much as she disliked her cousin, she knew that with her father gone, Fredo was vital to the workshop's continued output. "That's impossible."

"It's very possible. He left a note for me. Wouldn't even resign in person." Mattio seemed angry. "Coward."

"I saw him before he left, early yesterday evening." Emil

could barely make his timid voice heard over the rumble and roar of the furnaces. His hands twisted a moth-gnawed cap.

Risa felt shock as the realization hit her. "You're just leaving because of Fredo!" Her chest grew hot, her temper acting as bellows to the fire within. "You *wanted* him to be cazarro. You think I bring shame upon this house, don't you? You said so yesterday!"

"If... if you please... " he stammered.

"Go on, then. Get out! Fly with Fredo! Abandon ship with the other rats!" Either her yelling or her dramatic gestures made the slight young man cower before her and back away. She knew she must look mad, both to him and the others. "Go, I said. *Go!*"

Scuttling sideways like a rock crab, Emil fled from the room carrying only his cap and a bag of tools. The door to the courtyard fell shut behind him. Barely had a second passed than Risa took several long strides across the floor and opened it. *"You are never again to return to Caza Divetri!"* she shrieked at his back. She slammed the door again.

"Risa!" Mattio looked shocked.

"I don't want to hear it," she snapped. "We are better off without him. Without both of them!" The door opened again, admitting a servant. She turned away.

Milo wore the same chiding expression. "That outburst was not worthy of a cazarra," he said in a private aside.

"What do you know of cazarras?" she yelled. Her patience was pushed beyond endurance. "Why do you *constantly* remind me how a cazarra behaves? What gives you that right?" For a moment she was astonished at her vehemence. Immense satisfaction had welled up inside her. It terrified her that it was so easy to strike out at him—Milo, of all people. But she was angry. Angry at Emil, angry with Fredo for slinking away in the dark. Angry with Milo for acting like her father.

"Every citizen of Cassaforte knows exactly how its cazarri should behave—just as we know how our royalty should *not* behave."

"You're comparing me to the prince now?" Risa shouted. "Am I a tyrant? An ogre?"

Normally, in front of other members of the household, Milo assumed the role of the expressionless guard. With only Amo and Mattio present, he abandoned all pretense. "That's not what I said."

"That's what you *meant!*"

He held up his hands. "I don't want to fight."

"Please," said a quiet voice behind them all. It was barely audible over the workroom's sounds. All turned; finally Risa turned, to find Dom, the old servant. In front of him, on a worktable, sat a bowl filled with figs and pears and other fruit, obviously sent by Fita in apology for the inadequate breakfast earlier.

"What is it, Dom?" Risa's voice still trembled with anger, modulate it though she tried.

"Is—is something wrong?"

"Nothing's wrong," Risa lied as she continued to glare at Milo in challenge. "We're just having a discussion."

"You shouldn't ... "

It sounded very much as if the silly old man was going to give her advice as well. "I am *tired* of everyone telling me what I should and shouldn't do!" They all were conspiring to exasperate her! Her lips clenched, Risa stomped out of the workshop and through the door, leaving them all behind her.

A tired Camilla stood on guard outside. Risa dared not look to see how much of the argument she had overheard. As Camilla startled to attention and began to scramble after her, Risa marched swiftly across the courtyard toward the residence.

"Where are you going, Cazarra?"

"To my chambers!"

She heard the workshop door shutting once more, in the distance. That would be Milo, then. Or Mattio. Or all of them, chasing after her, telling her not to be so hot-headed. No words pursued her, however, nor did she hear any cries of apology.

Without looking over her shoulder, she pushed her way past the ancestral statues in their honorary nooks at the southern end of the residence and walked under the marble arch into the lower courtyard. Through the outdoor dining hall she hastened, and then through the grand hall and the vestibule. She had made a humiliating retreat along this route not even two weeks earlier, after she had failed the Scrutiny. But today was not the same, she told herself. This time she was seeking the sanctuary of her room, to get away from those who wanted to pry into and control her decisions.

It was not until she reached the upper hallway that Milo and Camilla caught up to her. She could see them reflected in the mirror at the hall's end, grimly following in her wake. She swung open her door, stepped into the room, and turned. "Leave me alone," she ordered before Milo could speak. She slammed the door.

Risa did not throw the latch that would have locked them out. After the previous night's events, both her guards would have made a fuss if they had heard that tell-tale noise. Truthfully, she did not care to lock them out. She wanted Milo to apologize. He owed her an apology. She perched upon the settee and spread out her skirts. For half of an hour she waited, fully expecting Milo to enter and beg pardon from her.

He did not.

You told him to leave you alone, a stern Risa thought to herself. In reply, an anguished part of her rejected the reproach. *I didn't mean it!*

She had not meant to shut him out. She had wanted him to implore her to be friends again, to try to make amends. She wanted Milo's attention. She needed his friendship, but her tantrum had made it impossible for him to offer. Merely for the sake of show, she had stormed off in a fuss rather than admit the fault of her own temper. If she had not over-reacted...

Of course he hadn't compared her to the prince. If she were to be absolutely truthful with herself, she had known what he was trying to say to her, even in the white heat of the argument. Everyone knew how a member of the royal family should and shouldn't act, just as she knew the duties and responsibilities of a guard.

Through the windows and balcony came the sounds of noontime activity in the piazza. Voices sounded in friendly conversation, though they were not as loud or as jovial as in the days before the fall of the cazas to the immediate east and west. Waters lapped at the canal walls. The occasional

sharp cry of a gull cut through the babble. They were soothing noises all, and Risa attempted to let them wash away the
ragged edges of her bad humor.

She had loved these sounds as a child. She wanted back
that childhood once more—a life free of danger and risk and
confrontation. More than anything, she wanted nothing but
to be happy and enjoy her home and family.

The thought of Dom intruded—the most frail and
dependent of all the household. Risa had been rudeness itself
to him. The memory brought a crease to her brow. Milo was
right—she was behaving not as a cazarra, but as a child.

What could she do? If she pretended that nothing had
happened, perhaps all the morning's drama would simply be
forgotten. The stern Risa inside her tried to insist she apologize first, but it was still difficult, even to herself, to admit
being in the wrong—much less voice the words aloud.

She looked around the room, feeling sad and hopeless,
until her eyes lit upon the glass bowl. She stepped lightly
across the stone and matting so her footsteps would not be
heard outside the door. The bowl was smudged and dirty
with fingerprints that were invisible in last night's dimness,
but which completely obscured her reflection by day. She
used a soft leather cloth and the moisture of her own breath
to wipe away the oils, and then gazed deep into the curved
pool of light. Why had her parents not again attempted to
communicate with her? She would give any number of lundri just to be able to see them face to face right now, and hear
their advice.

Risa startled out of her reverie at the sight of a face in
the blue-green depths of the bowl. Her eyes focused upon

the image—and saw that it was only her own. But it was no wonder she was confused. The stress of the previous days had made her face look drawn and thin. She had thought the face belonged to someone older—someone old and worn, the age of Ferrer Cassamagi.

Why had she not thought of him since his visit?

Within moments, Risa was opening the door to her room. Milo and Camilla stared at the broad smile that was transforming her face from a wilting blossom to a fresh bloom. "I've had the most marvelous idea!" she exclaimed, her heart leaping at the astonishment on both their faces. "We're going to Caza Cassamagi."

Neither Milo nor his sister seemed delighted at her announcement. "Why?" said Milo. Risa could scarcely read his expression. He seemed guarded and wary.

"The woman who founded his caza used many enchantments that the Seven no longer perform," she explained. "She could see and talk to people far away. That's what Ferrer Cassamagi told me yesterday. He might be able to explain my bowl, Milo. He might be able to make it work again."

They looked at each other. "It's a fine idea, Risa, but at the moment I am thinking primarily of your safety." Camilla looked grave as she spoke the words. "Someone was trying very desperately to hurt you last night."

"It's out of the question," Milo finished for her.

"That's ridiculous," she said flatly, but the siblings looked unmoved. "I insist."

"We just can't take a risk with your life," Milo explained.

"Anyone could attempt to kill you on the streets," added Camilla. "Someone's already tried twice."

"We'll go after dark, then," she said. "Like last night."

Her remark elicited a sharp bark of laughter from Milo. "No, we won't."

"It really is for your own good," Camilla added in a consoling tone.

"It would be for my own good to see Ferrer Cassamagi *today*," she said, surprised by the fierceness in her own voice. Anger choked her. A few moments before she had felt guilt for the way she'd treated Milo, but now she wondered if her instincts had been correct. He was a hindrance.

"We think it would be best to restrict you to the caza," Camilla said slowly. Milo nodded at her. They had obviously discussed the issue.

"And if I insist on leaving?"

"Then we've agreed we'll tell Tolio about last night's attack," Camilla said. "He's wanted to restrict you to the caza grounds since we arrived."

"You'll be reprimanded! You could lose your professions!" She was utterly astounded by the turn of the argument.

"But you'd be safe," Milo pointed out. "Keeping you safe is our duty. We could find other jobs eventually."

It was impossible to argue with them. "I thought we were friends," she told Milo. "You can't make decisions for me behind my back as if I was a child. You're not my father!"

Milo took a step toward her, his temper as frayed as hers. "One of these days, when you stop being such a little *baby*, you'll realize that your father isn't the only person in the world who gives a damn what happens to you!" His voice reverberated down the hallway until only a hollow echo lingered in the stairwell. He snapped his mouth shut.

"I despise you." At that moment, she meant every word.

With one hand he pushed his crimson cap back down over his lanky blond curls and looked her straight in the eyes. "Right now, I'm not that fond of you."

"Milo!" Camilla dropped any pretense of guard-like detachment. She looked plainly distressed at the shouting. "Risa, please—"

The door's slam cut off whatever reconciliation Camilla might have proposed. Seething with fury, Risa paced across the room and finally threw herself onto the bed. Baby! He had called her a *baby!* He was the stubborn one who had refused to listen to her argument. If they had been on the way to Caza Cassamagi, she might have solved their problems by sundown. *She* was not the baby!

A smile warped her lips. Even now, Camilla's extra guard uniform hung within her wardrobe. A *baby* could not have devised the plan that was animating her imagination at that moment.

She would show Milo how clever she could be.

26

A shrill cry of woe sounds into the night.
The city lies quiet in dread.
And high in the palace, a king in his robes
Lies quiet and still: He is dead.

A thunder as hoofbeats pound over the bridge—
Its echoes sound over the water
"Oh father, don't leave me!" resounds a soft cry—
The cry of the glass maker's daughter.

I *hate* that song," Risa growled to herself. Its singer was not very accomplished, either. His scratchy voice made her long, for the first time, for Ricard's. The people within the small taverna, however, shouted out their approval so loudly that panes of glass rattled. They were singing along with the minstrel lustily, banging their mugs on the tables in rhythm, unaware of the siege just outside the taverna's doors.

The shadows along the side alley of the taverna afforded her shelter, for the moment. She adjusted the sack over her shoulder, careful not to let it collide with the wall. It contained the most precious object in the world to her—her bowl of blue-green glass whose phenomenon she trusted Ferrer Cassamagi to explain.

It took only a little effort to peer beyond the building's corner, toward where the bridge leading to Caza Cassamagi's main entrance lay bathed in the light of two moons. Silvery light sparkled from the blades of two-score drawn swords.

It had been so easy, until that point. Risa had spent most of the daylight hours shut away in her rooms, scorning all company. She'd opened the door only to admit a dinner tray and later to emerge to perform the rite. Several times, when she caught him looking at her, she thought Milo might be trying to speak; when he did not, she hardened against him even more.

A cable of braided retas, knotted with a number of sashes from her gowns, had been all that was necessary to effect her escape after the sun had set. She had waited until all was quiet in the hallway, then had tied the makeshift rope to the sturdy iron grille of her balcony. Ridiculous, really, how easy it had been to lower herself down into one of the gondolas tethered at the servants' dock.

Everything had gone precisely as planned. No one saw her flight or questioned her when she punted along the canal route along Cassaforte's outer rim. It was not until she approached Cassamagi that she encountered any problems. She had planned to mingle among the guards encamped on the bridge, attracting little attention to herself until she could make her way into the residence. There had been a commotion upon her arrival, however, that caused her to scurry into the shadows. Scarcely had she climbed the old stone steps from the canal bank to the Via Torto, the street that led to a warren of homes and shops in this old part of the city, when she heard the clamor of shields and swords rattling against each other. City guards came running from all directions to meet in the center of the bridge, their swords drawn. Risa had made sure of her grip upon the padded sack containing her bowl, and scurried for the shadows by the taverna before any of the guards—the real guards—found her.

"There's commotion at the caza," someone murmured. Risa saw that a handful of people had gathered in the narrow alleyway with her. She hastily clawed her cap from her head and prayed that her uniform would be invisible in the darkness.

"These are sorry times we live in. Don't you think?" An old man was questioning a hooded figure next to him. The figure did not reply.

As she watched, a squadron in two columns poured through the gates from the caza, their march steady and swift as they kept pace with a vehicle between them. Some of the guards gathered on the bridge fell into the lead, while others waited until the procession had passed and took up the rear. As the assembly crossed the bridge, Risa could see that they were surrounding a carriage—the very copper-colored carriage in which she had conducted her interview with Ferrer Cassamagi two days before. Was Ferrer inside? Where in the world could they all be going, so late at night?

Instinctively she drew back as the regiment spilled from the bridge onto the Via Torto, turning westward and heading past her. The four or five others who observed the spectacle with her waited until the carriage and the last of the guards had passed, before stepping out into the moonlit street. As the noise faded, all save the hooded figure disappeared.

Questions battered Risa, as hopelessly as moths battered the lamp-bright windows above her. She stepped out into the street to catch a glimpse of the retreating forms. Should she follow the carriage? Had it contained the Cazarro? Or was he still within the caza itself?

"Rather late for you to be out, is it not?" She was startled to hear a voice address her; it was instantly familiar, yet she could not immediately identify it in her confusion. Oily and syrupy it was, and oozing with a sweetness that was as foul as the scent of cloves and pine oil and tobacco leaves that accompanied it. "Why are you so far from home ... cousin?"

The realization that the hood concealed Cousin Fredo made her gasp and stumble backward. "What are you doing here?" she asked in a choked voice.

"It is not so puzzling a tale." Though the rough fabric of his hooded cloak concealed his eyes, moonlight caught his lips and pointed chin in sharp relief. He smiled. "I happened to be passing through the Piazza Divetri when I noticed someone dangling from your balcony. Naturally, after what happened last night, I was concerned. So I took it upon myself to ensure your safety." He took a step closer to her and put his hand on her shoulder as Risa backed up against the taverna wall. His nails began to dig through the thick fabric of her uniform and pinch her flesh.

"You followed me," she accused him, trying to escape his clutch. "Stop that!"

"I followed you for the best reasons, my dear. Let me relieve you of your burden, so that I can escort you home. Shall I?" Before she could protest, he had scooped the padded sack from over her shoulder and put it upon his own.

"Give it back!" she protested. Fredo did not resist when, with a tug, she reclaimed her glass treasure. But his grip on her shoulder intensified; his pinch felt like it was drawing blood. It was the fierceness of his grasp that warned her, more than anything else, that Fredo had no intention of seeing her safely home. "You can't have known about last night," she said, finally understanding. Camilla had said her attacker smelled awful. She probably had gotten a snootful of his *tabbaco da fiuto*. "Unless you were there."

A breathy smirk escaped Fredo's lips. He shook his head so that the hood dropped onto his shoulders, revealing a face like a ghoul's. It took her several seconds to realize that the dark pools around his eyes were not shadows—they were the bruises that had formed after Camilla broke his nose the night before. "Perhaps I was. You must think you're clever!"

"You are my cousin!" she reminded him, fighting with all her might to escape. Fredo laughed and jerked her hand, burning her wrist. The padded sack fell to the ground, the glass bowl within crashing onto the stones of the street. Risa cried out at the noise.

"I *was* there, you little bitch." Fredo's voice was fierce and angry. His arms were around her from behind now, squeezing the breath from her lungs. Her legs kicked out, trying to connect with his knees or groin. "Of course it was me, forced to sneak around like a criminal! An outsider in my own caza! You wouldn't know what that feels like though, would you, Cazarrina?"

Despite her desperate attempt to wrench herself free, Risa could appreciate the irony in that remark. Instead of replying, though, she fastened her teeth onto one of her cousin's hands, chomping down hard until she heard him yell in pain.

She felt a blow against the side of her head that seemed nearly to swivel her neck past the breaking point. He had hauled off and struck her, stunning Risa so that she ceased kicking and struggling. "You'll not have the chance to best me again, either, you damned wildcat!"

Whatever substance was soaked into the cloth he thrust under her nose smelled sweet, but its pungent stench brought tears to her eyes. Pain shot through her shoulder blade as he wrenched her forward, forcing her to inhale.

Her throat no longer worked. It seemed choked and clenched. Around her the world reeled; her mind could form no words or pleas for help. Even if she could have cried out, who would have heard her? Milo was nowhere near … why hadn't she listened to Milo?

The last sensations she knew before slipping into unconsciousness were Fredo's hot breath against her neck and the sound of his triumphant laughter, as the men and women in the taverna launched once again into song.

The night passed, the moons set. The sun took their place.
No sign of her parents did greet her.
She wandered alone, her fair self not knowing
Another had plans to defeat her …

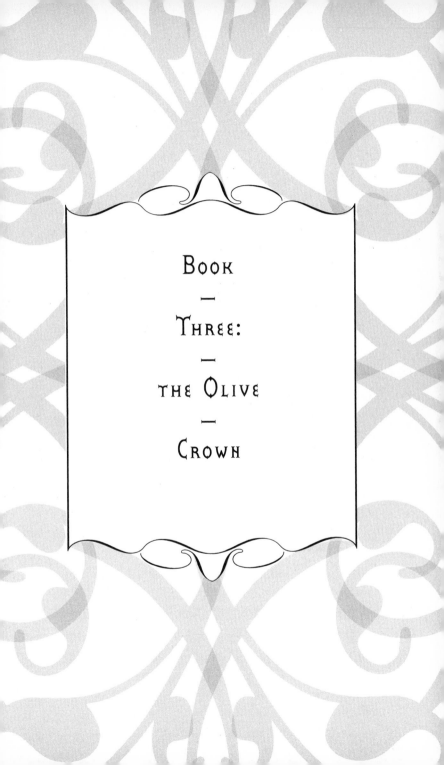

BOOK
—
THREE:
—
THE OLIVE
—
CROWN

27

—

The Palace of the Cassafort Citie was established at the high-est pointe of the swamplands on which the citie was established. Though it has been rebuilt several times throughout the centuries, a royal residence has always occupied that very spot.

—ANONYMOUS, A BRIEFE AND COMPLEAT HISTORIE OF THE CASSAFORT CITIE

They had piled rocks atop her. What other reason could there be for how she felt? Her limbs were so heavy that she could not lift them. Even drawing breath took more effort than it should.

"... glad to be of service ... from the bottom of my heart, I wish I could ... anything you wish ..."

Fredo, she thought to herself, recognizing the voice. The single word pulsed sluggishly through her brain, taking a moment to register. Why couldn't she move? Why did her eyes refuse to open?

A deeper and more deliberate voice rumbled in response. She could only hear a few words. "…risk…amply rewarded."

"I would gladly forego…merely for the pleasure…serving you…."

"…curious. How did you…"

She had to shake off whatever was holding her down. "…clever little music box…" she heard Fredo saying. His words now came in near-sentences, but she still had to struggle to capture their meaning. "It nearly worked, but the little bitch squirmed out of it. When I heard that you were looking for a way to get her, after you heard that ballad…"

Ricard's song was my undoing after all, she thought to herself, surprised at how slowly the words came to her. *Despite how hard we tried…*

"Why?" Fredo's voice continued, in answer to a rumbled question. "Because I hate them all! My father married outside the Seven and Thirty, and they have always looked down upon me, despised my tainted blood. What a fine thing it would be, indeed, to have them working for *me*. I know you make no promises, but you did say that you would consider me as the new…" She heard a clink of coins. Lundri had passed hands. She heard Fredo let out a hiss of satisfaction. "Oh. Oh!" he repeated, sounding astounded. "How marvelous!"

Deep inside her, a voice whispered a word of warning. It surfaced slowly, as a mud bubble might from the bottom of a pond. *There's trouble here, Cazarra,* she heard. *What are you going to do about it?*

Her lips parted, admitting cool air into her mouth and lungs. "Milo?" she said softly.

Across the empty space in which she lay, silks and velvets rustled. "She's wakening," Fredo hissed.

"Take care of it." For the first time, she clearly heard the other man's voice. Like a large bell it was, deep and resonant, tolling out her fate with deliberation.

Once again, aroma overpowered her, sending tides of scarlet and black to carry her back into their drowning depths.

When she awoke again, after what seemed like decades, her fingers tingled first, then her toes. Her extremities felt as if they were being warmed before a fire on a very cold winter's day. The tickle at the end of her nose spread to her cheeks, then to her ears, just as the rest of her body twitched back into life. She groaned, aware at how parched her throat felt.

"Do not move." The voice was masculine yet whispery, like the midnight speech of trees as they rustled to one another in a breeze. It was the voice of an old man, reassuring her. "All will be well, child. Yet do not move."

Her eyelids fluttered open, seeming to rip through a crust that sealed them together. It took a moment for her eyes to adjust to the brightness of the room. A face hovered over hers. "Cassamagi," she murmured.

Ferrer peered down at her through his double spectacles. Risa winced. The twin crescents of light they reflected reminded her of the moons. "You've been under the effect of camarandus seed oil. No, don't try to talk yet." She felt him apply something wet and cool to her forehead and cheeks. The soft cloth licked away the flames from her skin. "Camarandus is a flower of the woods, you know. Quite harmless in its native form. When the seeds are harvested and treated

232

with brine and pressed, however, they produce a sleeping philter that, while usually short-lived, is remarkably potent in its—no, do not sit up yet, my dear. You will be... "

The sensation of motion caused her stomach to churn. Fluids burned her gullet as her gorge rose. She sensed the cazarro thrusting a container into her hands. As she vomited into it, she was dimly aware that he was holding her hair, so that it would not fall into the slop.

There was not much left in her stomach, thankfully. After a few racking heaves, the uneasy feeling in her middle began to subside. She accepted the wet cloth Ferrer offered and dabbed at her sweating face and her mouth, mortified. "I'm sorry," she said, trying to blink back the tears that had formed during the contractions of her stomach.

"Youth today! So headstrong! As I was trying to tell you, the other effect of camarandus oil is a tendency toward nausea. Well, we learn by doing, do we not?" With the utmost gentleness he dipped another cloth into an ewer of water and handed it to her, taking the soiled rag and tossing it onto the hearth.

"Where are we?" she asked, looking around the room in wonder. They were in a space roughly half the size of her own bedchamber at home. Cozily furnished with four settees arranged in a square at its center, the room had been appointed with an excess of woolen tapestries, carpets upon the floor, and decorations of fine craftsmanship. It was plainly the parlor of some vastly wealthy citizen; even the table legs had been gilded. Its fireplace was a glorious thing of marble, carved with grapes and apples and an abundance of other fruit strung around columns that supported its deep mantel. A narrow window provided their only illumination. Daylight streamed in through its panes. "And who is he?"

Curled into a fetal position on the sofa opposite her own was a tall, thin boy. His hair was dark and limp, as if it had not been groomed in some time. He appeared to be sleeping, but his breath was so shallow and undetectable that for a moment she feared he was dead.

"If our view out the window is any indication, we are somewhere in the palace," answered the Cazarro. "And our companion, inert though he may be, is Baso Buonochio."

Risa stood up and took a few unsteady steps toward the window, feeling slightly dizzy at the motion. For a moment she feared another bout of sickness. After another moment, she realized that the feeling in the pit of her stomach was fear.

As she looked out the window, she realized with a sense of doom that they were near the very top of the palace; immediately outside the window were the statuary masks of Lena and Muro, smiling down toward the crowds. Below, Palace Square was filled with citizens going about their everyday business. When she tried the window's handles, hoping to open the vertical panels and let in the air, or even perhaps to cry for help, she found they were tightly sealed.

The sun shone brightly. She guessed it was mid-morning. A midsummer's day like any other to the people below, but to Risa it was the dark moment she had been struggling to avoid for some time.

"Baso Buonochio?" she asked, bewildered. "You told me he was acting as cazarro. That means..."

"Yes," Ferrer confirmed. "We are the three remaining

bearers of the horns. Allyria's ancient enchantment may allow others to complete the act of fealty for us, but our disappearances will make any candidates think twice about coming forward to risk their own lives. By nightfall, none of our cazas will be our own."

Struck by sheer panic, Risa looked toward the exit, half-hidden behind a tapestry depicting sheep tended by shepherds. "Guards stand outside," Ferrer said, guessing her intentions. "The door is sealed in a way that while it opens from the hallway to admit people, those of us unfortunate enough to be harbored inside cannot open it. The window is useless to us as well. Such locks are a common enough enchantment of Portello."

"It's unthinkable," said Risa. As the last of the weariness from the drug wore away, her anger flared.

"Not really, my dear. The primary function of a lock, after all, is to keep people out. Cassamagi's enchantments can only enhance the primary functions of everyday objects—"

"I know," she replied, failing to be patient. "What's unthinkable is that Prince Berto would *dare* to interfere with the country's natural order. You were taken from your own home in the middle of the night without even a chance to resist! I saw it!" The list of the prince's outrages seemed to grow longer by the minute.

The old man inclined his head. "To my shame, that is so."

"I was sold to him by my own blood!"

"Men will sell more than their kin for gold or for power, child," he whispered.

"I've learned that," she spat. She gestured at Baso, motionless in his slumber. "I'm sure the prince obtained him through equally devious means. He can't even confront us face to face!" Anger seemed useless, however. There was little she could accomplish in this confined space, and yet there seemed no escape. She noticed Ferrer's attention focused on Baso. "Why does he not wake?" she finally asked.

The old man shook his head. "Whoever drugged the boy used too much of the camarandus oil."

"How can you tell?" When Risa had partially woken under the influence of the oil, she'd felt as if she'd been flattened to the thickness of paper. She shuddered to think of how it would feel to receive an even larger dose.

"His sleep is too deep. I fear he has been poisoned. Without aid…" Gravely, the old man perched on the seat's edge, supporting himself with a wooden cane carved with vines. He sighed and shook his head.

Risa waited for him to say something further, yet he merely sat there, seemingly resigned to Baso's condition. For several more moments she waited for him to suggest a solution, frustration causing her to clutch the settee's velvet padding until she knew it was moist from her grip. "Without aid, what? He'll die?" she asked at last. The old man didn't have to say a word in response. "Then do something to help him! Can't you?" To her dismay, her question sounded harsh.

Over the top of his twinned spectacles, Ferrer peered at her. "What would you have me do?" he asked, brandishing his cane. His voice was perfectly reasonable; he asked the question as he might have inquired the time of day. "I have struck at the door repeatedly in the hope that someone would bring aid. They are not much concerned with our health or our comfort, my child. That is the sorry truth of it." It was not indifference that she sensed in his words, but a genuine sense of submission and acceptance.

"There must be something!"

"I possess no antidote. In every game of chess there comes a moment when one's priests and guards have been depleted, and one's knights no longer can defend one's king. Checkmate is never easy to accept."

"We're not yet in check," Risa told him, thinking hard. "You're the greatest of the Cassamagi enchanters. You must be able to ..."

"My girl. You compliment my abilities, but I am helpless." He gestured around the room. "My caza is known for its ability to enhance the natural function of objects. We can create perfumes that seduce, musical instruments that soothe even the most savage tempers, and also poisons so subtle that they work their deadly art weeks after their ingestion—though they cannot survive a Divetri-stoppered vessel charmed to keep a liquid pure," he added with a smile. During his speech Risa did not move. Though itching to escape the cage that held the three of them, she was held rapt by what he was telling her.

"We do not fashion objects with enchantments in their very structure, as does your family," the cazarro continued. "We cannot build walls with the blessings of Allyria embedded in every brick, as did Caza Portello. While Cassamagi's magics can be the most dangerous because of the sheer variety of objects with which we can work, they are also the most fleeting, because we do not craft the items themselves."

It suddenly came to Risa. "Don't you see? That's perfect! There must be *something* in this room you could use to rescue us." But even as she said the words, she heard a voice somewhere inside her murmur, *You're perfectly capable of rescuing yourself, you know.* For a moment she had a brief vision of Milo admonishing her. She banished it and returned her attention to the cazarro.

"My dear young child. Do you suppose I have not looked?" Ferrer gestured to the ornaments that crowded every flat surface. "This room contains gold and treasure enough for the average citizen to feed his family for a lifetime, yet it yields nothing suitable for my purposes. There are vessels aplenty." With some effort he raised his cane to jab the air in the direction of a case of beautiful glass, some of which Risa recognized as a style so old that they had probably been made by her grandfather and his ancestors. "Beautiful to behold, but how can purified liquid make a door open? There are pillows aplenty upon which I could lay enchantments to enhance their comfort, but how would they aid us? That mirror over the mantel I could adjust in such a way that if we stood in front of it, it would make us both seem like creatures of rare beauty. For you it would not be a novel experience—at my age it would be quite an oddity indeed. Yet doing so would not open that door, or wake young Baso, or aid us in any way. I am not unsympathetic to your desire to quit this incarceration, young Risa," he added kindly, smiling at her. "It is merely that I do not perceive any means of aid with which we can avail ourselves."

For a moment she stared at him, shoulders hunched. On the cushions opposite, Baso drew a sickly and shallow breath. She stared at the youth's skin, white against the burgundy silks. "He's so young," she said. "There must be something we can do for him."

"You are a year his junior." Ferrer's voice crackled like a winter's fire. "War is never kind to the young."

"Is that what this is?" Risa demanded. "A war?"

"It will be, once the cazas fall." The Cazarro's hand trembled as he reached up to remove his wire spectacles. He placed them on the seat and rubbed a nose speckled and red with age. "It will be one of the greatest wars that Cassaforte has seen, pitting citizen against citizen. Many of the people will not easily swallow the usurpation of the throne through the vile means the prince has used, and will rise against him. They will be opposed by the prince's favorites, the families of the Thirty that hope to replace the Seven. Guards loyal to the ideals of Cassaforte will find themselves pitted against guards loyal to the prince's ambitions." His voice grew louder as he continued to speak, and he peered so intently that it seemed he was seeing something far in the distance. "As King Alessandro named no alternate heir to the throne—oh yes, the kings of Cassaforte may do such a thing and sometimes have, in our history, when the heir presumptive was unsuitable—but since he hasn't, others will vie for the honor. The best men and women of our country will die, one by one, family by family, in a rising tide of blood so terrible that our descendants will regard this period as the darkest in our country's history. Oh yes, child. This is indeed a war."

Impatient for action, Risa took the old man's hand in her own, surprised at how light and papery it felt. In a low voice, she made her plea: "Then let us stop it before it starts."

28

*I couldn't help myself. Honestly! When I saw him in the square
below my window, I had to say something to him. He must have
thought me bold! If you had seen him that afternoon, shirt open
and smile broad, you too might have called out.*

—Giulia Buonochio in a letter to her sister, Sara,
a month before her marriage to Ero Divetri

🔖

As best she could guess, their prison was a parlor intended
for those waiting for an audience with the royal family. Every item was intended to impress the senses and dazzle
the eye. Her mother would have called it ostentatious. Risa
was conducting a thorough inventory of the room's objects,
in the hopes she could find something for the cazarro to
enchant. "Cherub?" she asked. The winged baby had been
formed with plaster and painted gold, and sat with its feet
hanging over the mantel.

Ferrer uttered a dry chuckle. "Dear girl, even my illustrious house can do nothing with a cherub. It serves no purpose whatsoever."

"A painting of King Paolo the fourth and his consort, Maria?"

"Ah. Pictorial art is an interesting area of study and one that too few of the Cassamagi pursue. An ancestral depiction's primary purpose is to be of pride to the family, and can easily be enchanted to enhance that sense of satisfaction in one's bloodline. Religious iconography, on the other hand, has the primary purpose of being the inculcation of solemnity and prayerfulness…"

Over the last hour, Risa felt she had received as much of an education in the primary purpose of common objects as she would during a year's education at an insula. Her head was already reeling from the overload of information. "Firewood?" she asked.

"…for example, the *Adoration of the Handmaiden Lucia before the Shrine of Lena* has unusual… Why, the primary purpose of firewood is to burn. You know well that Cassamagi-enchanted bundles of lumber keep your caza's furnaces at a hot and steady temperature." Ferrer seemed not in the least offended to have his monologue interrupted.

"Could you enchant it to blaze hot enough to set the room afire?"

"Easily, yet somehow I do not think it wise."

Risa sighed with frustration. She was aware the idea was not the best, yet she was quickly running out of options. "If we produced enough smoke, the guards might open the doors to see what was happening."

"We would be overcome and quite, quite unconscious

by that point, dear girl. I commend you on your creativity, however."

She scanned the items on the hearth. "Broom? Poker?"

"In theory it is quite possible to enchant a broom to enhance its purpose of sweeping up dust, though I have never seen it applied. I must test it with my maids, sometime, if I am granted that chance. Quite an interesting experiment. A poker's primary use is to cause a fire to burn more brightly. It can be enchanted ... "

"What if I don't want to use it for a fire?" she asked, losing all patience. "What if I want to use it as a weapon?" The old man stared at her for a moment. "The Dioro enchant weapons so that their blades are sharper and their arrows more deadly. Enchant this poker so I can use it against the guards!" With both hands she gripped the heavy instrument and brandished it in the Cazarro's direction.

"That's impossible," said old man mildly. "Destruction is not its primary purpose."

She gripped the poker so tightly between her hands that it felt as if the metal was tingling, changing into something cold and hard. "I *could* use this poker as a weapon. I could use a book as a weapon, if I wanted." Her memory flashed back to the night before the Scrutiny, when Petro had said the very same thing.

"But that is not their primary ... "

"Your enchantments are useless! What good is such power if it cannot be used in any but the most primitive of ways?" she cried, losing all temper. Her clench on the quivering poker was now so intense that it almost seemed an extension of her arm. "I am *tired* of primary purposes! Every object has more than one purpose, including this one!" Angry beyond belief, she hefted the poker over her head and brought it swinging down upon the low table in the center of the sofas.

She had expected nothing more than a loud retort from the impact. Making such a noise would feel immensely satisfying, even if for only a moment. When the poker struck the table, however, a cloud of marble splinters flew into the air, stinging her face with their needle-like points. The sound was immense, like a crack of thunder.

She gasped slightly, breathless from the exertion. There before her, the solid stone table had been roughly split in half. The insides of the marble top tilted in toward each other. A white pile of dust covered the carpet's pile and powdered the crimson of her dirty guard's uniform. On his sofa, Baso continued his soundless slumber.

Words of apology were the first things she tried to mumble when she saw Ferrer's expression of astonishment. Once again she had let her temper get the best of her—worse than ever. The old man was groping for his spectacles, then wrapped their earpieces onto his head. "My child!" he finally said. "Impossible. It's impossible for you to have done that!"

The shock upon his features inspired her. She had just done something unusual. Would it save them? Jutting her jaw out, she ran with the poker in hand across the room in the direction of the single window. With a mighty heave, she swung the poker at the wood-framed glass, hoping to shatter it as she had the table. The window's enchantment, however, was too strong; when iron collided with glass, the poker bounced harmlessly backward. The shock of the blow caused Risa to drop her weapon. Both her hands and wrists stung from the bone-wrenching recoil.

Ferrer still looked at her in astonishment. "It's impossible," he repeated again. For the first time since Risa had met him, he seemed utterly dumbfounded. "You should not have been able to break that table."

Her hands were red and swollen. Red welts were rising across her palms. It would fade in a while, she knew, but at the moment the pain was difficult to bear. "Tell me how I did it, then," she pled as tears rose in her eyes.

29

Every object has its natural and primary purpose. The blessings of the gods can certainly enhance that one natural purpose. But like the hands of the worker, are there not other and more versatile purposes to which objects may be put?

—From the private papers of Allyria Cassamagi
(from the Cassamagi Historical Archives)

🜍

Even minutes after Risa's feat with the poker, Ferrer's shock remained intense. It showed in the pallor of his face and the trembling of his hands; he had to help himself to several dippers of water from the bucket sitting just inside the door. Risa tended to him as best she could with her still-swollen fingers, all the while worried that he was angry with her. The guards in the hall had either not heard, or had ignored, the commotion within the room, for they never investigated the source of the noise.

At last the old man clasped both of his hands around the

top of his cane. "Who told you about secondary enchant-ments?" he asked.

"What? No one. What are they?"

"Someone must have. Your mother? No, she was never interested in the lore. So few people know. Who told you?" It took several denials before he seemed to believe that she had no idea of what he spoke. "I will put it simply for you. Allyria Cassamagi left few records of how she accomplished her enchantments, and they are incomprehensible to us. Many of our house, myself included, feel that her complex magic was the result of what we call secondary enchantments."

"What are they?"

"Hear me out, my dear. Every object has a primary pur-pose that the Seven can affect in their craft. The principle of secondary enchantments is based on the notion that objects can be utilized in other ways as well, and accorded enchantments as such. The purpose of a helmet or a crown is to protect the head, and can be enchanted to ward off injuries. Yet Allyria understood that a crown is a symbol of power, and a symbol of pride as well. She was able to enchant the Olive Crown on all those levels. Just now, when you grasped that poker—it became more than a poker. You wished it to become a weapon, and…"

"It became a weapon that could split a marble table in half." Her voice dropped to a whisper.

"Have you done such things before?"

"No, never."

"You must have. *Think*, child, think!"

Even as she denied his question, Risa knew that she had

indeed once performed a similar task. "My bowl..." she said. "My bowl. I saw them in my bowl."

"Explain. It is important!"

"I thought it was my father's enchantment! Not my own!" Hastily she told him how she had crafted her bowl, attempted to sell it, and later saw her parents' images dancing among lights caught in the concave surface. He encouraged her with nods and grunts until she reached the end of the story. "I was bringing it to you last night to see if you could make it happen again, when my cousin captured and drugged me."

His tone was low and reverent. "Oh no. I cannot make it happen at all. I have more knowledge of the craft than any, but I cannot. It is all in here." He pointed to his skull. "And not in here." He held up his hands. "Tell me, child. What were you thinking of when you saw your parents in the bowl?"

"We were arguing," she said. There had been a great deal of arguing with Milo. She would have given all the gold and wealth in that parlor at that moment for just one glimpse of him as he had been at Mina's taverna—strong, lively, confident. She would just as quickly have given her own family's fortune to erase the look of hurt she had caused during their final argument. "I had the bowl in my lap. I was touching it," she said, thinking back. "Then it started to show my parents' shadows."

"And the poker?"

"I was angry," she recalled. This was much easier to remember. "I wanted to hurt something. The poker seemed heavy. Then it grew heavier—as if it was changing beneath my hands."

At last Ferrer said slowly, "You've no idea what I would give, just to know how that sensation felt. If it can be felt, it can be manipulated. For a lifetime I have wished for such a blessing. Yet you do it instinctively, without even a single lesson."

His reverence alarmed her. "I don't understand."

"Don't be frightened. What happened to your bowl, the one you brought for me to see?"

"Oh!" Her sudden hope crumbled at the memory of the terrible and sharp sound of it striking the pavement. "My cousin broke it. He probably left it in the streets." Her shoulders slumped in despair.

"In what sort of conveyance had you stored it?"

"A brown sack padded with—that's it!" At the end of his cane hung the sack. While she was speaking, Ferrer had speared it with his cane's tip and withdrawn it from under the sofa. Risa immediately opened it to extract its contents.

"They obviously found it harmless, for they threw it in after you when you were brought in here," Ferrer said. "I tucked it away for safekeeping."

"It's in pieces." The impact from the pavement, or her cousin's rough treatment of it after she was reduced to unconsciousness, had broken the glass into a number of pieces. The largest of these was roughly one third of the bowl, a beautiful section where the blue and green glasses had melted into each other to form a rippling aqua. Mourning the loss, Risa assembled the shards on the sofa, laying them side by side as if hoping they might magically join edges and form a whole.

"Tell me about glass, my dear," said Ferrer. "What is it? What does it feel like? What does it do?"

It was an odd question, and obviously intended to draw her mind away from her loss. She reached out and touched the largest of the glass pieces. "It's really just sand and alkali, you know, melted together. And ... I don't know!"

"It's impossible to achieve an enchantment when the mind is in disarray." Ferrer's interruption was not in the least unwelcome. "There are ways we teach the insula initiates to clear their thoughts, but distressed as you are, it may be futile—"

"Oh! I can do that!" The old man rewarded her with a look of surprise. This was another thing for which she could thank Milo, she realized. She closed her eyes and breathed deeply, thinking of a box. With her hands upon the bowl's remnants, she mentally opened the box and withdrew a marble fashioned in the flames, streaked with red. She imagined holding the perfectly round globe in the palm of her hand. Her heart was gladdened at the sight of it. She felt at peace, and at home.

"I thought glass came from the moons when I was young," she whispered to him. "My father told me he would visit the moons and bring back glass for his workshops. I knew he was teasing me, but I liked pretending." Her voice grew dreamy as she talked. A curious feeling of stillness came over her. "I still think it's beautiful. Whenever I take one of my own works from the furnaces, I still marvel. It's wonderful to think that something so hard and smooth was born of fire." She heard Ferrer let out a loud exhalation, but she kept talking. "I love the colors—so pure. At the insulas they sprinkle metals over the molten glass to produce sheets, but the colors always seem so alive ... "

"Risa. My child, look."

She opened her eyes. The shards of glass flickered with light and shadow. They tingled to the touch, as if vibrating.

"Milo," Risa whispered. The largest, pie-shaped chunk reflected plainly the image of Milo standing by a balcony ledge, his face in profile. As she watched, scarcely daring to hope the vision was real, Camilla joined him and placed her arms around his shoulder. The faint image of a gondola drifted by.

The other shards were alive as well. Though she kept her fingers on the remnant that danced with Milo's face, she reached out with a gasp to see her mother reflected in one piece, her father in another. They both stared out a window at the sky beyond. Though it was difficult to see fine details, she thought she had never before seen them so careworn. She silently prayed that they had not yet lost hope.

In the smaller chunks she could see other people. There was Tania, wiping her face with a cloth, and Ricard, seemingly asleep on a pillow-covered bed. Mattio, sitting on a bench with his head in his hands. Amo, staring at something in her father's workshop she could not see. Mattio's mouth was moving—was he talking to the new craftsman? There was Fita, peeling fruit, a grim look upon her compressed lips. Her siblings—Romeldo, Mira, Vesta. Her lip trembled at the sight of Petro as he sat in a classroom surrounded by other youths.

She exclaimed in excitement as she pointed to the last of the pieces. "It's you!" In the curved splinter of blue and green, Ferrer was looking down at something out of vision—the very pieces of glass on the cushion before her.

"Remarkable," he breathed, and looked up directly into the mirror above the mantel. In the glass shard, he seemed to be looking directly at Risa. "I never thought I would see this day. And in one so young. It must be the secondary function of glass—as a reflective substance—that enables you to perform so remarkable, so rare a—"

"Milo!" she cried out, seizing the largest of the shards between her hands. Its knife-sharp edges bit into her palms, warning her that it would soon draw blood. She continued her scrutiny.

"I don't think he can hear you, my dear. There are limits."

"He must! Milo!" It was almost as if she willed the glass to carry her message to him. With fire, she had shaped the raw material into a thing of beauty; it was still hers to command.

The figure in the jagged piece turned in his place, suddenly alert. His mouth moved. A moment later, she heard her name spoken as if from a distance. Faint it was, softer than even her parents' voices when first she had heard them speak through the bowl. "Risa?" he said again. "By the gods, Camilla. It's—"

"Milo! You must listen. We're in the palace." His face grew larger as he moved toward her.

"You're in the glass!" he said. "I can see you in the glass!" She saw his fingers reach up to touch whatever was in front of him, momentarily blocking her view of his face.

Camilla's familiar form appeared behind him, her expression awed. "Don't," she chided. "You're smudging up her face."

Milo leaned forward and huffed on the glass to clean it. "I can't hear you well. Can you hear me?"

"*Yes!*" she cried. She looked toward the door guiltily, fearful the guards outside might overhear. "We're in the palace!" she repeated, saying the words distinctly. "Do you understand?"

His lips moved again, and a moment later she heard his

voice. It was as if it took seconds for the sounds he made to travel to her. "The palace," he repeated. He turned and spoke to Camilla. "We've got to get to the palace."

"How will we find her?"

"Look for me in a window!" she cried.

"Say it again," Ferrer suggested. His voice was breathy as he followed the drama.

She repeated the words. "In a window," Milo finally said. "It's so hard to understand you! I hope that's right."

"Yes!" she said.

"I vow I'll get you out of there! On my honor, Risa. Oh, thank Muro," she heard him say to Camilla. The shadows flickered. They were gone.

"Milo ... " There was so much she wanted to tell him. There was so much to apologize for.

"Who is this boy, Milo?" Ferrer's voice was gentle as he put one of his hands over hers. There was little warmth to his skin, but she felt comforted.

Like candles extinguished by a wind, the faces in the other shards of glass vanished. For a single tick of the mantel clock, she mourned the loss. The memory of how easily she had accomplished the feat emboldened her to a smile, how-ever. Somewhere inside her glowed a crystal marble, streaked with ribbons of red glass. "He is a friend."

"A city guard is your friend?"

She stood, irritated by the question. "Yes. He is not of the Seven and Thirty, but he is still my friend." Busying her-self with the objects in one of the cases enabled her to turn her face away. It would not do to show her frustration.

"My dear," said the old man. "I meant no censure. I have

always felt that if the Thirty were not as exclusive and, well, greedy for social distinction as they have become, we would not be as vulnerable to coups such as the prince is attempting! My own wife, may the gods have mercy upon her soul, was a physician's daughter. A *mere* physician's daughter, some said at the time."

This curious fact relieved Risa's fears. She would have very much disliked it had Ferrer shown contempt for the friendships she had made over the past few days. "Really?"

"Yes. She was working in one of the city's poorer sections, distributing medicines, when I first met her. A lovely creature she was. I think it was sixty years ago—dear girl, what are you doing?"

As patience-testing as she found the Cazarro's monologues, his last had inspired in Risa an idea. "We've a few minutes before my friend can reach the castle. We have to awaken Baso."

"He is deeply affected by the narcotic. It may be too late."

"Would you give up on him so easily? Let us try to help him if we can!" The sensation of her newly found powers both intoxicated and alarmed her. It felt as if she was a very small girl given a fortune to spend as she pleased—yet the gold was in a foreign currency, and no one would tell her where she could find markets willing to sell her the things she desired. She did not even know what she desired. Ferrer's mention of physicians had inspired her, however, and she would do what she could to aid the Buonochio boy. "If Milo manages to get to us, we don't want to have to carry him, and we can't leave him here at the mercy of the prince!"

"Do you really believe your friend can aid us?" The Cazarro's voice was low.

"I do." She was sure of it.

He rose from his sitting position. His spine gently bent forward as he took tiny steps around the split table. "I place my trust in you, child. You are the promise of eight hundred years fulfilled."

Risa flushed at the excessive praise. "No, I'm just a Divetri with a mission." It was a phrase her mother had used, more than once. "And a Divetri with a mission," she murmured to herself, feeling the force of new purpose, "is fearful to behold." She turned her full attention to the precious knick-knacks arranged around the room.

"Before you were brought in here, I looked high and low for objects with a primary purpose that might doctor him back to consciousness," mourned Ferrer. "There is nothing."

"There is something," she contradicted him. At last she found the object she sought: an ornamental silver spoon with a handle so richly encrusted with silver and amethyst roses that it looked as if it would be painful to grasp. It was protected inside a glass case. Without hesitation, she lifted a hideous porcelain elephant and smashed it against the glass, wincing to protect her eyes. Using two of her fingers and the utmost of care, she reached among the shards of glass and elephant and withdrew the spoon.

"A spoon's natural purpose is to deliver food to the mouth," sputtered Ferrer. Whether he was amazed at the object itself or the means by which she had obtained it, Risa could not tell. She wanted badly to grin, but felt he might mistake it for overconfidence rather than nervousness. "A Cassamagi enchantment could proof it against dripping…"

Risa marched over to the water ewer and carried it to Baso's side. Desperation was what made her so bold, she decided. They had little else to lose if she was mistaken, but much to gain should she be correct. "When my brother and I were sick, my mother would always dose us with tonic." He looked at her blankly. "Fed to us from a spoon," she explained. "A secondary purpose of a spoon is to feed the sick medicine."

Ferrer did not look as if he quite believed her reasoning, but he nodded. Did he doubt her? The old man was the expert on enchantments, after all. Was she merely playing at enchantments, and he humoring her? Biting her lip, Risa dipped the spoon into the container and drew up a dripping portion. Ferrer looked at her with expectation.

It wasn't right. She could feel that nothing was happening. The spoon was merely a spoon, with water drawn from the palace wells.

I've so much to learn, she thought to herself, nearly despairing. She closed her eyes and took a deep breath. Once more, from that most enclosed place inside, she withdrew the globe of glass that represented poise and self-assurance. It seemed to have grown since the last time she'd seen it, and the ribbons of red seemed alive with flame. She imagined Giulia hovering above her, balancing a spoon full of tonic.

Where it touched her skin, the metal began to prickle. Filaments of energy spread from her fingertips and wove around its length, delicate as a spider's web. She opened her eyes, and once more dipped the spoon into the ewer.

What had once been clear turned wine-red as she lifted it from the jug. The spoon was full of a dark liquid that smelled exactly like one of the more foul-tasting herbal stimulants in Giulia's cupboard of remedies—a mixture of willow bark, dried cone flower, spicy coriander seed, and fish oils. Within her, the glass marble flared as mentally she put it away once more. "Hold his head," she instructed Ferrer, trying not to spill her precious cargo.

Were those tears in the Cazarro's eyes? She could not spare even a moment to look. With trembling hands, Ferrer lifted the boy's head onto his knee and gently pulled down his jaw. Risa carefully moved the spoon forward and tipped its contents between Baso's lips.

For a moment nothing happened. Then, with great deliberation, the boy's mouth began to move. Briefly he choked, then swallowed. Breath escaped his mouth as his jaw opened in a violent cough. His eyelids began to flutter. A sob caught in her chest. She had done it. When she looked at Ferrer, there were tears among the wrinkles and folds surrounding his eyes.

It was painful to watch him cry, tears of joy though they might be. "I'll watch for Milo," she said. "Can you—"

As he cradled the boy's head and dabbed at his face with a moistened cloth, Ferrer was already waving her away. "You watch for your friend," he said, his face bowed low. "I can care for Baso."

It was not until she was at the window that Risa realized the old man had not wanted her to see how very fiercely happy she had made him.

30

—

Are we preparing our children well enough for the insulas?
They come in with knowledge of their family trade, the basics of
the sciences and history, and an eagerness to please, but in their
work I see little in the way of true innovation or thinking.
Why do we seem to be treasuring obedience and rote learning
more than exploration?

—Arnoldo Piratimare, Elder of the Insula
of the Children of Muro,
in a letter to Gina Catarre, Elder of the Insula
of the Penitents of Lena

"While you were still unconscious, I attempted every reversal available to my caza," Ferrer told Risa, just as distressed as she. "Nothing would make it open."

"But he's *out* there!" Risa said, frustrated. Milo and Camilla had arrived a good ten minutes before. From her high window she had spotted their twin uniforms, mere red blots, the moment they had stepped into Palace Square from the Via Dioro. After disappearing into the crowds around the market booths, they had re-emerged near the statue of King Orsino. By then she could see more distinctly; two large men accompanied them. Tears had risen in Risa's eyes as she recognized Amo and Mattio.

The old man was still sitting by Baso's side, having assisted him to an upright position. The boy was still stunned from the after-effects of camarandus poisoning, but at least he had been asking for water and seemed to hear their voices. "Can he see you?" Ferrer asked.

"I don't think so." Below, her four friends stood together on the bricks of the square, their heads turning to take in the sheer immensity of the palace wall before them. The palace's southern wall was the only side upon which the canals did not run; rows of windows reinforced with insula-made glass faced the square, each window recessed into the wall and surrounded by columns and statuary. Would they be able to see her on the top floor from so far away? They began to wander away from each other, continuing to study the stronghold's façade.

There had to be a way for her to open the window. There simply *had* to be. She reached out with her hands and once more felt beneath them the prickle of the enchantment's energy. Somehow she could alter those energies, if she could figure out how to redirect them. A window's primary purpose, as Ferrer would have said, was to keep out the elements.

What else could a window be used for? What other purposes did it have? To see through. To admit sunlight. To admit fresh air!

A sense of triumph filled her as she reached out to touch the metal frame. She calmed her mind, once again summoning forth the image of the flame-streaked marble. Like a Buonochio painting, her mind filled with a vivid image of the windows opening to admit a breeze that smelled of flowers and spice and canal waters. Empowered by what she imagined, she lay hold of the handles and turned.

They refused to budge.

"It's not fair!" Risa stormed, angry that it had not worked. On the ground below, Camilla was racing across the square followed by two new figures—Ricard in his gaudiest array and Tania wearing her full dancing skirts. All of her friends, there to help her. Her heart beat faster at the realization.

"Very little is fair, my dear," said Ferrer, with what Risa felt was an excess of practicality. For a man full of his caza's accumulated wisdom, he certainly knew how to make her feel crabby.

"Everyone else receives years of training in the insulas to learn enchantment, and I am expected to do it all in one morning!" The masks of Lena and Muro outside the window leered at her, seeming to mock her aspirations.

On the ground, Amo and Mattio finished a consultation with the guards and began running east. They were going to the other side of the palace, she realized. Milo remained behind, but would he stay for long if he could not find her? The prospect made her ill. Ferrer's stern drone only irritated her all the more. "Most of the Seven and Thirty have spent their lives behind insula walls studying tirelessly to hone their crafts. I suspect they would find it most unfair that their enchantments are substantially less remarkable than the two you performed in the space of less than two hours. Try not to try so hard," he suggested. "I suspect—" Baso leaned forward and put his face in his hands, distracting the old man from the rest of his speech.

His rebuke failed to comfort her. Milo was walking

back and forth in the square, once coming to a stop directly below the window against which she fruitlessly battered. Risa leaned her head against it. *Try not to try so hard!* She wanted to dismiss the advice, but she suspected Ferrer was right. The enchantment with the spoon had seemed effortless in its spinning, as if she had created a direct match between her goal and the manner in which she wished to achieve it. Trying to open the window for fresh air seemed like a cheat, almost. She had no need for fresh air—if anything, the room in all its splendor was almost too chilly.

"I wish I didn't have any of this responsibility! I just wish things were back to the way they always were!" Risa was almost embarrassed at the fury with which she spoke.

Ferrer's tone was gentle. "My dear, the first thing we wish for, in extraordinary circumstances, is our ordinary lives." It was the simplest thing he had said all afternoon. "We want the things we always want. It's simple human nature."

But what did she want? She looked at the window. What did she truly *need?* To call to Milo, to capture his attention. She might never see him again, if she could not open the panes and call to him before he walked away—just as years ago, her mother had called to her father from an upstairs window.

As she stroked the window's cold frame, Risa felt the metal thrum with energy. Absently running her hands over the marble sill, she once more noticed Lena's carved face, smiling at her from the column above.

It was so simple. Ferrer was right. She had been trying too hard. Her neck and face tingled as she realized that all she wanted was the same thing her mother, twenty-nine summers before, had wanted—to open a window to call to a boy in the streets below. To smile at him and attract his attention, and to keep that attention for the rest of her life.

She reached for the latches and pulled them inward, feeling energy surge through her fingers as the panels parted. Fresh air billowed over the sill, followed by the sounds of the square far below. Risa leaned forward, her hair tumbling down around her face. "Milo!" she shouted. In her heart she knew she called to the one boy she did not want to walk away from her. Not now, and not ever. "Milo!"

For a moment she feared he did not hear her. Sudden and sharp was her relief, however, when he looked up and his eyes met hers. His face lit up with the grin she had treasured over the last four days. She felt herself returning it gladly.

He raised a finger to his lips, warning her not to shout out again, then murmured something to his sister. Camilla too looked up and spied Risa, on the fourth and highest level of the palace. Milo was quickly informing Tania and Ricard of her whereabouts; when Ricard raised an arm to point, Milo hastily pulled it down.

Tania took a quick glance up, then leapt into the air. For a moment it seemed as if she was merely excited to see her, but when the girl pranced away with leaps and bounds, in the direction of King Orsino's memorial, Risa realized that Tania was dancing. From her waist she unfastened a tambour that she began to tap over her head in a lively beat; her skirts twirled as she began whirling in a swift tempo. Ricard strolled after her, moving his lute so that it no longer hung on his back but in a position to be strummed. Though she could not hear his music over the noise of the city below, Risa saw other people beginning to clap along to the poet's lively song.

For a moment she felt disappointed. Betrayed, even. She had supposed her friends had come to aid her escape. Instead, just as they had within hours after she had blown the Divetri horn for the first time, they were merely trying to earn coins.

She watched Milo turn his head to follow their progress. When Ricard and Tania reached the shadow of the statue, which was lengthening across the bricks as the afternoon progressed, he gestured to Camilla. Then, although he began to stride off to the west and the palace's rear, Milo stopped short and held up a flat hand with its palm facing her. Was it a goodbye? No—he was telling her to stop and to wait. *Patience*, she knew he would have instructed her. She nodded, and watched as the musical siblings scampered in the direction of the Royal Canal.

She was scarcely aware of how elated the silent encounter had made her until she drifted back across the room and sat down, still smiling. Although her stomach still felt knotted from the morning's events, for the first time in hours she felt optimism that the cazas might survive another night's test.

"That's three miracles you've performed this morning," Ferrer commented as he peered at her through his dual-lensed spectacles. "How many others shall we expect?"

"They're not miracles," she said, uncomfortable at the word. "It's just something that ... something that needed to be done." It was the best way she could explain it. "Cazarro, when you work your enchantments, do you *feel* anything?"

Baso, his hands over his face, appeared to be following the conversation although he said nothing.

"Feel anything?" Ferrer repeated. "In notes preserved by Cassamagi, Allyria wrote of the energies produced by objects when they are put to use, which she claimed could be altered and. ... my child, do *you* sense these energies?" When Risa nodded, his shoulders collapsed and he let out a mighty sigh. "What I would give to know how they feel! Allyria wrote that the energies between linked objects, such as the Olive Crown and the caza horns, can extend for many score of miles."

"Like a rope?" Risa asked, suddenly excited. "It feels to me as if the horns cast a rope in the direction of the palace as they complete the rite. Do you feel that too?"

Ferrer shook his head, astounded. "For how long have you sensed these things? You've never told anyone?"

She mirrored his headshake. "Ever since I was a child."

"The gods truly did not lie," he murmured. "You were never needed at the insulas. If anything, the insulas have needed you."

What a strange sensation, to be the tool of the gods. It was more frightening than any of the dangers she had encountered that week. Why was she so different? How would people treat her, if they knew? Realizing she was longing for earlier days, Risa reminded herself of what Ferrer had said—that she was merely wishing for ordinariness in the midst of extraordinary tumult.

But would she ever be ordinary again? The thought troubled her. Then again, if she was the hands of Muro and Lena, could there be hope that the gods might aid her in her quest to keep the city from a dark future?

From outside the window, the pound of drumbeats grew louder. Risa rose from the sofa and walked back to the open window. The crowd below had grown. Ricard still played, at the center of a circle surrounded by perhaps a hundred look-ers-on, but he had been joined by a number of lutists and jongleurs and drummers. A harpist—surely not the same harpist she had seen at Mina's?—sat plucking her strings near the edge of the impromptu stage. Tania had been joined by a number of taverna dancers, and they all shouted lustily as they leapt and twirled their skirts to the drum's rhythms. More and more people straggled from the market and from the palace to watch the jugglers and the flame-swallowers and the sword dancers who were entertaining the crowds.

When she saw a number of crimson-clad guards lope as a group in the direction of the revelry, casting looks of guilt over their shoulders, sudden realization shook her. Ricard and Tania had not begun this festival of music and dance for the sake of earning luni—her friends were creating a distraction! The pretty girls and handsome musicians were sure to lure a num-ber of the palace guards away from their posts, allowing Milo and Camilla a chance to work their way in. Their mother had been King Alessandro's own bodyguard—they had practically been raised in the palace, Milo had told her. Of all the people she knew, they would be best able to find her.

She looked out and up, to the left and right, where Muro and Lena's faces gazed down upon her and upon the ground below. Did they smile at her, or laugh? She could only pray that they wanted her to succeed.

31

You speak of our charges as if they were sheep, or at best, docile lambs led to shearing. My friend, these are the future leaders of Cassaforte that we educate. Innovation may not come easily to them, but by the gods, do they know how to fight for what is right.

—GINA CATARRE, ELDER OF THE INSULA OF THE PENITENTS OF LENA, IN RESPONSE TO A LETTER FROM ARNOLDO PIRATIMARE, ELDER OF THE INSULA OF THE CHILDREN OF MURO

A s the sun fell farther in the sky, its light slanted into the parlor. The reflected rays glanced off the mirrors and highly polished surfaces, creating a great deal of heat and brilliance, but none of the captives rose to close the window or draw the curtains. They would have been left with silence, then, and missed the pulse of the roundelays and jigs in the square below. It was very difficult merely to sit there, however, so for a while they busied themselves by helping Baso clean his face and hands. Then Risa guided him several times around the square of settees. He seemed weak on his feet, but grateful to be mobile.

Well over an hour and the greater part of another had passed by the mantel clock when they heard a scratch from the hallway. Risa immediately ran over and lifted the tapestry covering the massive oak door, her heart pounding as if it was a trapped animal trying to escape its cage. Ferrer also ventured over, leaning on his cane. Risa held up a hand to silence him.

The noise sounded again, from the crack between the door's bottom and the floor. She leapt back when the point of a blade suddenly protruded underneath, then retreated. The crack was too narrow to admit any more of the sword. She lowered herself to her knees and, keeping her face well away from the chink beneath the door, whispered, "Milo?"

The scrabbling with the sword tip ceased. She felt the tiniest whisper of air from the hallway against her cheek as someone on the other side lowered to the floor. "Risa!" Milo's fingers probed under the wooden door.

When she touched his fingertips with her own, her heart pounded madly. This morning they had been a city apart. Two hours before she had only been able to look at him from four stories up. Now they were mere inches away from each other. "Is it safe to talk?"

She could not hear his entire response, for it sounded as if he had turned his head at the beginning of his sentence. " ... Have to be quick," she heard him say. "This is one of the doors ... enchantment on it, I think."

"I know!" She found herself pronouncing every word more distinctly.

"We're going to try to break it down," she heard him say.

From behind her, Ferrer uttered an interjection. "My dear…"

"No!" Risa cried, ignoring him in her haste to stop Milo. "Breaking it in will make too much noise. Let me think of a way to remove the enchantment!"

"Cazarra," said Ferrer.

"That's impossible." Milo sounded as if he was holding his lips against the crack. "Just stand away from the door."

"Risa!" She turned, startled that Ferrer had pronounced her name so sharply. "Child! The Portello enchantment only applies to *our* side of the door. All your friend need do is to turn the handle and push."

"Oh." The simplicity of the solution caused her to blush. She repeated Ferrer's instructions beneath the door, then stood back to watch the handle tentatively twist toward the ground. The door eased inward, bringing with it a rush of air. Milo and Camilla stood just beyond, swords at the ready.

No amount of fresh air could compare to the relief that washed over her entire body at the sight of them. At first, Milo seemed surprised to see other people in the room with her. Then, recognizing the cazarro of Cassamagi, he gave him a respectful nod and sheathed his sword. For a moment he studied the prone form of Baso, and then turned again to Risa, seeming to drink in the sight of her. She felt she could bask forever in his gaze.

Yet she knew she could not. "We have to hurry," she told him, forcing herself to think of the dangers at hand. "How did you get rid of our guards?"

His smile grew more amused. "I convinced them we'd been sent by their captain to give them an hour's relief so they could go to the little festival outside," he explained. "They looked glad for the break."

"Very clever, young man." Ferrer had come up to stand beside her as Milo spoke.

Even beneath his tan, Milo flushed slightly at the praise. "Mostly it was Camilla's idea." He gestured at his sister, who inclined her head in modesty. She too seemed glad at the sight of Risa, but kept casting glances back in the direction of the long hallway. "She's the better strategist." Ferrer bowed in Camilla's direction, while Risa continued to stare at Milo. The fact that he was matching her grin for grin made her feel oddly giddy.

Camilla respectfully returned Ferrer's bow, recognizing his authority. With her hands, she mapped out their route while talking in a low and urgent voice. "We've gondolas at the lowest trade gate on the west canal." She led them into the hallway and pointed in the direction of escape. "Luckily our route is the shortest possible—down the stairs in the southwest turret and a short walk to the water gate. We've seen to it that any guards we might encounter were told to take a break at our little festival. I think we can have all of you back to your cazas by well before sundown, Cazarro." She sounded as if she was giving a report to Tolio, her captain.

"What about the cazarri?" asked Risa. Even as she had yearned for her own release, thoughts of her parents had never been far from her mind.

"Do you know where they are?" Milo gestured at the long hallway, upon which dozens of doors opened. It was one of scores of similar hallways in the palace, Risa knew, and one of hundreds of similar doors.

She shook her head. "You've probably not enough gondolas to rescue them all, anyway." Her heart sunk a little lower as she said the words. When Milo nodded in agreement, she made a decision. "I understand. Really, I do." It was still difficult to let go of her fantasy of a glorious rescue, but the afternoon was drawing to a close. They could not afford to waste time, or risk being caught, by searching for her parents.

Milo leaned in close. "We'll get them out soon. I give you my word." She nodded, believing him.

"This one must be returned to Buonochio. He is unsteady on his feet," Ferrer said, gesturing to Baso. His eyes, however, regarded Risa with sympathy.

"I am fine, sir," said Baso in a weak voice, struggling to rise. He stumbled slightly as he tried to gain his balance.

Camilla rushed to his side, draping one of his arms over her shoulder as she took a firm hold around his middle. She walked him out into the hallway as he protested mildly. "He can lean on me. Milo, you—"

Whatever she had intended to say was interrupted by the harsh grinding sound of a sword being drawn from its scabbard. They all turned at the clamor. Risa's pulse quickened when she saw a broad-shouldered guard running toward them, fire in his eyes and his mouth twisted into a scowl so savage she froze, unable to run. It seemed as if he was coming right at her, ready to slice off her head with a blade honed to a razor-fine edge, and all she could do was stand there.

A blur of crimson ran past her—it was Milo, throwing himself with abandon down the hallway. She heard the hiss of metal as he once more unsheathed his sword; an answering cry came from Camilla's own weapon as she tumbled after him. The pair of them stopped several arm-spans down the broad corridor, waiting for their foe.

Spit flew from the older guard's mouth. His foul oath echoed in the corridor. From his left side he withdrew a short dagger, so that he held a blade in each hand. Fully twice Milo's age and size he stood, hulking over the Sorrantos like a mountain looms over hills.

There was a silent, breathless pause as the three regarded each other. Though it lasted no longer than it took to draw in and expel a single breath of air, to Risa it felt as if time had slowed to a trickle. That one second seemed to last an eternity.

Steel began spinning madly without warning. Camilla and Milo battered away at him with their swords but he held them off, slowly backing down the hall. The sound of blade against blade echoed shrilly in the stone passageway, bringing tears to Risa's eyes from the sheer volume of it. Then the guard began to surge forward, driving the siblings back in their direction.

Behind her, Risa felt the bones of Ferrer's fingers pressing against her shoulder, drawing her away. She resisted, resenting his interference. Although part of her wanted badly to turn and run, she knew that flight might take them into an even worse situation. It was impossible not to admire the sheer artistry of the Sorrantos' athletic lunges and parries—it was like watching master craftsmen hard at work. Despite her fascination, however, she knew that upon the Sorrantos' skills rested all of their fates and lives. Even as she was unable to tear her gaze from the melee, she feared every blow dealt by the older guard's sword.

Camilla stumbled and fell onto a torch stand in her path. Like an acrobat, she turned the error into a tumble and somersaulted backward, using her blade to assist in the leap to her feet. Without even a sideways glance at her, Milo's rebuffs against the guard doubled in intensity, and he managed to fend off both of the attacker's blades without hesitation. He dodged and ducked and feinted, meeting blow for blow and even seeming to stop the man's onslaught.

Into action Camilla whirled, with a shout that welled from deep within. Her sword glittered as it swung in circles on either side. To Risa it seemed as if she passed her blade from hand to hand in a complex pattern that rendered her unapproachable from any angle; the maneuver certainly surprised the guard, who flinched and shied away as she came closer.

With the guard's attention distracted, Milo made his move. Like his sister, he began the same intricate sword-spinning and hand-passing pattern. It was bewildering to the eye; Risa was dazzled at its intricacy. Then, with the utmost of masculine grace, he suddenly stopped, twirled around, and balanced the point of his sword on the ground. He leapt up and kicked backwards into the air. The heel of his boot met squarely with the guard's jaw, lifting the heavy man inches into the air and sending him sprawling onto his back. There was a terrible crack as the man's head hit the stone floor.

With the same athletic polish, Milo landed back on the ground in a defensive stance, his sword once more at the ready. Camilla assumed the same attitude, ready to attack should the man try to rise. The guard, however, was utterly unconscious.

It was impossible for Risa even to breathe after such a spectacle. She had no idea that either of her friends had such extensive skills. Had she not witnessed it with her own eyes, she would never have believed that Milo could have overcome such a large and determined opponent. "How did you *do* that?" she breathed, all awe.

"That Catarre book on swordsmanship was a good read." He delivered the words with such understatement that Risa thought he might be joking with her. "It's the ugly one," he added, to Camilla. "I told you he was suspicious."

Camilla rose from her brief inspection, panting as hard as her brother. "We'll shut him in the parlor. A just reward for imprisoning three cazarri in there for so long, don't you think?" She took hold of the guard's leg and with great effort began to drag him in the direction of the Portello-enchanted room.

Milo sheathed his sword and moved to assist her. "What if the other guard is on his way back from the square? He'd be coming up the southwest turret."

"We'll have to take another route." Camilla looked grim as she pronounced her decree.

Risa once more felt her skin squirm in alarm. "What other route?"

Milo twisted open the handle to their former prison and grinned at her. "Don't fret," he said. "This is just the part where it gets a little dangerous."

32

Of the rumor that the current line of Cassafortean monarchs are descended from a dog thief, I could find no hard evidence.

—THE SPY GUSTOPHE WERNER, IN A PRIVATE LETTER
TO BARON FRIEDRICH VAN WIESTEL

🙂

Four men could lie lengthwise across the treads of the Petitioner's Stair, point their hands over their head, and still not touch the feet of the man lying ahead of them. So broad was each step that the same men could spread their arms wide and still not touch the edges. The Petitioner's Stair sloped upward from the first floor of the palace's grand entrance hall, passing through floors of gilded splendor until it reached the famed formal throne room at its peak.

Each of its tall risers was carved with a relief illustrating historical and mythical figures, their grandeur increasing with altitude. Fully visible from a full story below was the monarch's glorious gold throne. Even the most disheveled of beggars, when seated upon that engraved and radiant seat, would look like the most powerful of men. Those desiring an audience with Cassaforte's monarch would arrive at the summit of the Petitioner's Stair much awed and humbled and—as Risa had long suspected—too out of breath to present themselves with anything but humility.

Sunlight still fell through the massive throne room's glass dome. At this time of day, with light sparkling on its panes, the dome could be seen from leagues distant. Risa's group, however, was wrapped in darkness. In the tiny enclosure in which they stood, breathless and silent for fear, the only light came from the tiny slits cut slantwise into the richly carved surface of the Legnoli gilded-wood screen that encircled them on the uppermost dais. Lines of white like brushstrokes fell upon their faces.

With the utmost care not to jar the shards of glass that lay within the sack slung over her shoulder, Risa leaned forward so that she could peer through the nearest opening. Beside her, Milo and Camilla already peered through slits cut into the eyes of smiling cherubs. The room had once been a place of concealment for the king's bodyguards, so that they could watch over their charge and spring in an instant from hidden doors to defend him with their lives. Now the chamber held five renegades just trying to cross the palace to the northeast turret.

The prince's long fingers tapped on the arm of the throne, his nails striking the surface with the beat of a snare drum. "I grow tired of waiting," he announced, every syllable clipped.

"You need be patient only a while longer," said another

man, dressed in the raiment of the Thirty. Risa did not recognize him. "Then the Olive Crown will be yours to command."

"To the demons with that! What good is a thing when it cannot be grasped?" Prince Berto held up his left arm so that it was visible in Risa's limited view. She barely suppressed a gasp—at the end of his limb, the prince displayed a hand withered into a claw, its skin charred and blackened beyond recognition or use. The sight sickened her. She knew there had been a reason he'd concealed his hands that morning at the Divetri docks.

The prince's minion recoiled as well, then rallied. "Your Highness, the crown and scepter's healing powers will—"

"No more promises of miracles! It was the crown's curse that so afflicted me. Cassamagi's dissolution will be my revenge." Behind the screen, every word was audible. Risa felt, rather than heard, Ferrer shift uneasily behind her.

"One hour more only," said the man, bowing low. "Then all will be yours." As he moved closer to the prince, the courtier moved out of Risa's view, revealing the pedestals holding the country's two most sacred objects: a crown of gold fashioned to look as if it had been woven from olive branches, and a staff shaped to represent a heavy branch from a thorn tree. Beside them lay a horn—an exact duplicate of her own caza's. It was the palace horn, which for centuries had been blown on the rooftop above them to signal the rite of fealty. Rays from above made all three objects shimmer with light. Risa could feel their energies even from a dozen arm-spans away; they seemed to call to her with a song she felt certain none of her companions could hear. It gladdened her heart, that song. Its joyful refrain seemed to reassure her that all was right and as it should be.

Yet all was not right. She should have been well on her way back to the caza by now. Instead she was stuck inside this dark and depressing closet of a room, shoved there by Milo and Camilla during their flight across the Petitioner's Stair when they detected gallery noises from the direction of the prince's private chambers. The plan was sheer insanity. It was only thanks to the guards' lightning-fast reflexes and familiarity with the palace that they all, including the slow-moving Baso and Ferrer, managed to hide before they could have been spotted.

"But where are the other guards?" Risa had wanted to know.

Milo had told her that there were few guards remaining within the palace, and those that were there seemed to be concentrated at the entrances and within the prince's own chambers. "The prince is not popular," he had whispered. "Those who disagree with what he is doing simply disappear, most by their own choice. The ones still here would do anything for a chance of promotion or power. *Anything*," he had repeated with meaning. Risa was reminded of Ferrer's prediction that in the upcoming war, if the prince had his way, guard would fight against guard for the future of the country.

"That fellow who brought me that chit of a girl. The sycophant. What was his name?" The prince's tone was so cold that it chilled Risa from her own thoughts.

"I do not recall, your highness. He was a Divetri."

As she listened through the face of a carved cherub, her

heart skipped a beat at the sound of her name. "Yes, the bothersome one. From a most bothersome family. Presuming that I would name one of *his* kind to the new Seven. Have we shown him the hospitality he deserves?" Risa did not like the nasty undercurrent to his words.

"We stripped his body before disposing of it in the canals." The courtier's voice was smug. He reached inside a pocket of his coat and withdrew a familiar silver box. Opening it, he recoiled at the scent of the *tabbaco da fiuto*, then tossed it on the floor. "It will be difficult for anyone to identify him ... should they wish to."

"Very good." In the dark she felt a hand grope for her own. It was Milo, trying to give her sympathy. It was the last thing she needed or wanted, though she appreciated the comfort of his touch. The news of her cousin's death only filled her with a steely determination to succeed and to thwart the prince at his own game. Fredo had betrayed her, it was true, and had she the power to get rid of him herself she would have—but through exile, not summary execution.

The prince was only an arm-span away from where she stood within the enclosure. It would have been so easy to step out and attack him, right then.

Something in her movement must have betrayed her thought. She felt Ferrer's hand restraining her shoulder, and Milo squeezing her own fingers more tightly. Relaxation was difficult, but she managed to release her shoulders while determining inwardly that she would succeed against the prince at any cost. "And the Buonochio servant who so kindly helped us find the boy?"

"He has also been taken care of," the minion said smoothly.

Corpses plundered of their valuables and clothing were not uncommon sights in the canals in some areas of town, Risa knew. It was only by her intervention that the old beggar, Dom, had avoided a similar fate.

The prince chuckled without humor. "Very good. One hour, then. I can wait." He rose from his chair, his purple cloak rustling as it collected around him. She noticed that he kept his shrunken arm well concealed within the long left sleeve, curled close to his body as if he nursed it. "See to it that the cazarri are given what remains of their hospitality provisions for their evening meal. I want the stubborn fools to enjoy full stomachs as they watch the last of their precious houses fall." With a look of aversion at the Olive Crown, he moved in the direction of the long gallery leading to the east wing. "I think they should enjoy their last meal as cazarri. Does that make me a sentimental old fool, like my father?" The prince's laughter, as his minion began to scurry down the Petitioner's Stair, sounded like the mirth of a madman. In the dark, Milo squeezed Risa's hand. In her fear for her parents, she clutched his with equal strength. They all had to get back to their cazas, so that the imprisoned cazarri would not lose all hope.

A door slammed in the distance. Its echoes reverberated down the painted stucco ceilings of the gallery and faded into silence. They all waited in the close air and darkness for a moment, scarcely daring to draw a breath. At last Camilla cracked her panel and peeked out. "We have to move quickly." It was an order, not a suggestion. "There's no predicting how much time we have."

As they had been the last to gain the safety of the darkness when forced to hide, Baso and Ferrer were the first to follow Camilla from the bodyguards' closet. Perhaps the stress and agitation of their flight had expelled the last of the camarandus poisoning, for the Buonochio boy moved past the throne and in the direction of the northern passage without once stumbling. Ferrer moved as fleetly as he could upon his cane and old legs, while Camilla walked ahead of them both with her blade drawn and at the ready. Milo and Risa slipped out last. With a barely audible chink of metal, the elaborately decorated screen snapped shut. The silence of the throne room made Risa's stomach queasy. They began to tiptoe across the marble floors.

How many years had she gazed upon the palace, night after night, and wondered what lay beneath its vast dome? After the cramped closet, her city's throne room seemed to be the most vast and silent space into which she'd ever stepped. Story upon story it towered, its upper reaches higher than any temple. At its farthest side, down the stairs, were the famous gold doors which, when opened, admitted formal audiences; they had been cast centuries before with the visages of the gods, visible even from their distance. A woven carpet of royal purple ran from the entrance in their direction, up the incline toward the throne. Flanking the entrance, on walls the color of lapis, projected the balconies from which the Seven and Thirty were allowed to observe court events, perfect half-moon balustrades extending over the floor below. One of them closest to the floor, Risa knew, was assigned to her own family. She had never stood behind its white marble balustrade, however.

Neither Milo nor Camilla nor Ferrer seemed as overwhelmed by the throne room as she. No doubt they had seen before its banners—dozens of yards of brown and purple silks hanging from standards that ran nearly the chamber's entire height—and studied the statuary in its many alcoves. What other explanation was there for the way they seemed not to be awed by the sheer scale of their surroundings? Risa's head began to spin as she gaped at the dome above them, painted around its edges with a mural of both Lena and Muro reaching from the heavens, fingertips outstretched to touch the hand of a lowly mortal by the water. In the dome's center was a rounded apex of leaded glass, so distant overhead that she couldn't even make out its intricate pattern. One of her own forebears had fashioned that window, she realized, and she'd never known it was there.

"Careful," said Milo in a whisper, steadying her with a hand at her back. She jerked her head down, blinking rapidly. "Are you all right?"

"Yes." Some sensation fluttered in her chest. For a moment she worried that she'd given herself vertigo. Dizziness wouldn't leave her feeling so exhilarated, however. What was it, tugging her in its direction? "I'm fine."

"This is the opposite of *quickly*," Camilla hissed as she marched onward. "Come on!"

Once Camilla had turned around, however, Risa looked back. Behind her stood the king's throne, impossibly large in scale. Its back alone was taller than Ferrer, and fashioned with an ornate and beautiful relief of massed branches. Anyone sitting upon that mighty chair, she realized, would look almost as if he was framed by an orchard of golden olive trees. A smaller chair sat nearby at an angle, gilded and sumptuously cushioned. Risa guessed it belonged to the prince.

On the pedestal before the throne, however, lay the Olive Crown and the Scepter of Thorn—the symbols of the king of Cassaforte. She didn't know how, but they thrummed joyfully at her as she passed by. Even after centuries, their golden brilliance had not dulled or faded. She stopped to stare at them, enthralled by the vibrations they seemed to be sending her way—vibrations much like those of the window frame and her shattered bowl, but abundantly stronger. What she would give to be able to study them! Though more valuable than all the gold in the country, these two objects were not covered or concealed—the palace did not fear theft. Only the rightful king could seize either object and remained unharmed. Memory of the prince's ruined hand made her shudder. And yet...

"Risa!" Milo's shock drew her back to reality. His hand gripped her arm, which was outstretched in the direction of the crown. He had stopped her only a finger's length away from it. "What are you doing?"

"It's too much to explain," she told him in the lowest possible whisper. "Things have changed since last night, Milo. I'm different now."

He shook his head. "Think, Cazarra. You saw what a single touch did to the prince!"

The Risa of the day before would have resented his interference, but at that moment she only admired him for it. Like a buried spring of cool water released to the ground above it, joy sprang up from deep within her. She wanted to sing it to the world. He honestly cared for her! "I'm not the same person who argued with you yesterday," she told him once more, holding both of his hands with hers. "You saw me in the glass this morning—I *did* that, Milo. I made it happen. There's so much I can do now. I know why I was kept from the insulas! I know why the gods brought us together, and I know I want you worrying and fretting over me for a long time to come."

"You do?"

"Yes. But right now you have to believe in me. Do you?"

Her confidence seemed to amaze him. His face softened as their hands pressed against each other. At last he nodded. "Just—" He stopped speaking with a shake of his head. "I believe you. I do."

With a smile to reassure him, she reached out for the crown. After only a moment's hesitation, she took it into her hands.

The shock sent a jolt throughout her body. Her arms felt as if they were on fire, but they did not burn. She saw the crown as it originally was: a brown, crude circlet of branches snapped from an olive tree. Centuries of visions flashed before her eyes. In the flash of a second she saw dozens of grave-faced men and women—some young, some old, some scarred with battle and others fat with feasting—seated on the high throne as for the first time they seized the crown and placed it on their heads. Phantom crowds in rich attire, bowing low in obeisance before their new monarchs, bewildered her eye. She recognized the late King Alessandro at the very last of the lightning-fast procession: a hale youth in the full flush of his manhood, his curly brown locks appearing as they did in the portraits she had seen throughout her entire life. His face was not a portrait, however. He was *real,* just as every other monarch she saw was real, though they all had been laid to rest decades and centuries before.

She held the crown in her hands and studied it with a sight not of her eyes. It was a fascinating work of art. It reminded her of one of her mother's stained glass windows—thousands upon thousands of cut pieces, a jumble of color and shapes laid out and held together by channels of lead. In her training she had learned the theory behind window construction and had often made small panels of her own. She understood how her mother's windows were made, but their sheer scale dwarfed her own tiny labors.

The crown's energies struck her the same way. She knew instinctively that with time and study she could make sense of how Allyria Cassamagi had woven them into a remarkable enchantment. She also sensed that what she had accomplished that day was tiny in comparison. Ferrer had considered them all miracles, but the object she held in her hand was the true work of miracle. She would master it, in her own time. *One day,* she swore to herself. *One day.*

"Risa." Milo's voice was a whisper.

"It's all right," she told him, breaking out of the trance. From her shoulder she unslung the padded bag and opened its drawstring. "I was meant to have these."

"I don't understand. Are you—are you meant to be queen? Is that what you—oh gods!"

"No." She shook her head. "I am only meant to take them until we find the next true king."

"You can't take—" He closed his mouth as he thought better of the remark. Her immunity to the crown's destructive powers had dumbfounded him.

"I have to," she said simply, placing the crown in her sack. She reached out and added the scepter to her treasure trove. "I'm thinking ahead, Milo. If Prince Berto appoints a new Seven, they cannot award him the Olive Crown if it is not here." He smiled at the simplicity of that statement, then waited until she once more closed the drawstring to take her hand. "Don't tell the others," she warned him.

"We'd best hurry," he told her. "Camilla's probably having a fit by now."

The elder Sorranto indeed seemed none too happy at the delay when they finally caught up with the others in the anteroom. "Can't you two wait until this is all over to have your happy little romantic reunion?" she complained, spying their clasped fingers.

"I'll remember that when we see Amo downstairs," Milo snapped back, but without a trace of resentment. "I bet you'll be happy to have his mutton hands all over you." He subsided at his sister's fierce glare, but winked at Risa. For the sake of peace, she held a finger to her lips to silence him, and followed Camilla into the northeast tower.

Their trip down the stairs was blessedly uneventful. Camilla forged the way, her ears listening for the slightest noise, her muscles tensed and ready for confrontation. They stopped at each landing to check for possible sentries as they circled their way down the tight spiral of stone. As Milo had predicted, there were none, not even at the lowest level of the castle.

"This is spooky," he commented in Risa's ear as they stumbled down a low-ceilinged and dark corridor of brick. "It's almost *too* easy."

"The prince is living in a deserted castle," said Ferrer. Already hunched with age, he was finding the low passage less cumbersome than they were. "Very few guards, even fewer servants, and little concept of how palace affairs are to be run. Berto is not a man of forethought, but of fiat."

"I didn't say I wasn't grateful, Cazarro." There was a good deal of humor in Milo's response. "After the day we've all had, I'm grateful the gods blessed us with a safe exit."

"We've not exited yet," Ferrer reminded him, reaching out to steady Risa as she tripped over an uneven brick. On her back, her bag's contents jostled with a clink of metal.

Camilla cracked open an ancient, arch-shaped wood door that was reinforced with iron bands across its width. She looked out, then opened it wider. "We very nearly have," she announced, grim triumph in her voice. Sunlight from outside poured down the long arched corridor of water and walkways that lay before them. The glare nearly blinded Risa's light-deprived eyes. After blinking several times, she spied two gondolas moored near the iron gates at the end, beneath a low overhang of wet and moss-covered stone. Amo and Mattio stood in them, poles at the ready. She and the other escapees had reached the old water gate onto the Royal Canal, beneath the eastern bridge.

Relief at being once more in fresh air made Risa giddy with confidence. They had escaped the castle. She was amused to note the polite coolness with which Camilla greeted Amo. Had the guard exhibited any enthusiasm whatsoever at the sight of her love, Milo would have been sure to make more comments about the size of the glass worker's hands. Risa could not show similar restraint at the sight of Mattio, however. When she stepped from the water-smoothed steps into the gondola, she hugged him fiercely around his middle.

"You've cut it close!" he whistled, a broad smile on his face. Then, more seriously, he hugged her back with a strength that cut her breath short. "I was worried sick," he told her. "Your father would have had my life if I'd let anything happen to you."

"I missed you too," she told him, settling into his vessel with Milo. The others climbed into Amo's craft. She noticed for the first time the sounds of distant strains of music from the direction of the square. "Are they still performing?" she asked, amazed.

Mattio nodded. "I suspect that Ricard boy will play his fingers to the bone to make amends for what he did. He took the news hard when he heard you had disappeared." It was a touching thought. Risa swore to herself that she would think less harshly of the Poet of the People in the future.

"Gods," cried Camilla. Her gondola rocked violently as in one swift motion, she pulled her pole from the water and dropped it into the boat with a thud. A hiss cut through the air as she drew her sword in a glittering arc from its scabbard. Baso and Ferrer and Amo all reached out to balance themselves. The others stared at her in astonishment.

Risa turned to see what had alerted Camilla. Her spirits sank when she spied the outlines of two guards running toward them down the corridor. "Halt!" one of them ordered, his voice echoing against the brick. Risa looked around wildly. The others seemed just as taken aback as she.

"That's it, then," Mattio growled, pushing his pole against

the canal floor to propel the gondola forward. Amo heaved and grunted as he too began to punt.

Milo, at the stern of Risa's craft, brandished his sword. He stood unsteadily on guard, using his free hand to balance as the long boat lurched forward, out of the corridor and into the canal. Only Amo's barked warning saved his head from colliding with the sharp prongs of the raised water gate. With nimbleness, he ducked just in time. Then, looking back at the passage that still echoed with the shouts of the guards, he held up a hand. "Stop the gondolas."

"We cannot!" said Ferrer. "We must make all haste!"

"Stop!" Milo commanded. Mattio dared not disobey, and he and Amo braced themselves against their poles, slowing the two boats nearly to a standstill.

Risa had been speechless during the exchange, but not now. "We can't—!"

Milo cut off her protest with a hand. "I know how these guards think. Believe in me, Risa. Believe in me even as I believed in you."

The bellowing of the pursuing guards made Risa want to leap into the canal waters and swim all the way home. But anxious as she was to put as much distance as possible between herself and the palace, she fought down the urge to argue. It nearly killed her to keep silent, no matter how much faith she had in her friend and in his judgment. She clung to the sack in her arms, held her breath, and tried not to panic.

"They were probably just on a corridor sweep before shift change," Milo was saying to Camilla.

"If that's the case, there will be only the two of them."

In the other gondola, Camilla crouched in a defensive position, muscles tense.

"We have to time this just right." Milo held up his hand to indicate they keep the vessels still. Their gondolas were only a dozen arm-spans from the gaping entry. To Risa, he explained, "If we punt out too far, they'll just run back and summon more bodies, and then we'll be lost. If they think they can catch us..."

As if on cue, the two guards appeared at the water gate. The first was running so quickly that he couldn't stop himself; he stumbled upon the rounded bricks at the edge and toppled into the water with a cry of dismay. The other cursed audibly and looked back down the corridor, as if trying to determine what he should do.

"Wait." Milo crouched low and held out his hand.

The first guard sputtered and surfaced for air. His cap spun beside him in the water. Chin-length black hair covered his eyes. He blinked and spied the gondolas nearby, but when he tried to flail out and swim toward them, he found his arms tangled in the waterlogged, heavy fabric of his cloak. Gargling water in his fury, he began clawing at the golden rope at his neck that held it on.

"Wait..." said Milo again. The others looked anxious and white. Risa choked down her urge to speak, holding her breath until purple spots formed before her eyes.

The other guard, a large and muscular man, cursed at the ineptitude of the first. He also removed his cloak, undoing the knot with a single hand. His sword belt fell to the bricks with a clatter. Still looking over his shoulder for assistance that didn't seem to be arriving, he hopped up and down as one by one he pulled off his boots. Seconds later he was in his stocking feet. The first guard, in the meantime, called his companion's name as his soggy cloak finally sank down into the depths of the canal.

"Wait."

The second guard seemed to find no solution at the end of the corridor. His shoulders tensed. Without hesitation, he dove from the water gate into the canal. Water plumed into the air where he struck.

The two guards instantly began swimming toward the gondolas. They were only a dozen arm-spans away. Ten. Eight. Still the party sat in the boats, motionless. Risa realized they were acting like ducks in the water, unaware of the canal serpents targeting them as prey. Six spans away. In a few more strokes, either guard could lunge forward and haul themselves into the gondola's stern. When they were a mere four spans close, the second of the guards raised his head and shook water from his face, preparing to shout an order.

"Now!"

At Milo's word, Amo and Mattio heaved all their weight upon their poles. The twin gondolas resisted at first, then with an even motion began to slice through the water. Inhaling caused Risa's lungs to ache and her head to spin. She hadn't realized that she'd been holding her breath for so long. "They're stopping!" she said, pointing back.

Most of the others were already staring in that direction. Waterlogged by their uniforms, the two guards had ceased trying to swim after them. They were merely two rapidly diminishing spots of red bobbing on the water's surface. Only Mattio and Amo kept an eye ahead as their strong arms punted through the water, carrying the party away from the palace.

Over the pounding of her heart, Risa did not even hear, at first, the clanging sound from the uppermost reaches of the palace. The metallic sound, faint at first, grew into a raucous crescendo as windows opened and heads began to poke out. "Alarm bell," Milo said abruptly.

"But why?" Camilla sounded exasperated. She had crawled over the two cazarri in her gondola and stood as close to the aft as possible without interfering with Amo's punting. "They can't have found anyone missing yet. The two in the water didn't cry panic. How could they *know?* Give me that," she commanded Amo, seizing the punting pole angrily. Amo seemed relieved to have ceded his position; his lungs heaved as he tried to catch his breath. The splash of water drowned out the last burbled curses of their pursuers.

"Maybe we disturbed something," said Milo. He looked back at Risa, an apology in his eyes. With a flash of panicked understanding, she clutched her precious cargo even closer to her chest. He didn't want to give her away.

Anxiety gnawed at her as she suddenly realized how her foolhardy impulse had endangered them all. How could she explain to them that the abduction of the crown and scepter had been something she simply had to do? "I'm sorry," she said aloud.

"For what?" Mattio wanted to know. Risa might have told all if Milo hadn't shaken his head at her. Maybe it was better to keep quiet about the contents of her satchel.

They were finally leaving the nearly empty waters of the palace district and heading toward one of the many marketplaces on its outskirts; as they glided beneath a trade bridge, Camilla and Mattio were forced to slow their pace in order not to collide with the gondolas moored at the sides. A solitary beggar dropped the armful of gourds he had scavenged from one of them, astonished to see them pass.

"Are we safe?" asked Ferrer, looking up at the clusters of people on the walkways above them. Most of them were looking in the direction of the palace, from which the distant clamor of the alarm bells could still be heard. The air seemed full of excited babble, and no one was paying the least bit of attention as their crafts sliced through the water. "Relatively safe, I suppose I should ask?"

Risa wondered the same thing. Baso was leaning so far from the other boat's prow that for a panicked moment Risa thought he might fall out. He was only listening, though. "Hoofbeats," he explained, his eyes wide.

They all heard them, now. Clattering on the stones and echoing between the tall residences behind them. Risa craned her neck to see, but their gondolas once more passed beneath a bridge, deeper than most and likely under one of the smaller market squares for the neighborhood. It was maddening, not being able to see anything more than lichen hanging from the stones overhead and the lowering sun on the waters at the bridge's far end. Every sound was dampened save for their own strained lungs and the splash of the punts as Camilla and Mattio propelled them forward.

Into daylight they emerged once more. A horse's whinny cut through the air. Risa's head whipped from side to side, and at last she saw a white steed skidding to a halt near a handcart at the bridge's edge. All she saw next was a flash of dark red as the rider leapt from its back and dove into the water, nearly taking the small cart with him. The guard landed in the canal in a massive belly-flop, sending water cascading everywhere. Like their previous pursuers, he quickly found himself too tangled in the formal uniform of the palace guard to follow, and floundered helplessly.

None of them had any time to celebrate, however, because two more mounted guardsmen followed, pausing only briefly to edge past the horse abandoned by the first. The walkway balustrades were crowded with the citizens of Cassaforte, startled and scampering to safety as the mounts pounded relentlessly forward. Milo pointed to a weather-worn, carved stairway leading down to the water at the bridge ahead. "We need to go faster," he called. "We're going to get some visitors."

"I see that," Camilla grunted. Her face was red from the exercise, but she continued punting. The two guards had already gained the advantage, reining in their beasts and shouting out orders to nearby tradesmen. Their capes billowed behind them as they clattered down the steps toward another cluster of parked gondolas. When Risa's boat passed them, flying into the shade of the overpass, she could see their faces twist into snarls.

Amo had regained his wind. "Let me," he urged Camilla, trying to take over the punting once more. She shook her head, only once, violently. Ferrer's lips pressed together as he tried to peer through his spectacles through the darkness beneath the arched bridge.

"Faster!" Milo urged Mattio on.

"I can't keep this up forever, lad!" warned the older craftsman. His curly hair was soaked from the sweat streaming from his temples.

He kept punting, though, perhaps frightened as one of the parked gondolas broke away from the others and began to gain on them. There was no way they could maintain their lead. Not with the combined power of two strong guards punting a single boat.

Milo's sword glinted in the sun as they coasted out from under the bridge and began to round a curve in the canal. "Keep back," he warned Risa. "They're going to catch up. What can we do?" he called out to his sister.

"Nothing good," she growled back, glancing back at the pursuing craft. "Stay ahead of us. But not too far ahead." The two boats had been keeping pace as they traversed their way southward on the Royal Canal, but now Risa found herself gliding past her friends in Camilla's gondola—first Amo, then Ferrer, and finally Baso at the boat's front. Camilla grappled to keep her footing as she used her pole to slow down her gondola.

Risa turned in her seat, worried at their sudden change of pace. "What's she going to do?"

"I don't know," said Milo with a shake of his head. Even at this tense moment, he still managed to spare her a grin. "But I'm sure it's going to be good."

Camilla's voice rang out across the water. The chasing craft was closing in fast. "Let us pass," she begged, her voice surprisingly weak. She even sounded as if she might cry, which to Risa's ears sounded strangely out of character. "Please. We didn't mean to do anything!"

"You should have thought of that earlier, traitor," snarled

the guard at the gondola's prow, letting the other guard slow down their craft. "Lay down your arms and halt in the name of the prince!"

"Fine, fine!" Her right fingers still wrapped around the gondola's punt, Camilla reached to the hilt at her left side and, with her free hand, pulled out her sword. She dropped it behind her in the bottom of the boat. Milo took her cue and knelt down, dropping his sword into the unoccupied space between himself and Mattio. Then he stood up unsteadily, showing his empty hands. "We're unarmed."

"She's easier than you thought she would be, Vercutio," said the guard at the other gondola's stern. They were a mere arm-span away from Camilla's gondola at this point, and inching closer.

"The women always are," said the guard who had addressed them first. When he smiled with triumph, Risa saw that one of his incisors was made of gold. She also thought she noticed Camilla bristle silently at his next remark. "Pretty things. Shouldn't be made guards, though."

"Or given swords," laughed the other.

The iron ferro at his gondola's prow nudged against Camilla's boat. Obviously intending to board, the guard swung a foot out. Risa suddenly understood, from his gleeful expression, that he did not realize Camilla had deliberately allowed them to catch up. He began to pull himself into her gondola.

Suddenly, Camilla's heavy wooden punt cascaded up and out of the canal. Droplets of water formed a perfect arc in the air as she arched the pole over her head and brought it straight down on the guard's arm. The loud crack of wood against bone made Risa squeeze her eyes into slits.

"I don't *need* a sword," Camilla declared. The guard toppled into the water and began screaming in pain—a piercing squeal like a pig being led to slaughter. With both hands clutching the center of her pole, Camilla drew it up into the air again. Without hesitation, she plunged the end of it squarely against the middle of the man's forehead.

The squeal ended instantly. For what seemed like an endless moment, the guard swayed up and down in the gentle motion of the waves, stunned. His eyes rolled back in his head.

"Go," Camilla shouted to Mattio, urging him to punt at full speed once again. A circle of cherry red puddled on the guard's brow where the pole had struck him. His eyes were sightless and dulled. Then, with one smooth motion, his body slipped beneath the water.

Camilla looked sick to her stomach. Choking on bile, she handed her pole back to Amo. When she reached her seat, she leaned over the edge of the gondola and vomited into the water. *She's never killed anyone before*, Risa realized. Even in the name of duty, it could not have been easy to end a man's life. A chill crept over her. How many more lifeless bodies would there be before day's end?

"That's one down," Milo said to himself, his words grim.

33

A country is more than its standards, more than its fortifications.
From the highest to lowest, a country is its people.

—ORSINO, KING OF CASSAFORTE, DURING THE AZURITE INVASION

🜚

"We need a new plan." Milo pointed to the south, where the Temple Bridge loomed before them.

Had Risa been looking at it from her familiar perch on the caza balcony, surrounded by family and the men of her father's workshops, this longest and broadest of all the spans in Cassaforte would have been beautiful in the fading sunlight. But she could not now admire its five graceful, ornate arches, for she was astonished by what she saw underneath: dozens upon dozens of gondolas had been moored under and around the arches, completely obstructing the waterway.

Risa's first panicked thought was that the guards had

managed to outprint their party and were conspiring to block their route. As she looked at the collection of boats, however, she noticed that they were filled with huddled people wearing worn shawls and cloaks. Ropes tied between the gondolas' ferri had been hung with drying laundry. Even from a distance it was impossible not to hear the squalling of infants in their mothers' arms, and sounds of laughter and argument from the people crowding the floating island of boats.

Risa looked back at Milo in shock, but he seemed unsurprised. "You must never have traveled this way near nightfall," he told her, still looking over the stern to keep an eye on the one determined guard still in pursuit. "The gondola people moor here for the nights. It's a nuisance."

"Gondola people?"

Ferrer had been tense and quiet for the last few minutes, but he spoke across the short distance dividing them. "Many of the city's poor and outcast live in their boats, my dear. I had no idea there were so very many of them." He shook his head.

"But how can we get through?" Risa knew she sounded hysterical, but there was simply no clear passage ahead. They drew nearer, speeding toward the bridge at a rate alarming to some of those in the stationary gondolas. Several men were already standing up and shouting angrily at them, warning them to slow down.

"We can't." Milo set his jaw. "We're going to run across the flotilla—yes, jump boat to boat—and commandeer a vessel on the other side. Camilla, you take care of the old man. No offense, Cazarro," he added with respect.

"None taken," said Ferrer mildly.

"I'll do the best I can to guide us across, but everyone, keep your eyes open. Hold on tight." Grabbing the pole from the exhausted Mattio, Milo thrust it against the canal bottom. Their gondola began to sweep into a circle, spinning out of control toward one of the bridge's stone supports. His sister followed his example. Dizzy and confused, Risa watched as Camilla's gondola began to rotate away from them. Behind them, the guard still giving chase cried out in astonishment and furiously attempted to slow down his own craft.

A great outcry arose from the assembly of boats beneath the bridge. From behind her, Risa heard the shrieking of women and the angry bass shouting of men. "Hold on tight!" Milo cried again, with such command that Risa immediately braced herself.

As their boat collided into the outermost of the moored mass of gondolas, the impact nearly knocked her off balance. Its force spun them once more, into another craft, jarring Risa so thoroughly that it felt as if she were an insignificant bundle dropped from a very great height. Finally, their gondola smacked into a stone pillar. The hostile guard's craft rammed into theirs, which sent him sprawling, face-forward, into its bottom. They all fell forward at the impact.

An angry man with a thick mustache was shouting at them when they rose to their feet, all trying to keep their balance low so the gondola did not tip. When Milo drew his sword, the man stopped shouting, noticing for the first time that both Milo and Risa wore uniforms of the city guard. Only when Milo leapt into the man's gondola from their own did he object. Milo leaned over and held out his hand to Risa. "Come on," he urged, ignoring the man's astonishment. "Just follow me."

Risa had crossed from one boat to another many times, but never so many and never under such tense circumstances. Each of the gondolas was stacked with a bewildering variety of clothing, bundles, boxes, and even coops of chickens or rabbits. With every step, Risa feared trampling on a family's entire possessions. "Sorry," she told a woman eating a pepper, who swatted at her legs with a towel as they stepped into her boat. "Sorry!" she repeated to a dirty-faced girl who sucked her finger and impassively watched the three of them lurch over the plate of bread that was her dinner.

As tightly parked together as the boats were in the dark of the bridge, there was little chance of them capsizing. In many spots it was easy to hop from one planked seat to another, but often some of the leaps they took were perilous. Risa found herself cringing when she stepped into a basket of eggs and received a lifetime of curses from the old woman who had just set them down. They were moving slowly enough that she could see the others. Under the next arch, Camilla and Amo were assisting Ferrer through the maze of people and boats; they would intersect with Risa's party in a matter of moments. Baso seemed to be picking a path of his own, behind the rest of the group.

From behind her Risa heard a woman's scream, followed by a splash of water. "Muro's toe," Mattio cursed, several vessels away. "He's close."

The hostile guard had dragged himself up and into one of the gondolas. Water from the bottom of his craft had soaked his uniform. Anger fueled his every move. With amazing strength he scrambled across several seat planks in one desperate leap. A deep-chested man rose and began to shout at him, but the guard dealt him a savage blow to the middle and kept stalking toward his prey.

"Now we can deal with him," Milo growled. "Get down." He pushed Risa onto a seat, where she found herself face to face with a girl who regarded her with barely veiled hostility. Though the girl was obviously her own age, Risa was astonished to see that she had a baby suckling at her breast. Milo vaulted in the guard's direction.

"I'm coming," Risa heard Camilla cry. She shouted an order for Amo to keep Ferrer moving toward the southernmost perimeter of the bridge. Milo grabbed a gondola pole from its crook at the boat's side and held it with two hands, close to its center. The girl across from Risa glared at Milo, and then at Mattio as he scrambled to snatch a punt from the next gondola over, and then back at Risa. She continued to nurse the baby, jostling it up and down in a gentle rhythm, not seeming to care about the impending clash a few boats over. Risa wondered if brawls were a common occurrence among the gondola people.

At the sound of the chasing guard's cocksure laughter, Risa tore her eyes away from the girl's smudged and pockmarked face. The guard had grabbed a pole of his own. He feinted at Milo. With dexterity that dismayed her, he twirled the pole, stopped suddenly, and thrust it forward so that its ends nearly struck both Milo and Mattio's faces. Milo ducked in time, but Mattio had to dodge to the side, his head banging a pillar. He clapped a hand to his face, groaning. Risa turned to the girl. "Help us," she begged.

"Help you?" The drab scoffed. Her voice was hard as flint. "There's a laugh. What you're wearin' don't fool me. I've seen you. You're one of the Thirty, ain't you? You've never helped *me*. Why should I help *you*, high and fine as you are?"

Swiftly, Risa made some calculations in her head. These people were unlikely to aid them, and she could understand why. They had invaded their only homes, trampled their food, and endangered their few possessions. Her group was on their own. "Fine," she snapped at the girl, with more severity than she intended, and seized a hefty fishing rod from the bottom of the gondola. "I'll bring this right back," she spat out, ignoring the girl's yowls of protest.

She hopped toward the center of the underpass. Clack after clack of wood resounded as Milo and the larger guard began a barrage of blows and blocks. Her fishing rod was made of a sturdy length of wood; she hoped to get close enough behind the guard to prod him off his equilibrium.

"You damned fool," Mattio barked, behind her. Risa turned to see him removing his hand from his nose, blood staining his fingers. "She's not one of the useless Thirty. She's Divetri. Cazarra of Divetri!" The girl mouthed the words after him: "Cazarra of Divetri . . . "

When she heard a high-pitched shriek from Milo's direction, Risa for a moment feared he had been injured. But the noise came from a young girl who cowered behind him, crying and covering her head. Milo, too, heard the scream, and swiftly turned to see.

His attacker took advantage of his momentary distraction and delivered a forceful shove with his pole—a shove that sent Milo toppling and nearly made Risa shriek. But before

Milo landed on the helpless youngling, he thrust one end of his punt against the gondola's bottom, did an acrobatic flip into the air and over the girl, and landed in the next vessel over.

Although the motion set the girl's boat bobbing, she was out of harm's way, Risa noticed with relief. A woman snatched her from an adjacent boat and scampered out of their path.

"Cazarra of Divetri? Risa?" She was so astounded to hear the dirt-encrusted girl pronounce her own name that she nearly halted in her progress toward the guard. "Tessa!" the girl called to a woman in a nearby gondola. "Did you hear that? I had Risa the glass maker's daughter in my boat!"

She was close enough, now. Could she do it? She quailed for a split second—fighting was not something she was used to. Then again, she had already spent a morning performing impossible tasks. One more should not be beyond her.

The guard's bulk eclipsed Milo from view. Risa waited until he had lifted the punting pole. Using as much force as she could muster, she rammed the fishing rod into the small of his back, as hard as she could, with a mighty grunt.

"You don't say!" replied the woman, two boats over. "The one from the song?"

It was like trying to topple a palace wall with a blade of grass. The guard did not fall forward. He merely leapt sideways, keeping both Milo and Risa in his sights. With a grin, he used one hand to seize her rod and twist it from her hands. She yelled out in pain when the rough wood left scrapes across her palms.

"The very same. In *my* 'dola." The girl sounded smug at the fact.

"Risa! Get back!" Mattio was scrambling toward her now, his face bloodied and wet. He tumbled into the young mother's boat, his leg tangled in rope. Risa had no intention of backing off, however. She began to look around for some other weapon, so that she might try again.

Camilla had managed to cross closer to them, but was still out of reach. Risa could barely watch as Milo and the guard continued to do battle with the wooden poles; both guards seemed equally skilled. They alternated attacks in a manner determined to bash skulls or pierce the other's mid-section.

"Risa of Divetri? I love that song!" added a man several boats away. He leapt from his own gondola into one closer. The short sleeves of his tunic exposed brawny forearms. In each hand he clutched a tomato. "You shouldn't be picking on Risa, the glass maker's daughter," he shouted at the guard, throwing one of the vegetables with great force. It hit the side of the guard's head, catching him unawares and sending him reeling. With great satisfaction, the man hurled the other tomato so that it exploded in a juicy mess against the guard's cheek.

A pepper flew through the air from a distance away, then an egg. Without warning, the air was filled with shouts and heckles and a bombardment from every direction. Fruit, vegetables, eggs, mugs, candles, stones—all soared beneath the Temple Bridge arches in the pursuing guard's direction, causing him to cringe and attempt to ward them off. The pole dropped from his hands and clattered into a neighboring gondola as a second wave of artillery was launched from all sides. These items were cheap to her, she knew, but precious to these people who had next to nothing. Risa felt a catch in her throat to see the dirty girl, baby still pressed to her breast, rise to her feet, and with a great jeer, toss a wadded-up roll of old ribbon.

With the guard defenseless and unable to see, Milo took the advantage to bring the pole crashing over his head. The guard clutched his skull and fell to his knees as Milo brought it down once again, harder. The guard fell face-forward, arms outspread, in a heap over the side of the gondola. A great cheer went up from the immediate vicinity, though from the outlying areas of spectators vegetables still flew, pummeling the man's unconscious body.

Instantly Risa began to make her way back toward Mattio, so she could help him disentangle himself. The girl regarded her as if she were an old friend come to pay a call. "I know it weren't the fancy magic you people of the Seven do, but that was right fun for us common folk," she said, jiggling the baby.

Risa could only gape at her words. In the last hour alone, they had all experienced more fear and danger than most people encountered in an entire lifetime. She had witnessed one of her friends kill a man. She had witnessed utter strangers, those who should have despised her for her wealth and title, defend her. Though full of wonder at how they had all risen to her aid, all she could feel was a bittersweet sadness that events had come to this sad state.

As she stood, she felt the power from the Olive Crown and the Scepter of Thorn still humming in the sack she carried. All around her, however, she sensed power of another sort—intangible, yet equally compelling. Some came from Camilla and Milo, so brave and willing to fight for what they believed. More came from Amo and Mattio. And from the crowd came even more energy, strong and as palpable as any enchantment. It was fearlessness. It was devotion.

"No, you're wrong," she told the girl. "What each one of you did just now was magic." In a sudden impulse, she reached out to take the girl's hand in her own. She vowed to herself that when all this was over, she would not only remember the girl and all the brave people without homes who sheltered at night under the Temple Bridge, but she would see what could be done to help them. "Magic is just easier to take for granted when it's there all the time."

34

It is a pity that these strange people, these Cassaforteans, with all their indulgences and easy reliance on enchantments, sadly lack the qualities we in more civilized lands take for granted: resolve, determination, and the ability to see right from wrong. For these reasons, primarily, it is unlikely that they will ever become a major nation.

—CELESTINE DU BARBARAY, **TRADITIONS & VAGARIES OF THE AZURE COAST: A GUIDE FOR THE HARDY TRAVELER**

W have to make a decision, and now," Camilla announced in her brisk, efficient manner. One of the boat people at the southernmost edge of the flotilla had offered them the use of his gondola, a large vessel with enough room to hold them all. "If we'd been able to move more quickly," Camilla continued, "we might have been able to return you all to your own cazas. After the trouble with the guards, and since there are three of you … "

"What my sister is trying to say is that we have no more than twenty minutes until sundown," Milo interjected, his expression grave. "It will be difficult enough to return to one caza, much less three. You must choose."

There was a short silence as they bobbed upon the waters. Around them, the boat people who had heard the speech began to murmur. Risa's hope of homecoming jelled into nightmare. Again she had that sure and terrifying vision of all her family's windows shattering as their enchantments were freed: her mother's workshops becoming a death trap of razor-edged projectiles, her father's furnaces erupting into an inferno that would be seen for miles. Centuries of craftsmanship, ruined, if they did not return to Caza Divetri.

She looked at the other cazarri, surprised at how suddenly resentful she was of them both. Her friends had gone to enormous trouble to aid *her*, not them. It should be Caza Divetri that they chose!

It felt as if history, past and future, swung upon this single moment. Through the padded sack she could still feel the complex energies that pulsed through the Olive Crown and the Scepter of Thorn. All around her, as well, pulsed the powers she had felt from her friends and the people of the Temple Bridge.

No, she thought to herself, almost laughing at her own absurd selfishness. *That's not at all right.*

The poor and the outcast did not know her except through Ricard's song—they had not attacked the guard to protect her interests. Camilla and Milo had not risked their own lives and careers to rescue insignificant Risa Divetri, but to uphold what she represented. Liberty. Defiance against tyranny. All her friends had gone to enormous risk to preserve Cassaforte's freedom.

It was for Cassaforte that they all struggled at that moment, uniting their energies to avoid Ferrer's prophecy of war and doom. An unfettered country was a greater thing than an individual or even a family, Risa realized.

Milo had known that all along. In that moment she admired him, and his allegiance against the darkness, more than ever. "Caza Cassamagi," she declared, not at all regretting that she said the word. "We should save Cassamagi and its records."

The others all looked to Ferrer. For a moment he seemed relieved, as if he too had been struggling with the same demons. Then he shook his head. "Cassamagi is an old house," he said slowly, "run by an old man who bores sons and servants alike with his chatter. Our records are nothing. You are Cassaforte's destiny, young woman." With a hand that trembled as he reached out to cup her chin, he sighed. "Let us save Caza Divetri. I think Baso agrees with me, don't you, lad?" The boy nodded without hesitation.

Tears sprang to Risa's eyes at the declaration. Her skin flushed with chills and goose pimples. The old man smiled at her. "Thank you," she said.

"You are most welcome."

"Caza Divetri is the closest," Milo admitted.

"I can't say I'm not glad of the choice," Mattio said, obviously relieved.

"But what will we do when we get there?" asked Amo, ready to punt. "We need a plan. Milo? Camilla?"

Camilla shook her head. "It is not for me to decide."

Milo also declined responsibility. "A matter this grave requires the decision of a true cazarro." He nodded with respect in Ferrer's direction. "Or a true cazarra," he said, looking at Risa with hope in his eyes.

He believed in her, Risa realized. He did not feel the need to instruct her—he simply believed in her. At that moment, she felt as if she could do anything.

"I have a plan." It had sprung, fully formed, from her joy in his confidence in her. "We will return to Caza Divetri and make it our fortress. There are countless people in the city who would have us succeed against the prince." She gestured to the gondola people around her. They responded with vigorous cheers and applause. "There are others who will stand with us against the prince, all of them true sons and daughters of Muro and Lena! If we must, we shall make guards of them and stand them at every caza bridge and door and window. Night after night I will raise my caza's flag and sound the horn, and night after night my city will know that against a corrupt usurper, Caza Divetri and the people stand proud." Her determination had arrested the crowd's attention. She felt the golden load on her back invigorate her further. "We will stand against him for weeks and months. Years, if we must! We have to! Are you all with me?"

The ovation that arose overwhelmed her. Yet amidst the tumult, she only had eyes for Milo. In his shining face, she could read his response as clearly as if he had yelled it at the top of his lungs.

"We'd best be on our way," Mattio said, casting off from the Temple Bridge. "Amo, you take the other pole."

The canal waters appeared motionless, but when their party left the Royal Canal for the narrower waterway that would take them to Caza Divetri, the gentle course of the water's flow toward the sea hastened their journey southward. Risa was surprised, when she turned in her seat, to find scores of gondolas from the Temple Bridge following in their wake. Strong men's chests were puffed with pride. Women with kerchiefs over their braids punted too, as did youths eager to catch up to Risa's gondola. Some of them sang out Ricard's tune as they soared through the water.

It should have been a sight to gladden Risa's heart. Yet with every glance to the west, all she noticed was the heavy and swollen sun as it sank lower to the horizon. It seemed an ominous red as the last fingers of light began to dance across the rippling surfaces of the canals. Inwardly she began a silent chant as she watched the punters heave: *Hurry! Hurry!*

So fixated was she upon the sun and its relentless descent that the sound of boots trampling in unison startled her. Milo stopped in mid-punt to point up to one of the bridges crossing at a diagonal overhead. All singing ceased. They could see a squadron of guards running in formation to the south. It felt as if the prince's withered claw clutched her from afar at that moment, compressing her lungs and bowels. They were heading toward Caza Divetri, she was sure.

"We can outpunt them," Camilla assured her. Risa did not feel much comforted.

As large and heavy as their new gondola was, the combined efforts of the punters and the water's natural current enabled it to glide swiftly. Within a moment she could hear that they had caught up to the running guards; it took only seconds more for them to pass them entirely.

The buildings visible from the low surface of the water became more and more recognizable to her. Many were those she saw from her window every day. After so many unfamiliar and hostile people and places, the sight of the familiar buoyed her spirits. She would arrive with time to spare, surrounded by people determined to fight by her side for city and country. There was hope. She would succeed.

The gondola's prow jolted against the stone berth, and it shuddered to a stop. Instantly Milo was on his feet, helping Risa to be the first to set foot on land. "Go!" he told her, his hand on the small of her back as he guided her up.

She did not need his encouragement. Without looking back, she ran across the public dock and up the rough staircase that led to the Piazza Divetri. As she took the steps two by two, she plotted out in her mind the fastest route through the caza to the great balcony at the top. *It would be fastest*, she thought, breathing heavily as she gained the highest stair, *to take the upper bridge and then to—*

Then she stopped and stared, not comprehending what she saw. Across from her, blocking the bridge's entrance, twenty guards stood at attention. Shoulder to shoulder they ranged, swords drawn and crossed, an impossible barrier. She turned in the direction of the lower bridge, a short run to the east. But in the long shadows of dusk, she saw another team of guards in similar formation.

The lower edge of the sun was slipping beneath the western horizon. In the distance, from the center of the city, she heard the cry of the palace horn. Long and low it sounded against the purples and reds of the sky before fading into silence.

There would be no answering cry from the sweet horn of Cassamagi that night. *I'm so sorry*, a part of her mind spoke as she thought of Ferrer. She was dimly aware that Camilla and Milo had both reached her side. Their muttered curses of disappointment brought her back to the moment.

Though she had much to fear, she also had everything to lose. She was the acting Cazarra of Divetri. All depended upon her. Risa steadied her roiling emotions and marched up to the line of soldiers, feeling every eye upon her. She could tell that they would not hesitate to beat her down.

Captain Tolio stood before the men with his arms crossed. As she marched closer, he took two steps forward and halted her with a hand. "That's far enough," he said. "I don't want my men to have to hurt you." Flanking her on either side, Camilla and Milo reached for their swords. Instantly four of the guards stepped forward and stopped them in mid-gesture, ready to strike.

"You're a traitor, Tolio," Camilla growled.

"The three of you are under arrest by order of Prince Berto," drawled Tolio, obviously enjoying himself.

"A prince cannot order arrests," Milo countered.

"This one can, when he is king. I gather it won't be long." In the distance Risa heard the sound of fireworks. She mourned to know that the popping and fizzles she heard was the self-destruction of the enchantments in the oldest of the seven cazas. "The rest of you are under arrest as well." He nodded in the direction of those who had just come up from the dock below. Risa's heart ached to see Ferrer sinking to his knees, clutching himself as he heard the distant sounds of his home's devastation.

"I can't believe you would stoop so low." Camilla's rage was so fierce that she charged forward. Two of the guards grabbed her elbows to restrain her. "What has he offered you, a promotion? You were a hero against the Azurites!"

Out of instinct, Tolio raised his hand to the old scars that criss-crossed his face. "Heroism buys nothing. A man has to know who butters his bread," he said. "Take them away."

"No!" Risa did not know which emboldened her—sheer panic, or the positive energies emanating from the sack she carried. With a mighty leap she catapulted forward, ducking under Tolio's arms. She dove for a space left by one of the guards restraining Camilla, intending to slip through and run as quickly as possible to the balcony. Had she been more quick or lucky, it might have worked, but one of Tolio's men grabbed her by the hair and yanked her down, sending her flat to her back with a crash. The sack landed on top of her.

It felt as if her entire head were on fire, and her eyes filled with tears. But what pained Risa most was the certain knowledge that within moments, Caza Divetri would fall. With it would fall the entire country. The explosions of glass and fire that would soon deafen her would only be the opening salvo in a century of war. Guard would fight against guard and kin against kin as darkness struggled for dominion over the land.

She looked around, blinking away tears. Evening clouds like lace drifted above. Serene and slow-moving, despite the noise and the confusion around her, they parted to reveal the two moons. Muro and Lena, brother and sister, looked down from the heavens upon her, and only she could see them.

Brother and sister, the closest of kin—like Camilla and Milo, she realized. Like Tania and Ricard, or herself and Petro. Once more her eyes filled as with wonder she realized what a fool she had been. *You never deserted me. You sent brothers and sisters, like yourselves, to help*, she thought, gazing at their luminous forms. The sea winds blew wispy clouds, shrouding them once more. With despair, Risa watched them disappear. *The gods have been watching me all this time. If only I'd realized… maybe I wouldn't have failed.*

A single note cut through the commotion. Rich and soft it was, like velvet. It flew overhead in the direction of the palace, silencing every voice around her. She felt the power in that tone. It soothed her pain. The crown and scepter within her sack thrummed in response, approving. As if grabbing on to the invisible rope of the tone, cast from caza to palace, Risa rose from where she lay. She blinked away the sorrow in her eyes and craned her neck to see.

In silhouette, at the top of Caza Divetri beneath the family's blue and green banner, stood the lonely figure of a man. The horn's cry faded as he lowered the instrument back to its pillow. He stepped back down as a cheer of approval arose from the gondola people behind them, who were still filtering up from the docks below.

"That can't be," said Tolio, his voice angry. "There's no one left in the house who could possibly… only the cazarri or the king himself can sound the horns!"

Only the cazarri or the king himself could sound the horns of Cassaforte.

Even a child knew that.

There was elation in Risa's heart and courage in every atom of her body as she clutched the country's treasures to her chest. Taking advantage of the confusion, she dashed through the line of guards and ran across the great bridge, hearing Tolio's irate shout and cries from Milo and Camilla. Halfway across the span, she looked back and saw that the gondola people had rushed the guards, overpowering them and giving her time for a head start. Sparing only a look of thanks to the heavens, she dashed toward the residence, her mind puzzled to bursting with half-solved riddles.

When she mounted the last of the residence stairs, flushed and out of breath, the man who had blown the horn was sitting at the edge of the balcony. At first he did not even notice her approach. It was not until she sat down beside him and reached out to touch his spotted, translucent skin that he slowly turned to regard her.

"So much has gone wrong," he said simply. Those had been the first words he'd said to her after she'd pulled him from the canals.

"Why didn't you tell us?" she asked. Hours earlier, the Olive Crown had shown him as a youth—a vibrant young man with thick and curly hair. Here he sat, decades older, a skeleton of his former self. Wrinkled. Aged. A few white strands of hair were his scalp's only adornment.

He shook his head. "No one believes the ramblings of a ragged old man. Who would believe me even now?"

She knew that he was right. Had the old beggar told her that he was her king, she would not have trusted him. "They will believe you now," she promised.

With great reverence, she lowered herself to her knees. From the sack she withdrew first the scepter, which she placed at his feet. Using both hands, she removed the Olive Crown and lifted it to the sky. Once more the clouds parted, and they were bathed in moonlight. The relics seemed to shine as if struck by the sun.

315

"It has been such a very long time since I last saw the crown," Dom said slowly. He looked at it with longing. "When I had my first illness, my son locked me away from it and told the world I refused to see anyone save him. He knew that without the crown I would weaken and wither. He did not suspect that even at a distance, it would keep me alive for nearly two years. Many times I wished it would let me die." His gaze caressed the golden branches as he continued to speak in his weary, whispery voice. "But he was careless. I escaped, meaning to seek aid from one of the cazas. Then I learned he had announced my death. When I heard—when I heard the rumors he had kidnapped the cazarri, I knew they had refused him the crown because there was no body."

"I'm sorry," she said, unable to find words to express the pain his story inspired.

"I prayed," he replied, staring at her in the same dazed way as had Ferrer during their incarceration. "So many months I prayed to the gods to send me help. I prayed for them to send a miracle. And you...you have brought me the Olive Crown."

"It is rightfully yours." Risa stood and helped him lift it to his head, gently settling it down until it rested there. He closed his eyes and sighed, as if feeling the same tremor of energies as she.

When he opened his eyes once more, they were brighter and less weary. He was no less aged than he had been as Dom, but he seemed to have the beginnings of new energy and authority. He reached out to her. With a feather-light touch, he took her hand in his, pressing it to his mouth in a kiss.

She was not unaware that a crowd had begun to assemble

on the balcony behind them. Milo was there, and Camilla and Amo and Baso. Someone had helped Ferrer up the many steps. Tolio was there as well, his hands bound, surrounded by a number of people from the Temple Bridge flotilla. A baby cried somewhere in the back; Risa could not see if it belonged to the girl who had helped her. Those who had arrived early enough had witnessed her coronation of the old beggar. Those who were still crowding in now quickly caught the solemn mood and respectfully remained quiet.

The gods had set her aside, yes, but it was to achieve this moment. As if she had suddenly inherited Ferrer's gift of prophecy, she could see how narrowly they had all averted the darkness. She could see that the authority of the enchanted crown and scepter would return the monarch to his palace. He would exact justice for the treachery of his son, and appoint a new heir to take his place. The cazas would be rebuilt and the besieged insulas freed of their barricades. There would be no war.

Her mother and father would return home, and Petro and Romeldo and her sisters would come. She would greet them with open arms and a story to tell.

Happiness caused a lump to form in her throat, but pride in her king and country banished it. She drew in a breath and spoke to the crowd. "I give you Alessandro!" She was proud to see that Milo was the first to fall to his knees, followed quickly by Camilla and the rest of the assembly.

It seemed to her ears that the joyfulness in her voice was no less musical than the horn that rested within reach. "I give you your king and the bearer of the Olive Crown!"

epilogue

🝆

In the Piazza Divetri, over the sound of a hundred hammers, it was difficult for Risa to hear what the old woman
said. When her words ended in a clasping and kissing of
hands, Risa knew she had received another wish for good
fortune and a long life. She had received many of those
lately from people she had never before met. Old or young,
wealthy or poor, she always returned the blessings with a
smile, and a kiss of her own on both cheeks.

As the old woman trundled off, waving her farewells, Milo
approached with the last of her parcels on his shoulders. Into
the cart it went, atop the other bundles. "Poor old donkeys!"

he whistled, pretending to be disturbed. He patted a per-fumed hide as he joined her by the balustrade overlooking the canal. "They'll keel over on the way, with everything you're making them haul."

On impulse she took his hand in hers, and together they leaned against the stone rail of the piazza. Beyond the lower bridge and over the canals, scores of men and women labored over the shell of Caza Portello. No bigger than water bugs were they from this distance, but their hammers and pry bars glinted in the morning sun as they went about their construction. "Urbano Portello told me last night that he's almost glad his caza has to be rebuilt," Milo told her. "He said that enchantments can't make up for the shoddy archi-tecture of his ancestors. Besides, it gives the insulas some-thing constructive to do with their time."

At the royal banquet the night before, Milo had been a popular guest. All of the seven cazarri had treated him as their own son. Michele Catarre had presented both Sor-rantos with beautifully illuminated books on weaponry and swordsmanship; the cazarro of Piratimare had prom-ised Milo a specially made gondola of his very own. During Ricard and Tania's after-dinner entertainments, Urbano Por-tello had monopolized Milo's attention, and Dioro's cazarro had pledged to provide Camilla and Milo with the finest weapons they could desire, throughout their lives.

Most mortifying, however, was when Dana Buonochio made both Risa and Milo promise to pose together for a painting Alessandro commissioned for the throne room—a depiction of the pair kneeling before the recrowned king on the Divetri balcony. "Ah, but Cazarra, I must commission two," the king had interjected after his announcement. "For I wish to have a portrait of my new chief bodyguard as well." Camilla had turned white at the news, and struggled hard for the rest of the evening to maintain her composure.

"You're thinking about that painting, aren't you?" asked Milo. A gull cawed overhead as it swooped down to retrieve some garbage on the canal waters.

Surprised, she turned to him. "How did you know?"

"You're covering your nose again." Hastily she jerked her free hand away from her face. "Honestly, Risa. I don't know what you're worrying about. You don't have a duck nose. You're very pretty." His voice turned low and earnest. "I thought so from the first time I saw you."

"No you didn't," she said, blushing and hoping that he would contradict her with more flattery. It was a luxury to stand there with him in the sunlight, holding hands with no fear of the day ahead. It had seemed, over the past week, that the simple things had given her the greatest happiness. The sound of her mother's laughter. Her younger brother's clownish antics. Fita's grousing. Milo's smile.

"Yes, I did. I even said so. You've got a ways to go on accepting compliments." His wry tone made her laugh.

Behind and over them came the sound of a deep-voiced man clearing his throat. "I trust I'm not *interrupting* anything?"

Giulia's rebuke followed quickly. "Now, Ero!"

"I don't know, wife. We don't know a thing about the boy who will be taking our daughter away." Her father sounded stern, but Risa could tell that he was only teasing. Moments after his release, Ero had lifted Milo off the ground and hugged him like a son, and then had spent the rest of the week attempting to convince him to quit the city guards and become a glass blower in the Divetri workshops, like Amo.

"He's only taking me over to Caza Cassamagi," Risa pretended to complain.

"I don't know if I'll be able to sleep nights, thinking of you there," Giulia fretted. "The residence is in ruins. Ferrer's an old man. Does he even know whether there's still a roof on her chambers?" Most of the worry lines on her mother's face had been erased since her release from the palace, but she still seemed to have aged during her captivity. A few gray hairs even streaked through her dark tresses. Were they recent, or had Risa simply never noticed them?

"Not all the cazas are as badly damaged as Portello, my beautiful worrier," Ero assured her, his bass voice rumbling in amusement. "The freeing of Cassamagi's little enchantments did little damage. Even Piratimare's damage was concentrated on the piers outside its sea walls and its dry docks. Our daughter will not be sleeping under the stars."

"I just wish she didn't have to go." Though she smiled, Giulia moved to her husband's side for comfort and laid her head on his shoulder.

Last night, both King Alessandro and Ferrer had made the public announcement that Risa would divide her time between their residences. She would spend the next few years living at Cassamagi, attempting to decipher the earliest records of the caza and the handwritten notes of Allyria Cassamagi herself. As she chose, she would also be studying the oldest manuscripts in the palace's libraries, searching for keys that could unlock the power inside herself that was as yet mere potential.

At first, she had greeted the news with a wrinkled nose; even at her most enthusiastic, Risa had never been much of a bookworm. The image of dusty tomes and sunless days had been relieved, however, by the king's talk with Milo.

"For your future, I have in mind a special position," he had said to Milo when he had taken them both aside for a private audience. Light danced in the monarch's eyes, as if he held a secret. "A very special position indeed. It will require a knowledge of diplomacy and history, of war and of peace-keeping. I think it is a position suitable for a young man such as yourself, a young man of a fearless nature and a swift mind and a keen sword—but you will have to study." When Milo had asked where he was to study and who would teach him, Alessandro replied, "There are texts in the palace librar-ies I will ask you to read. I will serve as your tutor ... for a while. In the years after I am gone, however, you will have to rely upon experience and instinct. Just as I have."

King Alessandro had smiled at them both, then, and was preparing to send them back to the banquet, but Milo had one question more. The most important question. "Will I be able to see Risa?"

His expression caused the king to laugh loud and hard. When he had calmed down, he shook his head. "As if I could keep you two apart! She will be here in the libraries often enough, lad, and Caza Cassamagi will be but a short punt away in your fine new Piratimare gondola. You will see enough of the girl, if she'll have you."

Afterward, Milo had been wild with curiosity about the

position King Alessandro had in mind. Was it as ambassador to Pays d'Azur? A diplomatic post in one of the frontier countries? All that night he had invented increasingly wild scenarios, even at one low point speculating that the king was embalming him in the dusty old library merely to keep him out of trouble.

Risa had her own 'suspicions about what position King Alessandro had in mind, but she vowed never to voice them. Her brief contact with the crown and scepter had brought her closer to the thoughts of those who bore them. Though she professed not to be a mind-reader, she felt warm inside at the certainty that Milo's future would be both bright and glorious.

"One thing, love," said her father, drawing her aside as Milo hopped into the Divetri cart. "I've a present for you." He withdrew, from the back of the cart, a box he had hidden there a few moments before—one of the padded boxes in which he sent Divetri glass to Pascal's in the Via Dioro.

Feeling like a child on the day of the Feast of Oranges, Risa unlatched the box. She gasped. Her father had blown for her a slender vase of the deepest blue and green glass. The colors undulated like waves. "It's beautiful," she told him in a whisper, drawn by the beauty of its colors.

"It is a flower vase, with the primary purpose of keeping flowers fresh. They will not last forever, but they will bloom for a long, long time. Do you not recognize it?" He smiled when she shook her head in puzzlement. "Mattio gathered up the scraps you had abandoned on the balcony, the night you returned our king to us. It is your own bowl, my little lioness."

Her mother quickly took the box as Risa threw herself

into her father's arms. More than at any time before, it struck Risa that she was leaving them both. Often had she longed to, in the past. Now that the moment had come, more than anything she wanted to stay. Ero's whiskers tickled her ear as he lifted her up. He whispered, "You will always be the true cazarra here, little one. More so even than I. No matter where you are, no matter what you become, you *are* Caza Divetri. I, or anyone else who blows our horn, only stand in your stead. Do you understand?"

She nodded as he put her down, too overwhelmed by his admission to speak. Tears filled her eyes while her mother kissed her with a soft and heartfelt goodbye. Milo had the decency to find the Sorrendi house fascinating as she climbed into the cart and wiped the streaks from her face. Then, with a flick of the reins, he set the donkeys into motion.

After the last few waves to her parents, Risa spent a moment composing herself. "Well," she said finally, finding herself almost ridiculously excited at what the rest of the day would hold. "I suppose now I can finally do something *important* with my life."

Milo laughed, just as she'd hoped he might. "You've already done a lifetime of important things and everyone knows it, from the king to that little old woman in the street!" He still seemed amused at her joke. "What was she saying to you, anyway?"

"Who?"

"The little old woman."

"Oh. She wanted to give me the gods' blessing," Risa replied, remembering how the woman had murmured over her hands before pressing her lips to them.

"You've had plenty of hand-kissing this week!" he said.

They turned from the piazza into the street that would take them along the city's eastern coast. One of the Portello workmen, a boy wearing the robes of the Penitents and carrying a basket of bricks, waved cheerfully as they passed. On the canals below, birds squabbled for floating scraps of bread. Above the sound of the donkey's clattering hooves, Milo began to whistle a tune. It was Ricard's song, written for her.

No matter what might happen to her, no matter what she became, she was Risa, the glass maker's daughter. She always would be.

For a moment she rested her head on Milo's shoulder, enjoying his warmth and the clean smell of his skin. There was only one answer she could give him:

"That's because I am abundantly blessed."

The Song of the Glass Maker's Daughter

A shrill cry of woe sounds into the night.
The city lies quiet in dread.
And high in the palace, a king in his robes
Lies quiet and still: He is dead.

A thunder as hoofbeats pound over the bridge—
Its echoes sound over the water
"Oh father, don't leave me!" resounds a soft cry—
The cry of the glass maker's daughter.

"The caza's so empty, my brothers are gone.
No sisters I have I can turn to!"
Tears fell down her cheek, so pale, soft, and fair.
To stroke them away, men would burn to.

She stood 'neath the moons. They cast down soft rays.
A goddess in white, yes, I thought her.
"Yet no harm will come here. Oh gods, hear my vow!"
Cried Risa, the glass maker's daughter.

The night passed, the moons set. The sun took their place.
No sign of her parents did greet her.
She wandered alone, her fair self not knowing
Another had plans to defeat her.

"The caza is mine!" said a cousin of hers,
"Every room, every chair, every quarter.
Cazarro I am, and I'll prove it this night
To all, and the glass maker's daughter!"

The sun settled down ever close to the ground.
Of countenance glad she is shorn—
Our Risa, she shudders, she startles with fright
At the sound of the palace's horn.

"Blow now, my cousin!" she cried with alarm
To the man determined to thwart her.
"We'll all come to doom and the house will be harmed!"
Came the plea of the glass maker's daughter.

A rumbling shook poor Portello that eve.
Foundations were rocking like thunder.
And Risa's poor cousin and servants took fright:
The girl spoke as they looked on with wonder.

"I'll not let my caza see such dire fate!"
And just as her father had taught her,
She took up the horn. Everyone marveled
At the brave, fearless glass maker's daughter.

A blossoming tone deafened all who stood round
As she blew in the marvelous horn.
"Cazarra am I!" she cried loud, without fear,
And she looked at her cousin with scorn.

The caza she saved, that night of dark fate—
Every brick stayed firm in its mortar.
And the masses sang loud, round the beautiful maid,
This tale of the glass maker's daughter!

ala dri
28)
7093102

About the Author

V. Briceland wanted to be an archaeologist when he grew up. Instead, he has worked as a soda jerk, a paper-flower maker in an amusement park, a pianist for a senior citizens' show-tunes choir, an English teacher, and a glass artist. He likes writing novels best of all. He lives in Royal Oak, Michigan, where there is a sad lack of ruins to be excavated.